il

Miranda Seymour is a novelist and
biographer who lives in north
London, the setting for this novel.
Her books include an innovative
study of Henry James in England
and a widely acclaimed biography
of Lady Ottoline Morrell,
published in 1992. She is married
and has one son.

Also by Miranda Seymour

MIRANDA SEYMOUR

The Reluctant Devil

A Cautionary Tale

Mandarin

A Mandarin Paperback
THE RELUCTANT DEVIL

First published in Great Britain 1990
by William Heinemann Ltd
This edition published 1993
by Mandarin Paperbacks
an imprint of Reed Consumer Books Ltd
Michelin House, 81 Fulham Road, London SW3 6RB
and Auckland, Melbourne, Singapore and Toronto

Reprinted 1993

A CIP catalogue record for this title
is available from the British Library
ISBN 0 7493 1579 2

This novel is a work of fiction.
No resemblance to actual events, places
or living or dead persons, their thoughts or
emotions is to be inferred. Any such resemblance
would be entirely coincidental.

The quotation on page 200 is taken from
Walden by Henry David Thoreau (1854).

Printed and bound in Great Britain
by Cox & Wyman Ltd, Reading, Berkshire

To Anthony

I would go fifty miles on foot,
for I have not a horse worth riding on,
to kiss the hands of that man whose
generous heart will give up the reins
of his imagination into his author's
hands – be pleased he knows not why,
and cares not wherefore.

Laurence Sterne

Last Reprieve

'Say at last – who art thou?'
'That Power I serve
Which wills forever evil
Yet does forever good.'

Goethe

It's a long walk to the last gate and the heat in the metal tunnel is intended to remind those who are rash enough to disobey orders that there are greater discomforts in store. Clegg is sweating in his heavy earth-clothes and not just because of the temperature. All very well being bold and resolute when you're down there. Lucky for them that they don't know what comes next.

Moistening his lips, he stretches them into a cheerful smile. Just in case. There's always a chance that the porter could be one of the old gang ready, in exchange for a wink and a joke, to let a pal slip through one of the side-doors and into relative peace. He peers through the bars. No such luck. The boy is young and hard-faced with the shining stare of the new recruit. They're always the worst, desperate to show off their professional detachment.

He adjusts his expression to one of sad humility.

'Not too late, I hope?'

'Never too late for us, sir.' Not a flicker of interest in the words or the eyes. He's going to do the job he's been trained for. 'Clegg, isn't it?'

His hands are starting to twitch. He hides them in his pockets. 'You don't need me to tell you. You've got my case history.'

The porter's white lips lift in a sneer. 'I can see you know the ropes. Well, I suppose you would. Quite a record, Clegg. Quite a little history of treachery. I wonder why the master's put up with you so long, Cleggie, I really do.' He lets a moment pass before he steps forward, pressing his face against the bars. 'So, you let the prisoner go three days before they put him in the chair. It's not a bad way to die, you know. I've seen worse. I don't understand it. You got him convicted, didn't you? What went wrong? Lose your nerve?'

He raises his shoulders and lets them drop before remembering that the idiom of a shrug has no meaning here. 'He was innocent.'

'Nobody's innocent,' the boy says flatly. 'Remember the basics. And it's not up to you to make judgements like that. You had your orders.'

He bends his head.

'Tell me,' the boy says, 'did you enjoy it? Doing – good?' He spits out the last word with such venom that the man flinches. Trying to remember how it felt, he can recall nothing, only the whiteness of his own ending as S. terminated the mission.

'See,' the boy says, grinning. 'Threw it away, didn't you? And look what you could have got for being a naughty boy.' His fingers slip between the bars, dangling the keys. The man turns his head away.

'Don't play games with me. You know I can't make use of them any.' The words are going wrong. He forces himself to concentrate. It isn't easy. 'I can't,' he says faintly, 'use them.'

'You're fading,' the boy said, withdrawing his hand. 'Well, let's see what he's got lined up for you. Twenty-fifth misdemeanour, eh? Trouble time, I'd say.'

Don't let them rile you. You never can tell who the new favourite may not be. 'Whenever you're ready. Hundredth System?' He feels better saying it straight out, naming the worst.

The boy holds the card up, squints at it and grunts. 'Not exactly. S. must have a soft spot for you, Cleggie. Can't think why. I mean, you're not what I'd call a live wire.'

'Get on with it,' the man says.

'Laugh a minute, aren't you,' the porter says sourly. 'Right. He's sending you back. London and Paris. Twentieth century, so no re-education. Young and handsome – that's going to take some doing. You're a lucky one, Clegg, no doubt about that. No revolutions. No murders. All he wants from you is a bit of grief for a few people on a street in London. Selena Street. Particular attention to a woman called Calman who's been messing up our communications system.' He peers through the bars. 'You've gone very quiet. Don't tell me you're complaining.'

Clegg is struggling against the familiar waves of giddiness and nausea of the transfer period. It's an effort now to shape the simplest words.

'Name?'

'Fancy. Raphael Sartis. Thirty when you move in, starting at Paris. And there's a note on the card from the Master. "In honour of Honoré, but try not to be too much of an ass." Whatever that means.' His manner is conciliating. The softness of the assignation and the tone of the message hint at a privileged relationship with S.

The glimmer of a smile twitches Clegg's lips upwards. *La Peau de Chagrin*, one of the few earth-books S. never wearied of reading. Rastignac, he liked to say, was one of their few adequate presentations of Himself. Was he to take it that he, like poor Raphael de Valentin, would pay with his life if he dared to exert his own will, to use his supernatural powers on his own behalf?

'Don't bother with the revealer. I'll go straight through.'

'Please yourself. There's plenty of attendance-room if you want a break.'

'No point.' He turns to start the long walk back down the tunnel. 'Thanks for the help.'

'My pleasure. I'll be keeping in touch with you to see how you're doing.' Reassured by the man's meek manner, he raises his hand in sardonic salute. 'Remember Rule Three of the originals, Mr Clegg.'

'Quite so. "If you can't be bad, be nothing." ' It gives him a moment of pleasure to see the boy's uneasy stare. 'I should know. I helped to write them.'

The Raising
of Hopes

Selena Street is not easily distinguishable in the lattice-work of homely terraces, crescents and squares of which it comprises a modest half-inch in the London directory. It is a residential street with the usual supply of acacia and cherry trees to shade its pavements and the usual timid aspirations to individuality in each of its gabled redbrick properties, a front door of seasoned and panelled pine for one, a brass knocker representing a yawning lion for the next. The houses on the north side of the street bear the masks of philosophical-looking gentlemen over their doorways, while those to the south are ornamented with round-cheeked cherubs. The significance of the distinction has interested few and been solved by none.

Modest in its appearance, Selena Street is not without its social aspirations. Lying on the boundaries of three small boroughs, it unabashedly declares its affiliation to lie with the grandest, regardless of the fact that the residents do their shopping and catch their buses in the other two. Their nearest church, St Giles's (into which few of them have ever set foot), is unquestionably in the grandest borough, and on this they rest their claim.

Estate agents tend to describe Selena Street as friendly. This is not strictly true. Selena Street residents keep themselves to themselves. Reluctant members of the neighbourhood-protection scheme headed by Miss Millicent Press, the oldest inhabitant of the street, they do not share Miss Press's lively interest in the activities of her neighbours. Each for himself is the street's unspoken rule. It is one which has, until now, been observed without discomfort.

2

One of S.'s greatest charms was his unpredictability, Raphael thought as he lay back on the pile of exquisite eighteenth-century cushions and idly stroked the supple, still more exquisite shoulder of the young Vicomtesse de Grèves, audacious, sensuous and madly in love with him. Who could have guessed from his performance as Clegg that this would be his reward?

Strolling the crimson length of the savonnerie carpet which had been the Vicomtesse's latest gift – so casually bestowed as to suggest that she was even richer than rumour's report – he paused to glance at himself with cool satisfaction in the window's pale reflection, before he drew the grey curtains across his view of the Tuileries.

The sated Vicomtesse slept and could be relied on to slumber for some hours. It was time to apply himself to a study of the task ahead.

'Ready, then?' The porter's voice crackled through the spirit transmission system.

He yawned. 'Whenever you are. Where did you say this place was?'

'North London. And S. wants you to get things moving, so I suggest you tell your lady-friend you're going on a little holiday. Got it?'

Raphael did not deign to answer.

'Right,' the voice said. 'We'll start feeding you the images. You know what you have to do. Pick on the flaws. They've got plenty of them and that's what you'll be working on. And Sartis –?'

'I'm listening.'

'Don't go soft on us this time.'

He closed his eyes, giving the faint images a chance to develop. They came confusedly at first, twittering and only partially visible, like an old film seen through a heavy veil of gauze. Patiently, he waited.

He was looking at Fay Calman.

Behind the glazed panels of the basement door, Fay Calman saw the familiar peak of Lucy Medway's yachting cap and groaned. In the kitchen, music tinkled out over the credits and magnified faces on the television screen. It was the one programme of the week which everyone knew she couldn't miss. Everyone included desperate would-be adulteresses. Fay decided to stay where she was, quietly crouched among the cats, eyes directed to the screen.

'Oh please, Fay. It's really important.'

'So's Charlie Everest. It's just started.'

Lucy's voice rose to an implacable shriek. 'You're going to put a television programme first, with someone dying on your doorstep?'

One more scream like that and Miss Press would be hobbling across the street to complain. Resigned, Fay turned down the volume and went to open the door. Forgetful of courtesy and even for a moment of Charlie Everest, she grinned. Not just at the miniature cap sitting askew on Lucy's froth of blonde curls and not entirely at the gilded sailing boats which were still rocking wildly under Lucy's ears from the speed of her dash down the steps. It was the uniform that did it. Gold braid on the shoulders, a silver whistle swinging from her canvas belt and, embroidered in pink silk on the breast pocket, Trixibelle Dancer.

'Miss P & O?'

'Not another word,' Lucy said. 'It wasn't my idea. John gave it to me. Birthday present. You know him and boats.'

'Trixibelle's the new yacht?'

'Oh no,' Lucy said. 'Trixibelle's just what I'd have emblazoned on my front for fun, isn't it. Well? Are you going to let me in?'

Fay looked at her with a hard and critical eye. Rosy cheeks. Clear eyes. Doused in a scent that had nothing to do with life on the ocean wave and a lot to do with Lucy's weakness for availing herself of the tester bottles in chemists' shops. 'Dying?' she said. 'Don't make me laugh.'

Lucy pressed a white-gloved hand to her heart. 'Thank God I've always been able to put a brave face on. And God knows I've needed to. Silent slipstream exhaust systems. That was yesterday. Electric bonded circulation systems. That was breakfast. And now he's off somewhere talking about track pods and navigational overlays. I don't know how I manage to keep going.'

'You have,' Fay said, preparing to shut the door. 'And you will. Free prediction. And that's all you're getting.'

Lucy's oddly round blue eyes turned to saucers of incredulity. 'You wouldn't do this to me? Twenty minutes, Fay. That's all I'm asking.'

'Ten.' But Fay knew Lucy far too well to hope that she would leave until she had taken her money's worth of false hope. Money's worth? The woman never brought along so much as a packet of biscuits by way of a thank you. 'Come on then. In the bedroom and I'll get the cards out.'

'You aren't missing anything. It's a repeat episode.' Plunging into the womb of curtained darkness which was Fay's bedroom, Lucy stared at the four squat red pillars standing around her hostess's mattress. 'That's new.'

'Elemental four-poster. Very calming.' Fay looked at her defiantly. 'Carl did them.'

'Oh, Carl –' Lucy's voice grew cautiously respectful. Carl was Fay's lodger, her substitute for the son she had never had. 'He does have original ideas, doesn't he? And – and that? Fay?' Her voice had dropped to a whisper of horror. 'He's not alive, is he?'

'Who? Oh, Uncle Eric. Sorry. I keep forgetting to tell people. We had him stuffed. He was very psychic, you know. He helps me concentrate the powers.' Fay gave him a thoughtful glance. 'It's a pity they didn't do a better job on the eyes. They do stare a bit. Still, what do you expect for a hundred quid?' She shuffled the cards. 'Ready?'

'You're such an angel.' Perched on the hard little sofa at Fay's side, Lucy peeled off her gloves and stretched out plump well-manicured hands to take the pack. Deftly, she selected twenty-one and handed them back. 'There's got to be something here. He gave me the sign last night.'

'John?'

'Gareth,' Lucy said with a tight smile. 'You know perfectly well I wouldn't be here to ask about John. No, listen, Fay. I just happened to be driving by Gareth's home last night – '

'I thought they lived in Essex.'

'Well? It's less than an hour when there's no traffic about. Fay, he twitched the bedroom curtain. I promise you. It's what he used to do. It was our signal.'

Fay failed to suppress a yawn. 'How long is it since you slept with Gareth? Three years? And you're telling me he's still out there twitching the curtain for you? Come on.'

'True love never dies.'

'This isn't true love, it's obsession.'

'Talk to me about obsession!' Lucy gave a loud mirthless laugh. 'I'm married to a man who can't get an erection until he's seen me dancing a bloody hornpipe round his bed and you're telling me about obsession. I love it.'

'We've all got our weaknesses. You knew John had a thing about boats when you married him. It didn't bother you then.' Fay stared down at the cards. 'I can see a bit of a problem around that boy of yours. Mark.'

'Max.' Lucy took out a cigarette, snapped a lighter. 'He's fine. Nothing else? Maybe Uncle Eric's got something to say?'

'I doubt it.' Fay handed over a tissue as Lucy's eyes filled with tears. 'I'm sorry, Lucy. That's all I can see.'

She prodded the cards with an angry finger. 'What's this one, then? Water. That's travel. John's trying a new boat out in Sicily next week.' She gave Fay a hopeful stare. 'You don't see anything – well – tragic around that, do you? I keep having these dreams about shipwrecks.'

'It's not John.' Fay put on her spectacles to peer closer. 'It's a man from over water. A stranger. He's very near us.'

'Don't tell me, I've guessed it already,' Lucy said bitterly. 'Mr Wonderful strikes again. Why is it that whenever I ask you to read my cards they always end up by being about you?'

'Mr Wonderful's Pentacles, not Swords,' Fay said automatically. 'I don't know who this one is, but I don't trust him.' She swept the cards together. 'That's it. One spread. Charlie Everest time for those of us who like real life.'

Desperation lent Lucy a bold agility. She trapped the hand in which the magic cards were clasped and wrenched it towards her. 'I'm taking out Gareth,' she said, 'and you are going to give him all you've got. I want the full picture.' Triumphant, she plucked out the card and whirled her yachting cap through the darkness to repose on Uncle Eric's knees. 'Maybe that'll perk his psychic waves up a bit. Come on, Fay. The truth. I can take it.'

She couldn't, and Fay knew it. Lucy had dragged her every step of the way of her forlorn pursuit of perfect love with Gareth

Lloyd-Evans. She knew his car number and that Lucy had drawn hope from the fact that it began with the letter L. She knew, too, that Lucy's last holiday in Tunisia had been booked after hearing that Gareth was scheduled for a business trip there. (Lucy had returned home with sunstroke after five days of storming the foyers and beaches of every Hilton, Holiday Inn, and Highway Motel on the coastal strip to learn that his trip had been cancelled.) She also knew that Gareth had agreed to have tea with Lucy once a month only after Fay, under tearful pressure from Lucy, had telephoned him to extract this miserly concession. Gareth had not needed to be told that rejection was a word Lucy had never understood.

Something must be said. Lucy was chewing rather than smoking her cigarette and her eyes were frantic with apprehension. Looking down at the cards, Fay had one of her insights. Closing her eyes failed to block the embarrassing vision of Gareth locked in violent motion with a handsome young woman. By no strength of imagination could she convert Lucy into a tall and coffee-skinned brunette. The unclad Lloyd-Evans was not an appealing sight, but it wouldn't do to tell Lucy that. Honesty would not earn her a peaceful night.

'Well, there's a woman here,' she said at last. 'A very passionate woman.'

Lucy's smirk acknowledged that the description was acceptable. 'What's he thinking about? You can be absolutely frank. But you must see something!' she wailed as Fay shook her head. 'We're having our tea on Monday. He'll be thinking about that. He tells me everything, you know.'

'Then you don't need to ask me. He's certainly thinking about this woman, oh, definitely,' she added quickly as Lucy's face hardened. 'I've got your meeting. Wear something red and don't ask too much about his plans for the future. And Lucy?' She retrieved the cards and put them out of reach. 'Forget the weedkiller. Poisoning John isn't going to make Gareth marry you. I know I told you that I didn't see the Lloyd-Evans marriage lasting, but it's better to let these things take their own course.'

'I don't know what you're –' Lucy's injured stare gave way to alarm as the bulging ceiling creaked and dipped. 'It's not going to come down, is it?'

Fay had changed her mind and was dealing out the cards again for herself. 'I wouldn't be surprised. Grendel's got one of his playmates up there for extra tutoring. Evening courses in destructuralisation. How to break the bedsprings in three easy lessons. Well, his house, his love-life, his problem.' Frowning, she bent over the cards again. 'King of Swords. I'm picking him up now. Tallish, darkish –'

'Handsomeish.' Lucy, having got what she wanted, was ready to be benevolent. 'It must be your Mr Wonderful. You do deserve him, Fay. We all need a little happiness.' She stirred and sighed and waited, but Fay failed to respond to her cue. 'Right, I'm off.'

'Don't let the buggers get you down,' Fay said, but without her usual cheerfulness.

'Anything wrong?' Lucy looked at her anxiously. 'You don't look well. It's not a cold, is it? You know how I suffer when I get colds.'

'You won't catch this. I just feel a bit odd. Something about that card.'

'Nothing Charlie won't be able to deal with,' Lucy said brightly, but Fay's face was blank.

'Charlie? Oh, that.' She pulled one of the cushions on to her knees and huddled behind it, waiflike. 'I don't think I'll watch, after all.'

'Next one,' said the porter's voice. 'Forget she's got a pretty face. Sloth and envy are what we've got on her card. Ripe for the picking.'

4

At eight o'clock on a warm spring evening, Lily Tremain sat on the cropped grass of Camomile Hill, brimming with quiet satisfaction as she sipped red wine through a straw. She had toyed with the idea of buying a celebratory bottle of champagne but had baulked at the absurdity of carrying it all the way up here to drink on her own. Champagne was a sociable drink. People might laugh at her and there was nothing which Lily feared as much as the idea of being an object of ridicule. A further attack of self-consciousness had driven her to pour the wine into a Coca-Cola bottle in case anybody should mistake her for an alcoholic. All they would see was a pretty well-dressed girl admiring the view.

Lily was celebrating a new home and the end of a short marriage. 'It's not that I don't like him, I just can't stand him,' had been her father's verdict. Divorcing Nigel had, he said, been the first sensible decision he had known her to make. He had bought her the house in Selena Street to show his approval. He hadn't seen it himself and had done his level best to get her into a Chelsea flat, but the estate agent had assured him that it was a good investment. Besides, Sarah, the older and stronger-voiced of his two daughters, had bluntly told him that it was time he stopped bullying Lily. 'Just so long as you can promise me Mr Tremain won't be oiling his way in on the strength of a bunch of cheap roses,' he said as he signed the cheque.

'To freedom,' said Lily, waving her bottle at a friendly-looking skyscraper as it twinkled up through the city murk. 'Here's to the end of being told what to do and what not to do and how to make love and not to wear jeans in restaurants –' She yawned. No point in getting worked up any more. It was all, beautifully and thoroughly, over. And she had barely begun. Decline began at about twenty-five, which meant that she had three years in credit during which to arrange her destiny.

She liked making time-plans. In three years, anything might happen. What mattered most was that it should be something which would enable her to outshine Sarah, an ex-literary agent who now wrote irritatingly successful How-To guides. (How to arrange your life. How to be a career woman and a wonderful mother. How to give perfect parties.) How to give younger sisters inferiority complexes was more to the point, in Lily's view, although she had to admit that Sarah always did her best to encourage her. 'I thought I'd try writing a novel,' she had said when Sarah took her out for lunch after the divorce was finalised and told her how to set about getting a job. And Sarah had beamed and said in her new American-English voice: 'Oh Lily, that's a great idea. You were always so imaginative. I'll be back in London in a couple of months, so maybe you'd like me to show the manuscript to a few editors.' She had looked more surprised than hurt when Lily said that real books took a lot longer than that to write, and that she didn't want any help.

Writing a novel had turned out to be more difficult than she had imagined. She had brought her notebook along with her, just in case a moment of inspiration should occur. She picked it up and opened it, looking about her for objects worthy of record. 'Kites strain and fall on the buck of the summer wind,' she wrote carefully. 'Elder bushes put on their lace dresses and bow to each other like ancient dowagers.' She sucked the end of her pen. 'Camomile Hill – good place for the climax,' she added hopefully. She was not yet sure what the climax was going to be. So far, her heroine had done no more than wake up and realise that her lover had gone. What she was going to do next was anyone's guess.

She could, of course, be discovered and become a star. This was Lily's own favourite fantasy, one that often kept her idling in the bath until the water turned cold enough to shiver her back to reality. She had drifted through her schooldays in a haze of boredom, shutting herself in the lavatory for hours on end in order to practise film-star expressions into the mirror. Her photogenic quality had often been remarked on by the family and Nigel, to be fair to him, had always been telling her she ought to do a screen test. It wasn't, she knew, as easy as that. You couldn't just ring up a film studio and ask them to discover you. Sarah seemed to know a lot of film people now that she lived in Pasadena, but to be sponsored by Sarah and then rejected would be a good deal worse than nothing at all. Easier, really, to go on dreaming. Her slow, voluptuous smile was, she couldn't help thinking, particularly effective. Ideally, the film would end on that just after she had stabbed her lover. Panting, she bent over his spread-eagled body. Enigmatic, she raised her head. Slow, voluptuous smile. Then, suddenly, regret. The music swelled, the camera focused on her eyes as they filled with tears. She had loved him so much. A knock at the door! The police? Already? Calm and exquisitely fragile in her white silk dressing-gown, she confronted them, a heroine. Eyes again. Queen Christina going to her doom. Real tears started to roll down Lily's cheeks as she blissfully contemplated the effect of her mesmerizing beauty. The camera crew were in floods. Even the great director, brutal, tyrannical, had taken his handkerchief out.

'Cheer up, darling. It may never happen.'

Lily jumped. An ancient, winking troll was leering down at her from the path.

'Young women shouldn't be up here on their own,' he said. 'Never can tell. Or maybe you can. Maybe you're looking for something, hey?'

Lily decided not to answer. She adjusted her expression from Queen Christina to a great painter drawing inspiration from nature. The troll drew nearer.

'Buggers' Wood, that is,' he remarked with a nod at a pretty little clump of elders. "I don't mind what you do, it's where you're doing it," I tell them. Stands to reason. They've got bedrooms like the rest of us.' He sidled closer. 'Not fit to think about, the things they get up to.'

Lily did not like the way he smacked his lips after this observation. Unfitting thoughts clearly excited him. She stood up, brushed the grass off her skirt and gave the old brute her best tea-party smile. Nobody had ever been able to accuse her of being impolite. 'I'm sorry to interrupt you, but I have to go now.' She flinched as he made a sudden lunge, but it was only to offer her a crumpled sheet of paper. 'Poetry,' he said. 'I give readings if you're interested. Watts Road, Mondays. Outside the hospital, Tuesday mornings, and it won't cost you more than a pint of bitter.' He held his hand out expectantly.

'But it's T.S. Eliot,' Lily said indignantly. 'Why should I give you money for somebody else's poem? Oh, all right, 20p.'

'Fifty – here, you bring that back. That's stolen property.'

'Stolen from who, I'd like to know?' She dropped it on the grass as she ran forward down the hill, spreading her arms to the rush of wind, all the way down to the smooth silver peace of the twin ponds where a few children were comparing the day's catch of tiddlers and tadpoles.

Peace. Drifting from a balcony, high up, came the full, sweetly rounded notes of a flute, invisible, piping to the elegant sickle of a bleached moon. Higher still, as she raised her head, was a line of silver light streaking towards her, hovering over Selena Street. An aeroplane wing? A meteor? Puzzled, she stared at it, watching it shrink to one intense point of light before it faded into the dark.

Time to go home.

5

Raphael looked round nervously as the Vicomtesse stirred and murmured before nuzzling her face deep in the pile of cushions.

'I think she's –'

'Same time tomorrow, then,' the voice said. 'And don't waste any time about telling her. S. says he wants you in London this week.'

'But that's out of the question.'

'Question? There is no question. We'll take care of the flat. And Sartis? You'd better take this on board. You go alone. Playtime's over.'

Glumly, Raphael looked at the Vicomtesse as she sat up and stretched her arms out towards him, beckoning him back.

'*Ecoute, Madeleine, petit trésor, ange de tous mes rêves –*'

Her pretty face grew tight and narrow and small as a pilfered wallet. It wasn't, he reflected, going to be easy.

6

Millicent Press walked stiffly down the stairs (she refused to use the stick which the nice young doctor at the hospital had given her after the last operation) and plucked back the curtains from the kitchen window to make sure that the street was behaving itself. Her new role as head of the Selena Street Neighbourhood Protection group (she had proposed herself and nobody had dared to gainsay her) had made a pleasant duty of her daily treat. Today, even the sparrows looked bored. Not a sign of movement in the new girl's house. Curtains all drawn. Dustbin brimming with bottles and cartons, some of which appeared to have been thrown out untouched. Millicent pursed her lips. Good food or bad, it should never be allowed to go to waste. Deadheads hanging like old lace all along the fence, spoiling the look of her street. Perhaps she could take the cutters across and do a bit of pruning. Good chance to introduce herself. She might offer her a drink, give her a few hints and tips, warn her not to go to the new butcher. Not unless she didn't mind what her mince was made of.

Miss Press's eyes brightened as the door of Professor Grenderlyn's house opened and Harriet appeared. Poor little Harry. Not looking her pink and rosy self this morning. Grendel must be up to his tricks again.

'Hello, dear! Hello, Harry!' she shouted, almost trapping her fingers in her haste to get the window open. 'We haven't seen you here for a bit. Been on holiday?' Not wanting to embarrass the girl, she dropped her voice to a conspiratorial whisper. 'How's old Grendel, then? Back on the straight and narrow? He had that American girl in last week, the redhead. I couldn't help noticing.'

There you go again, Milly, she reprimanded herself as the girl's face went from white to deep red. Well, best to know, especially with a man like Victor Grenderlyn. Poor child. She really did look miserable. No use telling her he wasn't worth it.

'I was just thinking how gorgeous your hydrangea is,' Harriet said in a stifled voice. 'Must rush or I'll be late for my lecture.'

Seeing the facial contortions of approaching sobs, Millicent restrained herself from pointing out that it was a rhododendron. She smiled graciously.

'Come to supper on Wednesday and we'll have a nice chat,' she said. 'No need to bring him. He'd only spoil the fun,' she carolled, happily aware that Grendel would be lurking behind the bedroom curtains, listening and not daring to show his face. Just let him try! She was, in fact, quite proud of her neighbour – an intellectual added tone to the street – but she saw no reason to condone his carryings-on with Harry or any other of the hapless stream of young women who had tripped so unsuspectingly in for tea and biscuits with their teacher. Academics! Brains like devils and morals like rabbits. Well, Harry was a dear little thing. Millicent was going to stick up for her and Grendel could see if she cared what he said about it.

'Seven o'clock and I'll get a nice bit of fish in.'

Harriet's head bobbed sad assent. 'That's very kind of you, Miss Press. Only I –'

'That's settled, then,' Millicent said. Folding her arms, she kept guard at the window, foiling Harriet of the chance to raise her eyes in the timid hope that Grendel might lean out to blow her a farewell kiss. 'Well, I mustn't keep you from your breakfast,' Harriet said.

'Had it,' Millicent said untruthfully. 'You'd best get going if you don't want to miss your lecture.' Her curtains suddenly snapped together, leading Harriet to suppose that she must somehow have caused offence. Rubbing her eyes with her sleeve, she turned to see a pale young man staring at her through the railings which led to Victor Grenderlyn's basement. His full mouth hung slightly open as he stared at her. He looked a little mad. Reluctantly, she took a small step towards him as he beckoned her to approach.

'Hello, gorgeous.' His intense blue eyes were burning into her as though he had never seen a woman before. 'What's the hurry? You're not frightened, are you?'

She shook her head, wondering if he was some nephew or cousin who was being housed by Victor. He hadn't mentioned anybody. The young man came up from behind the railings. 'You've been crying,' he said. She stood still, hypnotised by his oddness. Carefully, he lifted a hand to touch her cheek. 'Pretty,' he said. 'Pretty and sad. You aren't getting it, are you?' His breath was sweet and winey. 'I bet you like it up against the railings. Amazing. Oh God. Sorry. Sorry.' His expression changed to a look of loathing. 'Dirty tarts,' he hissed and walked on down the road, his head bent.

Puzzled and curiously comforted, Harriet watched him slink from sight. Victor would never say, or think, such things. The encounter only reinforced her sense of how great and noble a person he was. Difficult, but all great men were difficult and she had no doubt at all that Victor was great. He had collaborated with the great. He had written about the great. He talked like the great – and great was the honour he had conferred on her in allowing her to share his bed and to rest her head on his shoulder as they played recordings of Victor's radio talks with other great thinkers. And when he spoke to her of his loneliness and of the aridity of a fifty-year-old bachelor's life, Harriet's heart swelled.

For Harriet, at the age of nineteen and one month, life held no more glorious prospect than marriage to Victor Grenderlyn. In his own overweening ambition, she had instinctively spotted the perfect excuse to surrender and sublimate her own placid lack of aspiration. Living through him and for him, she would no longer need to make any efforts on her own behalf. She had, from an early age, accepted that she was unlikely to achieve any personal distinction – her grades at university were as respectably mediocre as had been her school reports. 'Well tried' was the verdict on her efforts now, just as it had always been, and nobody reproached her. 'Be good, sweet Harry, and let who can be clever' was the first thing she could remember her father saying to her; she had understood him to mean that there would be something less admirable than virtue in any sudden display of intelligence.

The only child of elderly parents, the dutiful daughter who was always home by ten o'clock (social life on the outskirts of

Radlett was so unruffled in its tranquil sobriety as to offer little alternative), her only previous experience of passion had been a disappointingly chaste relationship with a gym teacher called Tony. He had, towards the end of two years of frigid pecks at her cheek and long uneventful walks among the Saturday High Street crowds, caused her considerable embarrassment. The revelation of Tony's preference for men had been made in a loud voice less than a stone's throw from where her parents were taking their afternoon tea in the garden. He had, after an awkward pause, suggested that she might like to sponsor him on a walk for a homosexual sports centre in Radlett. She had refused. They had not met again.

Coming to London to study English under Professor Grenderlyn had been the most exciting experience that yet had stirred the quiet pool of Harriet's emotions. She had gone to his first lecture in her best pink candy-striped dress with her hair tied up in a matching ribbon, a chocolate-box sweetheart so ripe for consumption that the professor had wasted no time at all in suggesting that she would benefit from a little private tuition. Her virginity had been lost in a trice and so, alas, had poor Harriet's heart. She walked, she worked, she woke, in a state of anguished and unquenchable love. Victor Grenderlyn, flattered and amused by her puppyish devotion, charmed by this pink and pretty country girl who came to her assignations with baskets of home-baked cakes and who nestled at his side in a state of radiant adoration, had salved his conscience with a few mild remonstrances, a few well-timed murmurs about finding a young fellow of her own age. These, as he would have expected, had been repudiated with indignation, dismay and, on one or two occasions, with a showerburst of tears.

He had never mentioned marriage. But he had acknowledged that he was lonely. And he had told her that she made him very happy. Remembering his recent and most affectionate farewell before he shut her gently out of his home, Harriet shut her eyes in a moment of sublime joy, closing out the image of that peculiar, quite possibly mad young man. She would be there when Victor was ready for her, waiting and willing, his comforter, his cook, his consort.

Warmed by fantasy, she strode briskly towards the bus-stop.

7

Breathing heavily, Fay extricated herself from the yoga position of the crouching tiger which enabled her to squint under the bedroom curtain without having to acknowledge that she was spying on her lodger.

'Pervert!' She flung the word down like a challenge to a restless audience of three cats with breakfast on their minds. ' "Up against the railings!" With half the street listening? Would any normal boy do that?' She strode into the kitchen, an enraged Brünnhilde, with the pack prowling at her heels. 'The help I've slaved to get for that boy. The time I've spent. And listen to it!' Wrenching the top off the Kittimix tin, she glared down at the three ancient animals who looked in turn with sad and hungry eyes at their empty bowls. 'You! You're just as bad. Take, take, take. Leeches!' The cats squirmed forward, tongues trembling in anticipation. From force of habit, Fay took up her pendulum and hung the silver ball over the tin. 'Is this all right for the cats to eat?' The ball swung slowly from left to right, indicating that it was not. It was the last tin. Fay hesitated. Desperate, the cats rubbed her ankles, begging her to see that they didn't give a damn what the pendulum said. Fay shook her head. 'You want me to poison you? No way, my darlings. It's going in the bin.' This was not to be endured. Dora, oldest and boldest, was the first to spring forward and topple the bin. Colette and Sibyl, loyal acolytes, followed to help strew the floor with cabbage leaves and tea-bags while Dora salvaged the tin and defied any human being to put a finger near her clawed trophy with a low and expressive growl.

'Fine. Kill yourselves. See if I care.' Stumbling through a sea of rubbish (Lucy was right: she couldn't live like this), Fay reached the telephone and rang Carl's work number.

'Spiro? Fay here. Sick. No, not ill, just sick. What do you mean, aren't I always? I'm not a healthy woman. My body is the Holiday Inn of every virus in town and just now they've met for a punch-up in the foyer. Yes, that's exactly how it feels and yes, it has got to do with Carl. If he happens to get to work today – and I wouldn't bet on it – you can tell him I'm packing his things and renting his room out. Support! What about me? Who's supporting me? Yes, I'm sure your mother felt the same as you, but I'm not Greek and I'm not his mother. Sacrifice is not what my life is about. That's right. You tell him. He'll know why.'

Trembling, she put down the telephone. 'Don't look at me like that,' she said as Dora stared at her with regal distaste. 'I know he's always giving you extra food. You're an old whore, Dora, and that boy's worse than the hottest tom-cat in town. It's only with you that he's human.'

The doorbell rang.

'If that's you, Carl, I'm not letting you in.'

'It's me. Max. Mummy sent me over in a taxi.'

It always astonished her that two people as corpulent as Lucy and John Medway could have produced such a tiny son. Large brown eyes looked up at her from under the brim of an outsize version of Lucy's yachting cap. They were the most guarded eyes she had ever seen. In a seven-year-old's face, they were terrifying.

'Darling, what a lovely surprise.' She bent a long way down to hug him and felt him flinch. She had forgotten that this was a child who hated to be touched.

'Oughtn't you to be at school?' She led him in and, turning to hear the answer, saw the look of horror on his face. 'It's being cleaned up tomorrow. Here, you can put a piece of paper on the chair. Keep your trousers clean. Orange juice? Scrambled eggs?' She always wanted to feed up the poor little mite.

'I'm not hungry. There's a teachers' strike at school today and it's my nanny's day off. Mummy said to remind you that it's Monday. She said you'd understand.'

'Oh, I do.' Fay's face was grim. Putting her precious tea-time tryst before everything else and expecting her friends to do the same. Typical. Not a thought for the fact that she might be busy or going out.

'Just let me get a few things sorted out and I'll take you down to the ponds for a walk. We can go and feed the ducks.'

Max smiled politely. 'I'd rather just sit here. I've got a book. Mummy said she'd pick me up at six. After her tea with Gareth.'

Fay almost dropped her bottle of seaweed pills. 'What do you know about Gareth, Max?'

He smiled. 'He's in love with Mummy. Well, that's what she says. But it's meant to be our secret and Daddy isn't to be told anything about it. I think he does know, though. Anyone would. She's always telephoning him up.'

'Ringing him up. Probably about business. Your mother's a very busy woman,' Fay said.

'Business doesn't make people cry. And Mummy cries lots when she talks to him.'

'You shouldn't eavesdrop, Max. It's not a good thing to do.'

'I don't,' he said indignantly. 'It's not my fault if she shouts. Where's Carl?'

'At work.' She'd forgotten that Carl was one of the few people who could make Max laugh. God only knew at what.

'What are you cross about?' A gleam of interest came into his face. 'Mummy said you're writing a new screenplay. Are you going to be in the film?'

Fay sighed. 'No, sweetheart. I just write them. Mine's the name that comes up right at the end of the film, you know the ones, just when everybody's left the cinema.'

'Do you get paid lots of money?'

'I get paid. When I'm lucky.'

'But how much? Enough to buy a Ferrari?'

'Max –'

'Enough to buy a speedboat?'

She looked at the clock. She couldn't take eight hours of this. She had never been intended to be a mother. Carl proved it. 'Grown-ups don't talk about money. It's bad manners.'

'Daddy talks about money,' said Max. 'It's bad manners to be rude about other people's parents. Didn't anyone ever tell you?'

She gave up. 'Read your book, sweetheart. I've got things to do. The television's in my bedroom if you want to watch.'

She drained her coffee and went into the bleak little room at the back of the flat which had been Carl's since his return from the Retreat the previous year. He had made her promise to stay out of it and, until today, she had kept that oath. Expecting chaos, she was disconcerted by the emptiness which confronted her. A photograph of Father Gerard smirked down from the shelf above the neatly made bed. Beside it were two of the painted boxes which had inspired Father Gerard to lecture her on Carl's artistic genius. Fay took them down and examined them. The colours were crude and shakily applied. The draughtsmanship would have disgraced a six-year-old. 'Sure and I'm telling you the boy's got a remarkable gift,' she remembered Father Gerard saying in his soft treacherous brogue. 'It's encouragement and support he needs from you now, Mrs Calman, and I'm counting on you to give it to him when he leaves our little community. (And that'll be another £500 if you don't mind, Mrs Calman, and the Lord's blessing on you for a generous woman.)' Hopefully, she looked around the room for signs of Carl's much-discussed work-in-progress. A couple of paint brushes, caked and dry, stood to attention in a jar on the window-ledge. A felt-tip drawing of a one-eared rabbit pinned to the mirror did not qualify as art. The drawers held only socks and pants. The cupboard offered two suits, an old school scarf and a couple of tattered paperbacks on the interpretation of dreams. He must have done something. She knelt to peer under the bed.

'Can I have some milk, please?'

'In the fridge. Help yourself.' She hesitated as her exploring hand came into contact with a thick pile of magazines. Curiosity disguised itself as maternal concern and ordered her to pull them out. Dora, contemplating a possible expansion of territory, strolled through the door and stopped. Why was her mistress doing the crouching-tiger position here and why was she making that ugly noise? Best be off, thought Dora, and went.

'Oh, Carl,' Fay said. She thought of all the evenings when he had come in late and had barely paused to mutter that he'd had something to eat before scuttling into his room and closing the door. 'Doing a bit of painting' was the mumbled response to her offers of a bit of pie or some grilled fish. Secretly relieved (for she always felt uneasy when Carl joined her at the table in unsmiling silence), she had gone away with the feeling that she had done her best. And all the time he must have been lying in here on the bed, gloating over his hidden hoard, fobbing her off with those painted pillars round her bed.

Numb with shock, she leafed through the pages. Pictures. Cartoons. Photographs. She couldn't bear to look too closely. The titles were bad enough. 'Bonking in the sewers.' 'A Day in the Life of a Sleaze Empress.' 'Superscrew!' Hot tears of self-pity salted Fay's cheeks and dripped on to the flabby mound of magazines. Was this the reward for all her efforts? Hadn't she been the one to scoop him out of the cardboard-box camp down by the river and bring him back to a proper loving home? Encouraged him with his painting and salvaged his pride by letting him pay his rent in pictures? God only knew, she had tried. She had been his mother and his father, too, for the last five years. Money had never been spared when Carl was in need. Clinics, therapists, counsellors and finally, at ruinous expense, the Retreat run by Father Gerard, all had been employed in the cause of getting Carl into good shape. And this was her reward.

She couldn't keep horrors like these in her house. She would have to burn them.

'Who's that dead person in the chair in your room?'

'Out of the room this minute!' Flinging the magazines behind her, Fay rushed at the door, blocking his entrance. 'You are not to come in here, Max.'

His stare of polite surprise was astonishingly irritating. 'Why not?'

'Because – because there's a very important programme on television I want you to watch for me. Research. For one of my screenplays.' She hunted through the television columns for a plausible subject. '*Our Friends, the Animals*. ITV. I'd watch it myself, but I've got a bit of work to do in the garden. Burning rubbish.'

'Bonfires!' His eyes brightened. 'I'm good at making bonfires. Why don't you watch the programme?'

Blast the child. 'Because you are going to watch it for me, dear,' she said slowly and clearly. 'And you are not going to come out of that room until the programme's over. Understand?'

'*Ja, mein Führer.*' He clicked his heels and marched away. Baffled, she stared after him. How could she have known that bullying would have such a magical effect?

The telephone rang. Ignoring it, she scooped up the magazines and marched resolutely up the rickety iron staircase to the small portion of Grendel's garden which had ungraciously been allocated to her. On happier days, the contrast to its surroundings afforded her considerable satisfaction. Grendel's larger area was a triumph of order over nature, marching rows of chromatic dissonance, a plea to the Almighty to look down on discipline and say that it was good. Fay took the attitude that God and she need make no distinction between the weeds and the flowers. Nettles made a good cheap curtain for the bathroom window and she had always been fond of green. Squatting uncomfortably among the stinging leaves, she held a match to the incriminating pile. 'Oh damn!' she said as the feeble flame expired.

'I'm hopeless at lighting fires or I'd offer to help.'

Cursing herself for not having had the forethought to wrap the pile in newspaper, Fay crouched on top of them, spreading her skirts like a broody hen. A palely pretty young woman was staring at her over the garden wall. 'I'm Lily Tremain,' she said. 'Your new neighbour. And you must be Carl's mother.'

Long blonde hair and a tight black tee-shirt with the neck scooped low. The stuff of fantasy. She could expect the worst. 'Just his landlady. If he's been pestering you –'

The girl looked surprised. 'Oh, he hasn't. Not a bit. I thought he was sweet to be so kind. He helped me to move the furniture round.'

'Think yourself lucky if that's all he did.' She waited for the girl to go away. 'Well, nice seeing you, Lily. I'd better get on with this.'

Lily propped her elbows on the wall and peered down. 'Is it something to do with your work, Mrs Calman? They told me in the corner shop about you being a witch.'

Fay's eyes narrowed. 'A clairvoyant, dear, and this has nothing to do with my work. Just some old magazines I'm throwing out.'

'I'll have them!' Lily was pink with pleasure. 'I love magazines. Are there any with agony columns?'

'No, there are not!' Conscious of over-reacting, she smiled. 'They're – they're Official Secrets papers.' She hoped her skirt was protecting Miss Linda de Nova's ballooning bosoms from her neighbour's interested gaze. 'Isn't that your telephone ringing?'

'They'll call back if it's urgent,' Lily said. 'Official Secrets. Goodness.' But she showed no inclination to move.

Fay tried again. 'Well, I mustn't keep you.'

'You're not,' Lily said happily. 'I haven't got anything special to do and it's so lovely out here. I think a fire-lighter would help. I'll get you one. Back in a sec.'

As soon as she was out of sight, Fay seized the pile and rammed them into the largest clump of nettles, wincing as the leaves needled her fingers. 'All done,' she smiled as Lily returned, breathless in her eagerness to help. Now that the evidence had been hidden, she was prepared to be friendly. 'Thanks, anyway. I'd better get going. Carl's moving out today. I'm clearing his room. If you can think of anyone who wants to rent it, let me know.'

'Oh, I will.' Lily couldn't think of anyone who would want to live in Mrs Calman's basement. The man in the corner shop had said his boy delivered her papers in a space helmet so as not to catch a disease from all the rubbish. Still, a real clairvoyant was worth cultivating.

'Can you see things for anybody?' she asked. 'I've always wanted to know about the future.'

'Get rid of the past first,' Fay said briskly. 'You're still brooding over that husband. Well rid of him.'

Lily gasped. 'Amazing! How do you know?'

Fay grinned. 'Wedding-ring. New house. Young girl. And you're always well rid of a husband when he's gone. It doesn't take clairvoyancy. Just common sense.'

Lily hopped up and down like a child. 'Oh, would you – I mean I'd pay. And I'm sure I could find somebody for the room.' Desperate to please, she conveyed only the desperation.

A cat was yowling somewhere. Or it might be Max. Fay brushed the grass off her skirt and stood up. Neighbours were always the worst: they expected free readings and then used them against you. 'Another day. Just remember to ring before you come round. Nice meeting you, Jilly.'

Lily looked after her with faint disappointment. Jilly? She clearly hadn't made much of an impression.

8

Settled into a first-class window-seat with a pretty girl at his side and the stewardess running towards him before he had even managed to touch the summoning button, Raphael was beginning to resign himself to the loss of the Vicomtesse and the flat. He had always preferred London to Paris. It was only a shame that he was being sent there on such a dismal mission. He had done as they asked. He had concentrated on his victims and scrutinised their flaws. It was his own fault, he supposed, if he found himself wishing that fate had decreed that he could be on their side and not against them. That pretty little divorcee, for example. Why torment her when so much more pleasure could be had out of – no, he mustn't even think of it. His last chance, S. had said, and that meant the Hundredth System if he didn't do a proper job.

Selena Street. Pretty name, but where was it? Nobody in Paris had ever heard of it. He turned to his neighbour with an apologetic smile.

'I wonder if I could bother you.'

'No bother at all.' He still hadn't got used to the effect he had on women. Charisma wasn't in it: this one looked as though he had asked if he could possibly rape her. It was a moment before he realised that the look had nothing to do with him. Useful asset, telepathy. She was terrified of aeroplanes, bracing herself against their graceless jolting drop through the clouds. Defying the stewardess's scowl, he put an arm round her shoulders.

'Don't give it a thought. We'll be down in five minutes. What's your favourite music? No, don't tell me. Let me guess.' He hummed a few bars of a particularly dreary di-wah-wah-*chérie* number that even the delectable Vicomtesse had taken to humming as she tripped down the marble staircase. Ah, the Vicomtesse. . . .

'But you couldn't have possibly have known!' Eyes like blue pools, rose-petal cheeks. S. was certainly in a good mood.

'Ah, but I do. I know everything. I know, for instance, that you're on your way home to tell your parents about a charming young man.'

The wonderful eyes widened. Not a spark of intelligence in them, but did he want to be critical? 'But how –?'

'Seats in the upright position,' snapped the stewardess, slamming their tables back into place. 'No more smoking. Bags under the seats, if you don't mind, madam.'

'If I was you, my dear – you don't mind if I make a little suggestion? Ring this very charming young man before you tell them. Just ask about Sophie and see what he says.'

'Sophie!' It was the biggest lurch yet and she hadn't even noticed. 'How dare you say things like that when you don't even know me! Jean-Pierre loves me!'

He patted her hand. 'And who could blame him? I thought you wanted your mind taken off the landing. We're almost down, you see, and you haven't felt a thing.'

'Oh! And I thought –' He was just about to suggest that she might like to share a taxi when a stiletto heel impaled his foot, rendering him speechless with agony. 'And that's less than you deserve, you bastard,' she said.

Wincing, he turned towards the window to watch the pale sheds skim past. Evidently, not a part of the Selena Street plan. Or was it just a warning to him not to forget whose side he was on during this visit? Not the angels'.

9

Millicent Press was feeling strong and fit after the half tumbler of whisky with which she liked to wash down her breakfast. Old habits are hard to break and Millicent had no intention of giving up a pleasant indulgence which she had started in the blitz. Humming to herself, she prepared to set off for her daily chore of weeding the graves in St Giles's churchyard. She was not a religious woman, but it offended her propriety to see a neglected grave. The vicar had made the mistake ('a grave mistake', Millicent would playfully say when reminding him of it) of thinking she was a believer when he first saw her diligently clearing the Harrowby family's ornate tombs. 'God in his place, me in mine,' Millicent had told him. 'He certainly doesn't need me, and I get along very nicely without him. But I don't care to have all those foreigners' – she had jerked her head towards a young Japanese couple taking photographs of each other by the lych-gate – 'thinking we're letting our standards drop.' She had always believed in making herself clear. None of that 'God's little helper' nonsense for her, thank you very much.

'Oh, what a beautiful mor-ning,' Millicent warbled in her pleasant contralto. 'Tum-ti-tum-titty-tum-tum.' There was Grendel weaving down the hill on his tall bicycle. She smiled thinly. Nobody else had questioned Grendel's sudden decision to exchange his car for two-wheeled transport. 'I like the exercise,' he had said and they, silly creatures, had thought no more about it. She had. Well, it was obvious, wasn't it? The man had been banned for reckless driving and didn't dare own up to it. It always amazed Millicent that her fellow creatures should be so lacking in common sense.

Rather a mercy that the vicar was on his annual holiday, walking in the Holy Land. He would always stand behind her in that maddening way and talk about divine purpose when she was working on a well-rooted bit of groundsel. He got in the way of her pleasure.

There was somebody there. A dark young man. And what was more, he was standing beside the grave to which Millicent had given her best attentions. Sir Hubert Harrowby, what was left of him after two hundred years, lay at his ease under two Rosinas, a particularly fine Canary Bird and a healthy display of

pinks. Millicent had no idea who Sir Hubert Harrowby had
been, but she had come to think of him as her property. She
gazed, scarcely able to believe her eyes. The young man was
bending down. He was snipping off the roses, her roses,
purchased with her own money for Sir Hubert. It was not to be
borne. Bristling with all the rage of ownership, Millicent bore
forward.

There was no one there. Blinking and, for almost the first time
in her life, confused, Millicent peered and stared and searched.
Nothing. Only a line of lime trees by the wall rustled their
boughs in the light summer wind. But there was no mistaking
the fact that Sir Hubert Harrowby's grave had been robbed of its
finest flowers. Millicent took out her gardening mat and knelt
down. Absently, she patted the earth. 'There, there,' she said.
'Plenty more where those came from, dear.'

10

'Light! Sheathe yourself in the womb of night!' Harry Carpenter
bellowed over the roar of a passing juggernaut. 'Cleave to the
darkness, red wanton rose!' Twenty pence in the cap and only
an hour to opening time. Bloody housewives. Purses bursting as
they waddled past him into the supermarket. 'Ever thought of
trying to get a job, Harry?' 'Ever thought of offering me one,
duckie?' Well, they had tried, to be fair. Old Milly Press had
started him cleaning windows in Selena Street last year. Not a
bad line of business – amazing what people got up to in the
middle of the day. Harry's ancient eyes gleamed in recollection
of the feast they had been offered when he turned up a bit after
lunch-time to do the gent on the raised ground floor opposite
Milly's house. That freckled girl with the big bust and the long
red hair had been giving the gent a really good going-over, all
the works and, right in the middle, when he'd got his face buried
deep in the pillows, she tossed back her head and looked
straight at Harry. And gave him the most gorgeous wink. Legs
like jelly when he crawled back down the ladder. She must have
tipped the gent off, though. He'd been told he wouldn't be
needed again.

Then there'd been the day he'd had a drop too much and gone clean through the window of that American actress, straight on to her Ming vase. Well, she *claimed* it was Ming. Not a thought for the fact that he'd cut his nose to ribbons. No more window-cleaning in Selena Street after that.

'Grim is the reaper whose scythe keeps no season.
Grim is the heartbreak of love without reason.'

'Cheer us up, won't you, love,' said a fat flowered lady, dropping a dirty 5p in the cap. 'There you are, and don't spend it in the pub.'

'And where'm I going to get a pint for 5p, you bloody cow?' Harry bellowed as the doors of the supermarket sucked her in.

No respect for art, that was their trouble. Time to trot out one of the Churchill speeches. He fumbled in his pockets.

'Can you tell me the way to Selena Street?'

Harry's face brightened. Handsome young chap. Arms full of roses. An easy touch.

'Sure and it's a swate bunch of blooms you have there,' he said. 'Reminds me of my dear old mother's home in the Connemara hills when I was just a little lad. And shay the swatest flower of them all.'

The man just stood there, staring at him. 'Hull,' he said, screwing up his eyes as though it hurt to speak. 'Mrs Arthur Carpenter kept a sweet-shop in Hull.'

'Gerroff!' Harry said, alarmed.

'They said she'd died of asthma after your father ran off and you left home, but she did it with sleeping pills. Didn't want to live. Never went to Ireland.' He blinked. 'It's round here somewhere,' he said in a pleasantly conversational voice. 'Third on the right, they said at the post office. But that seems to be Fairlie Crescent.'

Harry was shaking. 'Next one down. How was I to know she'd do a stupid thing like that? Right as rain when I left. Knitting blanket squares and talking about giving the shop a new window-dressing. Next thing I knew they were telling me I was the deceased's next of kin. I was next of kin all right. She'd only got me when Dad took off with that peroxide bit. Never thought they'd let the asthma story slip past.' His eyes were wet. 'I had to get her buried right. Nothing else left to do for her.' He mopped his face, getting his breath back, ready to ask the man what else he knew.

He blinked. Nobody there. The street was empty. But in the cap at his feet was a newly minted pound coin, lying beside a single, yellow rose.

Harry lifted his head and shook it. Midday was striking and for the first time in years, he felt no desire for a drink.

11

Carl was on the telephone, whimpering with self-pity. 'You don't mean it, Mum. You can't do this to me. Father Gerard said I needed a secure home environment.'

'So do I, sweetie,' said Fay. 'That's why you're leaving. I have had enough. And I'm not your Mum.'

'I don't understand. I don't bug you. I keep out of your way.'

'Not far enough, you don't.' Conscious of Max's lurking presence in the next-door room, Fay dropped her voice. 'I saw you with that girl. I heard what you said. And I've seen that filth you keep under your bed.'

'Well?' Carl's voice was unexpectedly truculent. 'They're only comics. Nothing wrong with them. Everyone reads them.'

'Pornography.'

'Come off it, they're science fiction. They're going to be worth a lot of money one day. I've got the full run. You leave them alone.' He softened his voice. 'Listen, I'm going to get a take-away Chinese and a bottle of chianti on the way home and we'll have a nice early evening, just the two of us.' She could hear Spiro whispering in the background. 'I could stop at the video place and pick up the new Charlie Everest.'

Nice one, Spiro, she thought. She contemplated Charlie's slow smile, the hard lean body of the film world's most famous cop. For a moment, she was tempted.

'Nothing doing.'

There was a long hurt silence, then Spiro was back on the line. 'Fay, why you have to give the poor kid such a hard time? You been like a mother to him all these years. He is really upset. Don't you think you're being a little unreasonable?'

'I'm a very reasonable woman,' she yelled. 'He's upset? What do you think I am? How would you like to find you were sharing your home with a sex maniac?'

'Carl is not a sex maniac, Fay,' Spiro said carefully. 'He's a sensitive boy. I think this can have a terrible effect on him.'

'What about the effect on me?' She steadied her voice. 'I'm not a saint, Spiro. What kind of life am I meant to lead with Carl around? It's just too worrying. I've played mummy long enough, darling. He's twenty-two. It's time to call it a day. Tell him – no, I don't want to speak to him – I'm putting three hundred in his bank account. And that's it. I've got his clothes packed for him to pick up.'

She put the telephone down. 'What's a pervert?' asked Max.

She looked at him without affection. 'I thought you were watching television for me.'

'It finished hours ago.' He held a sheaf of paper up. 'I took lots of notes. It was pretty boring. Dora bit me. Can you get rabies from cat-bites?'

'Not when the cat's got no teeth, sweetheart.' Fay's eyes sharpened. 'I don't believe it! My new screenplay! They're sending a bike to pick this up at three and you've drawn bloody cows all over it.'

'Not all over it,' Max said. 'That's not a cow. It's the Queen of the Night for my art project. There wasn't any other paper and you said not to disturb you.' His brown eyes filled with tears. 'I don't like it here. I don't like being with that dead man. I want to go home.'

'And so you shall, my pet.' She telephoned Lucy at the Help the Sailors Fund where she did a light three days' work each week. 'Mrs Medway, please. Tell her it's Fay and it's urgent.'

'Ay'm afraid Mrs Medway isn't here just now,' said Lucy's secretary. 'She's just popped out to the hairdresser and she has an appointment at five. Perhaps Ay can help? Can Ay leave a message for Mrs Medway?'

There were a lot of messages which Fay would have liked to leave for Mrs Medway, but not with Max looking at her like a mournful grasshopper. 'Just tell her I called.' She hung up. 'Nothing doing, Max. We're just going to have to make the best of each other's company for the next four hours.'

Four hours sounded an unconscionably long time to both of them.

12

Harriet pushed her way through the crowd of students at the door and strode towards her usual desk, the one directly in front of the lectern.

'Hi there, Harriet. Seems I pipped you to the post this time.' Sally-Anne Quinlan gave that wide white smile which seemed to show every tooth in her mouth, and tossed back her long red hair. Today, she wore a brief gesture towards a skirt and a yellow silk vest against which her breasts strained for release. Tart, thought Harriet, dropping her bag of books by the adjacent desk. 'All the same to me,' she said. 'Didn't you see the notice about short skirts? We're not meant to wear them to lectures.'

'Catch Grendel objecting.' Sally-Anne gave a throaty laugh and twitched her legs an inch nearer to the lectern. 'Although you do need the legs to carry it off.' She contemplated Harriet's shorter, pinker limbs. 'You been working late again? You look wiped out.'

Harriet tried not to sound complacent. 'I had dinner with Victor last night.'

'Victor?' Sally-Anne gave a hoot of laughter that echoed round the room.

'I don't see what's funny,' said Harriet. 'I had dinner with him on Tuesday, too.'

Sally-Anne wiped her eyes. 'I'm sorry. It's just you calling him Victor. Where'd he take you, the Taj Mahal?'

'I'm very fond of Indian food,' said Harriet, untruthfully. 'As a matter of fact, Victor and I have many tastes in common.'

'Oh, Grendel's got common taste all right,' said Sally-Anne. Her pretty face hardened. 'So long as it's female and under twenty.' She leant towards Harriet. 'Beth Hardy told me he had every single one of the third-year girls. Randy bastard.'

Harriet stared at her desk. The tears were smarting and blurring her eyes. It wasn't true. Girls like Sally-Anne could never be of interest to such a man. She wished she hadn't called him Victor. She had meant to convey superior intimacy. She did have superior intimacy. Hadn't he stroked her blonde hair and called her his little witch and said he would be in touch very soon? But she had noticed that there were two breakfast cups in the sink when she went into his kitchen.

'Did you – I mean, have you – I suppose he's been to bed with you,' she said with a sudden rush.

Sally-Anne yawned. ' "Well now, shall we do a little lateral studying?" ' she said in an unnervingly accurate imitation. 'Yeah, you could say I've been on familiar terms with Grendel. But I know the ropes. With a man like that, you've got to keep him on the hop. Play a few games.' She looked at Harriet thoughtfully. 'Grendel isn't about to marry one of his students,' she said. 'Not now and not ever. Love's just a four-letter word where he's concerned. Banal, my dear, but true. Be warned.'

A discreet rustling of notebooks announced the professor's approach. It was a good ten minutes before Harriet felt able to lift her head and look at him. There he stood, her noble, beautiful Victor, gazing proudly into the distance as, with effortless authority, he directed his flock through the jungle of Blake's symbolism. Not for a moment did his eyes flicker towards Sally-Anne's languidly extended legs. Sally-Anne was such a liar. Harriet shivered with excitement as she remembered the little laugh with which he had steered her into the bedroom and said: 'I think you know the way.' Her hands were trembling. She would never be able to read the notes. She must concentrate, must succeed, for Victor's sake.

'Oh, that was such a wonderful lecture!' Breathless, she stood beside him at the university gate as he swung his long, elegant leg over the bar of his bicycle. 'I did so want to wave to you this morning,' she whispered, scarlet-faced. 'Only Miss Press kept talking. I thought about you all day.'

His escape secure, Grendel smiled upon her. 'And I of you, Harriet,' he said. 'I'll be in touch.'

Forlorn, she watched him go. He had to be discreet, of course. He had explained that. And he had to be alone a lot, to work on his book. Only she had hoped – perhaps she could visit him after her supper with Miss Press. It wasn't good for him to lead such a lonely life.

13

Sarah had come to inspect her sister's new house. She had told Lily how to give an impression of space in the bedroom by judiciously placed mirrors. Then she had told her how the bathroom would look much better if she ripped off the floral paper and cloaked the walls in glass panelling. The kitchen, apparently, was also in need of improvement. If only she had asked Sarah, she could have got it done by some German firm who gave you a free cooker and fridge.

'I prefer it the way it is,' Lily said defiantly. 'I like scratched pine. It's homely.'

'Certainly is,' said Sarah. 'God, will you look at this Formica! Pre-war! Where do you keep the saucepans? Oh, I see. Under the sink. Bit inconvenient, isn't it?'

'Not really.' Lily hurried her through the arch into the dining-room. She'd fallen in love with the dining-room on her first visit. It was small and demure with red wallpaper and an old-fashioned fireplace surrounded by green and yellow painted tiles.

'Ouch!' said Sarah. 'I mean, you don't like it, do you?' She didn't wait for answers. 'White. White on white. White trellising on the wall nearest the garden. White tiles round the fireplace, if you're going to keep it. Personally, I wouldn't. White curtains, and maybe a hint of gold.' She folded her arms. 'Yup. Lily, this is going to be just gorgeous.'

'I like red paper,' Lily said in a very small voice. 'And I like the fireplace. I don't want to change anything.'

Sarah stared at her. 'Suit yourself. I thought you wanted ideas.' She gave a sudden shamefaced smile. 'I'm sorry, Lil. I didn't mean to hurt your feelings. I do like the house. Really.' She leant against the despised fireplace. 'Nice neighbours?'

Lily toyed with the idea of fabricating a few exciting ones.

'There's a clairvoyant next door. She said she might read my cards.'

Sarah sighed. 'I thought you'd grown up. Oh, guess what! I forgot to tell you. I saw Nigel last night.'

Lily's heart gave an unexpected lurch. She bent to rearrange the vase of flowers on the dining-room table. 'I thought you went to the opera. Nigel can't – Nigel couldn't stand opera. I remember going to *Così fan tutte* with him and he made me leave after the first act. He said it was like being in a cage full of quarrelling canaries.'

'Well, he certainly looked pretty happy last night,' said Sarah. Don't tell me, thought Lily. I don't want to hear. I don't want to know.

'I don't suppose he was on his own,' she said, when it became apparent that Sarah was going to add nothing to her announcement.

'Don't you? It'd look good if you papered these alcoves, Lily. You could make a real feature of them.'

'What was she like?'

'Who? Oh, the girl.' Sarah wandered through to the kitchen and pulled aside the net curtains. 'You've got to get rid of these. She was OK. Thin, blonde, some kind of a cream silk dress. I saw her in the first interval. She was laughing a lot.'

Lily clenched her fists. 'Laughing? I've never heard Nigel make a joke in his life.'

Sarah was gazing out of the window. 'So? Don't get mad. Maybe he went out and bought a joke book. There's no point in being jealous. You're not his wife any more.'

Lily's hands dropped to her sides. Sarah was right, of course. Only it was so unfair that Nigel should be going to the opera with elegant, laughing blondes while she sat alone in her new home. It was barely two months since the divorce. He didn't have to flaunt his beastly new-found happiness for everyone to see. 'I'm really glad for him,' she said morosely. 'Maybe I'll send him a bunch of roses and tell him so. I mean, it's pretty wonderful that a fat, balding, middle-aged businessman with three false teeth can get a girl-friend like that just by clicking his fingers.'

Sarah laughed. 'That's more like it. For a moment, I thought you were missing him. You're missing nothing, Lily. I can promise you that. Men are nothing but trouble, and the sooner you realise it the happier you'll be.'

Lily hated it when Sarah talked like that. It was all very well for her. She didn't like sex, she ran a mile at the mention of babies and she was in the habit of offering newly married couples her commiserations. She had gone to bed with a man, but only because she disliked the idea of dying a virgin. Lily had once plucked up the courage to ask her if she liked women any better. Sarah, whose sense of humour was not strong, had laughed for a full five minutes before shaking her head. It seemed that all of her considerable energy was channelled into her work. Lily thought guiltily about her novel. That was what she ought to be doing, concentrating on her career.

'Talking of men –' Sarah said, picking up her bag. 'I promised to drop in on Daddy today. I'd better be off.'

Guilt consumed relief. 'Already?' cried Lily. 'But you've only just got here. Stay and have some lunch. I'll make an omelette.'

'An omelette!' Sarah looked as though she had been offered poison. 'You said you had a fried egg for breakfast. Don't you know anything about cholesterol, Lily? Two eggs a week is the absolute maximum.'

'Not for me it isn't,' said Lily. 'I eat chocolates, too. And butter. And all those things with additives.'

'You're crazy,' Sarah said with calm conviction. 'Don't you care about the way you look?'

Lily let her eyes slide towards the mirror. 'I look all right.'

'Inside,' Sarah said sternly. 'Read the diet books.'

Lily made a face. 'Worse than the air mags. No thanks.'

'Pity,' said Sarah. 'I'm writing one. I was going to send you a copy, but since you're obviously not interested –'

'Of course I'm interested if you're writing it.' Lily tried to hug her, but Sarah's body was resolutely unbending. 'I read all the others,' Lily said, releasing her. 'I even read the one about how to grow old gracefully. What are you calling it?'

'How to eat less and enjoy more,' Sarah said.

Enjoy more what? Lily wondered. What had Sarah ever enjoyed, other than showing off her superiority, 'Very good,' she said. 'Yes, I really like that. Clear, straight to the point, concise –'

Sarah looked smug. 'The series editor wanted to call it how to get more sex for less pecks, but I soon talked her out of that one.' She gave Lily a brief kiss. 'I mentioned your novel to her, by the way. Nearly finished?'

'Coming along,' said Lily, praying that Sarah would not delay her departure to inspect it. 'Well, I mustn't make you keep Daddy waiting.'

When Sarah had gone, Lily found she had left her white jacket behind. St Laurent. Nothing but the best for Sarah. Trying it on, she thought it suited her. From there, her thoughts moved unerringly towards the pleasant prospect of a clothes-buying expedition. Wasn't it the great beauty of being a writer that you could choose when to work and when to amuse yourself? This evening, there would be time enough to get on with the novel.

The doorbell rang. Guilty on two counts, Lily hurriedly unbuttoned the jacket before going to answer it.

'I was just going to rush round to Daddy's with it –' The lie expired on her lips. There, standing on her doorstep, was the most handsome man she had ever seen in all her life, smiling and holding out a bunch of roses. Could this be real life? Did such things happen? Absolutely not. She braced herself for disappointment.

'I'm afraid you've got the wrong house.'

Raphael was less astonished by his good fortune. He had been standing on the opposite side of the street for several minutes, in a position which afforded him an excellent view through Lily's window. He had watched the dark girl leave before making his approach. On closer inspection, the blonde divorcee was even prettier than he had thought. Tall and slim with eyes like cornflowers and a wide friendly smile. 'Wrong house, wrong house,' bleeped the voice on his spirit register. 'WRONG HOUSE!' Grinning faintly, Raphael took one step nearer.

'Actually, I was rather hoping it might be the right house,' he said and held out the bunch of roses he had picked that morning. 'Can you find a home for these?'

'I don't believe it.' Outraged, Millicent Press pressed her nose to the window. 'Right under my nose, he does it. Grave-robber!' Breathing heavily, she sat down to contemplate the best course of action.

Sergeant Fairweather was sympathetic, but unhelpful. 'I'm sorry, Miss Press, but unless these are rare plants, I don't think there's much we can do to help. Perhaps if you went across yourself and had a word with the gentleman. . . . Dangerous?'

'All criminals are dangerous,' Millicent snapped. 'Don't you read your papers? Haven't you heard about body-snatching?'

There was a pause at the other end of the telephone. 'I'm sorry, Miss Press. Just making a few notes. So you think it's Sir Hubert's body the gentleman is after. Well, that, of course, is a very serious matter. A very *grave* matter.'

Millicent did not care for the sergeant's jocular tone. The pun was, moreover, one she had come to think of as her own property. 'I'm glad that grave-robbing amuses you so much,' she said in her iciest tone. 'I'm sure I don't need to remind you that Sir Hubert Harrowby's grave is a monument of considerable distinction.' She took advantage of what sounded like a mumbled apology to press her point home. 'The flowers are only the beginning, you mark my words. You've had fair warning. If you choose to ignore it, at least it won't be on my conscience. The trouble with you lot is that you're so busy chasing after bedouin addicts that you can't see what's happening right under your noses.'

She replaced the telephone with a pleasant sense of having put Sergeant Fairweather in his place.

Lily, whose most pleasurable moments were spent in self-analysis, liked to think of herself as a woman of depth. When people told her she was superficial, she laughed with real amusement. How little they understood her. How shallow was their perception of the complex creature who lay behind the mask of careless gaiety.

She was, Raphael thought, as clear as a brook. He didn't need to listen to what she said: everything showed up in her face. Selfish, she certainly was. Spoilt, yes, and childish. So what was it that made him so dislike the thought of harming her? Her candour? Her –

'I don't think you've been listening to a word I've said. Well, I don't blame you. I've probably had too much of the wine. Anyway, divorce doesn't seem to have done him any harm. He's got a new girl-friend already.' She was pleased to find that she no longer cared whether Nigel went out with the Queen of Sheba or a belly-dancer or both. Perhaps that was the effect of the wine, too. It was a long time since she had drunk a bottle before lunch.

'And you?'

She gave him an evasive smile. 'You haven't told me anything about yourself yet. Your turn.'

'You know my name. And you know that I'm a helpless stranger in London.' He debated touching her arm across the kitchen table and saying something a bit bolder. And decided against it. One false move might lose him the game with this pretty, skittish creature. 'And you know that I'm hoping you'll change your mind and rent me a room.'

'Oh, I would like to!' This was not entirely true. She didn't for a moment believe that he was as helpless as he claimed. Or as lonely. Only supremely confident men made statements like that with a smile. Could she cope with the humiliation of finding herself in the role of his unloved landlady, cooking up breakfasts for a string of French girl-friends who would borrow her make-up and wash their hair in her bath? Gambol with him in the top bedroom while she lay below, wakeful and solitary? It was unthinkable. And, anyway, she wasn't thinking of herself. She had given her solemn promise to Daddy. No boy-friends until he'd had them checked out.

'Lily.' He leant towards her as she slowly shook her head. 'You know what I am thinking? Perhaps it was no coincidence that brought me here. I like you, very much. I feel so happy in your house. I think that this was meant to happen.'

It wasn't, and he had made a bad mistake in saying it. The spirit register rose to a demented shriek that almost pierced his ear-drums.

'You're ill.' Lily pushed aside a veil of hair to look at him with anxious eyes. 'I'll get you something.'

'No, no, I'm fine. Really.' It was like a bee in his brain, buzzing and whirring, demanding his attention. Under the table, he clenched his hands, digging his nails into his palms. Here he was, with the prettiest, most desirable girl imaginable – the Vicomtesse had, when he thought about it, been a trifle pudgy and more than a little dull – and all the register did was shrill 'Calman' at him. Calman could wait, and he was damned if he was going to cause any grief to Lily, whatever S. might say. 'Too right you're damned,' snapped the porter. 'I wouldn't like to say where he'll send you if you carry on like this.'

'So we're agreed?' He looked at her anxiously. 'I'll pay, of course. That's understood. Whatever you feel to be appropriate.'

She shook her head again. 'It's not the money. I mean, it is the money, but not yours. That's why my father agreed to the house. It was on condition, you see.'

He didn't. He wished she knew what he was risking for her sake.

'It does sound so awful,' she said despairingly. 'That was why Nigel married me, only I didn't know. It's all in trusts and things, so it doesn't mean much to me. But there's rather a lot of it and I suppose, after Nigel, Daddy was worried I might make another muddle.'

He nodded slowly. 'Take in an unscrupulous tenant, for example.'

'Oh, I didn't mean *you*,' Lily wailed. 'I always put things so badly.'

Did she, he wondered, or was she a good deal shrewder than he had supposed? No point in explaining that he had come to her door on a romantic impulse. Daddy had clearly trained her to see all strangers as fortune-hunters. So much the worse for her. He stood up abruptly. 'I'm sorry to have taken up your time. I'd better start looking elsewhere.'

'Yes.' She was numb with despair. No invitation, no mention of wanting to see her again. She couldn't blame him. She had bored him with stories of Nigel and now she had allowed him to see her as a spoilt little heiress, clinging to Daddy and her inheritance. No. She would be honest. To see her as she was. Selfish, cowardly and mean-spirited. And now he was going and it served her right.

'Here.' She lifted the roses out of the vase and thrust them into his hands. 'Have them back. I don't deserve them.'

'Don't you?' He put them back in the vase. Obeying a sudden impulse, he leant forward to kiss the top of Lily's head just as she tilted it back to stop the tears spilling from her eyes. His mouth met hers and, before he had thought what he was doing, his hands were on her shirt-buttons.

Another mistake.

'Look at the time!' Lily pushed back her chair and leapt to her feet. 'So late!' She turned her back on him, clattering saucepans into the sink with frenzied purpose.

'You don't know anyone who might have a room near here?' he shouted over the din. Lily swung round, scarlet-cheeked, furious at her own behaviour. Queen Christina would have known what to do. One enigmatic smile would have said it all. Not she. She had almost fainted with pleasure when he kissed her and now where was she? Nowhere. Unless –

'I do, actually,' she said. 'Next door. The lady downstairs told me to look out for someone. She's called Mrs Calman.'

He looked at her with an expression she found strange. 'Calman,' he said. 'Yes, of course. Well, why not?'

'And perhaps I'll see you,' Lily said with what she hoped was a careless smile. 'I – we – we'll probably see each other over the garden wall.'

Raphael picked up his hat. 'Dinner tomorrow night?'

'Oh. Now, what am I meant to be doing tomorrow?' So one's heart did give a bump. She had always imagined it was poetic licence. 'Yes, I'm sure I'll be able to put him off. Thank you.' She held out a prim hand. 'I shall look forward to it.'

Raphael smiled. 'And I to getting to know you better, my dear Mrs Tremain.'

It was only after the door had closed that Lily realised what had disturbed her about that last remark. She was sure, absolutely sure, that she had never told him her surname.

Five minutes later, the doorbell rang again.

'Yes? Can I help you?' Lily looked down with ill-concealed irritation at the bristling silver curls and stoutly brogued feet.

'Millicent Press. From across the street.' She lowered her voice to a conspiratorial whisper. 'If I could just come in for a moment?'

Lily remembered her manners. 'Of course. And I'm Lily Tremain. Would you like a cup of tea, Mrs Press?'

'Oh, plain Miss, but Milly to you dear, just Milly,' Millicent twinkled, settling herself into a chair. 'I'm afraid I never touch tea.' She gave a significant glance towards a promising array of bottles in the corner. 'If you did have a little whisky – doctor's orders. It's my bones.'

'I'm so sorry.' Proffering the medicine, Lily saw that Miss Press was eying her roses. 'Aren't they lovely?'

Millicent drained her glass before nodding. 'I just felt I ought to warn you, dear. I don't like to cause trouble. We're a friendly little neighbourhood here. Always popping in and out of each other's houses for a chat.'

'How nice,' Lily murmured, appalled by the prospect of Miss Press popping in for a daily chat. 'But I'm sure I shan't need warning. I always lock the house up before I go out.'

'I know you do, dear.' Miss Press looked mildly embarrassed. 'Living opposite, you know, I can't help noticing what goes on. I meant to have a word with you the other day when I saw you going off to Camomile Hill on your own. You really shouldn't. Very unpleasant things have happened up there to young girls in the past. I won't go into details, but I'm sure you follow my meaning.'

She found Lily's silence rather baffling. She wanted to get round to the subject of the flowers, but, having missed her first opening, she couldn't quite think how to get back to them. She decided to play for time. 'Grendel, now.' She leant forward with a confiding smile. 'Your neighbour upstairs. I dare say he hasn't wasted any time in making your acquaintance.'

Lily was finding it difficult to hide her annoyance. 'The professor? I've seen him in the street once or twice. He looked quite agreeable.'

'Agreeable?' Miss Press allowed herself a cynical titter. 'Oh, he knows how to be. You want to watch out for him, dear.'

Was that all she had come to say? Lily glanced at the door. 'It's very kind of you to warn me, Miss Press. And now, if you'll forgive me –'

Millicent stayed in her place. 'It's worse than that,' she said solemnly. 'Those flowers. I'm sorry to have to say it, my dear, but they're stolen property. My heart sank when I saw that man walking down your path. A man who could rob graves – well, Milly, my girl, I thought to myself, that poor child could be murdered in her kitchen and nobody the wiser.'

'Miss Press, please!' Lily felt her control beginning to slip. 'It's very kind of you to bother, but I really don't need help. Mr Sartis –'

'Sartis!' Miss Press sniffed. 'He made that up, I'll be bound. I knew there was something nasty about him the minute I saw him in the churchyard. You could have knocked me flat when I saw him carrying them in here, bold as brass.'

'He wanted to rent a room, that was all.' Deliberately, Lily bent to sniff the roses. 'And I don't see why a dead person should miss a few flowers.'

'It's not the dead I'm talking about,' Miss Press snapped. 'They're my roses. I planted them. And I certainly didn't put them there for Mr what's-his-name's benefit.'

Lily shrugged. 'Anyway, you needn't worry. He won't be moving in here.'

'Well, that's a relief.' Miss Press fanned her face with her hand. 'I couldn't have supported it, my dear, I'll tell you the truth.'

Lily smiled at her, savouring the moment. 'I'm afraid you'll have to,' she said. 'He's moving in next door instead.'

14

Lucy had been waiting for twenty-five minutes in the Silver Teapot. She had eaten two cream cones and four smoked-salmon sandwiches to ward the waitress off. He couldn't have forgotten. He could. No, there he was, handing his coat to the woman at the door, looking around with that gentle, anxious stare peculiar to men who know they look better without their spectacles. Lucy saw only his vulnerability. She had to squeeze her knees together to stop the trembling in her legs.

'Here, Gareth!' She fluttered her hand, showing off the long pearl-pink nails. 'Over here.'

'I thought we'd agreed not to draw attention to ourselves,' was his opening remark. It seemed to refer to the red-silk dress she had chosen with such care after Fay's hint about colour.

'Don't you like it?' Her eyes reproached him. 'You used to say it brought out the temptress in me when I wore red.'

Had he ever made such an idiotic remark? He never knew with Lucy. 'Lot of water under the bridge since then, old girl,' he said brightly.

Lucy flinched and then rallied. 'A lot of shared experience, let's say.' Her legs rubbed gently against his under the table.

'Well now,' Gareth said, trying to ignore this suggestive movement. 'Toasted teacakes for me. I see you haven't wasted any time.' That was the right note, he thought. Jolly, un-romantic, unconcerned. She'd put on weight again. Handsome woman though. Pity she couldn't settle for something uncomplicated. His eyes travelled with guilty lasciviousness over the generous bosom which Lucy rightly considered to be her finest feature. 'You're looking well.'

Lucy's face grew instantly mournful. 'I do my best. It's so hard for me, Gareth, being with him and thinking how happy I might have been –'

He was saved by the arrival of the waitress. Pretty little thing. Lovely legs. 'Just the teacakes,' he muttered, bending his head. He was always terrified that Lucy could read his thoughts.

'How happy I might have been with you,' she said softly, leaning forward to clasp his hand. 'There hasn't been a day when I haven't thought of you since our last meeting. You do read my letters, don't you, Gareth?'

'Letters? Oh, absolutely.' He smiled with extra warmth to cover the hesitation. 'Never known a letter-writer like you, Lucy.'

'And the last one – you weren't angry with me? You think I'm doing the right thing?'

Gareth nodded through a mouthful of buttered teacake. He had seen enough of Lucy's letters to guess what she was hinting at. They were, as he remembered, pretty hot stuff. There had been a time when he used to save them up to read at his desk during the lunch-hour and get a guilty thrill out of thinking about a younger, prettier Lucy acting out her lurid fantasies. But then a secretary found one and shared the contents with half the office and Gareth, after sacking her, decided it was wiser to throw Lucy's letters away unopened. He couldn't stand the idea of being a laughing-stock. Still less, could he stand the idea of someone telling Felicity, his wife.

Lucy seemed more nervous than usual, today. A trickle of sweat was running down her face and her hand was unpleasantly clammy. Menopause, he thought knowledgeably. Hot flushes. Poor old girl. He tried to move his hand away so that he could give it a discreet wipe, but Lucy's grip was surprisingly powerful.

'I'll get the girl to open the window a bit,' he said.

'Fancy her, don't you,' Lucy said sharply.

'A waitress in a tea-shop?'

'Oh,' Lucy said with dangerous sweetness. 'Is there a big distinction between waitresses and copy-typists? I hadn't realised.'

His head was beginning to ache. 'Melissa is a private secretary, not a copy-typist, and we have an excellent working relationship, nothing more. She is only twenty-two,' he added, unwisely.

Lucy's eyebrows turned into skipping-ropes. 'How reassuring.'

'It should be.' He looked at her plaintively. 'I've had a very busy day. Let's just enjoy the tea. Sticky weather, isn't it?'

Lucy recognised evasion tactics and felt a moment of pity for her beloved. Subtlety was not Gareth's strongest suit. She had always been able to read him like an open book.

'To get back to the letter,' she said firmly. 'Do you really think I'm doing the right thing?'

Thankful to have escaped the dangerous topic of Melissa, Gareth nodded vigorously. 'Oh, definitely. It's a sort of therapy, writing letters like that, I dare say. Gets it all off your chest.' He thought of adding a little witticism to this inadvertent allusion to her bosom, and decided against it. He didn't want her reading too much into anything he said.

Lucy stared at him, baffled. He sounded so cheerful, so matter of fact. The clairvoyants had all told her that they could see the situation coming to a head. Was this it? Had he at last accepted what she had known for so long, that their lives were inextricably entwined? Dizzy with hope, she readied herself for the next response.

'So you think Felicity will accept a divorce?'

Gareth froze. What could she have put in that letter?

'There'd have to be a gap, of course,' Lucy went on rapidly. 'I don't want scandal any more than you do. I've Max to consider.'

'Max,' Gareth said feebly. 'Oh yes. Yes, you must consider Max. And John, Lucy? What about your husband?'

'After he's dead, you mean.' Lucy looked thoughtful. 'Yes, I've thought about that. But I don't think it's a very unpleasant way to die. Spirits only come back when they've had a painful death. Weed-killer's quick. That's why I chose it. You've spilt your tea.'

'No,' he said faintly. 'I mean, yes, I've spilt the tea, no, you can't do it. Oh God, I think I'm going mad. And you wrote a letter to tell me you were planning to kill him? Christ, woman, don't you realise that's enough to make me an accomplice!'

Tears were pouring down Lucy's face and splashing on to the red silk. People were turning to stare, but neither of them noticed. 'You didn't even bother to read it,' she wept. 'You sat there saying how much you loved my letters and you didn't even look at it. You don't love me.'

The sobs were getting louder and it was no moment to point out that he had said nothing about loving her letters. 'I'm very fond of you,' Gareth hissed. 'We've had some very happy times together. But I am not going to leave Felicity and I am not going to change the nature of our relationship. I don't mind having tea with you once a month, but that's it.'

'You don't mind! I give you years out of my life and you tell me you don't mind.'

'You've every right to be angry with me,' Gareth said meekly. 'I can't blame you if you never want to see me again.'

Lucy rose to her feet, picked up her bag and looked down at him. Solemnly, she shook her head. 'No, Gareth,' she said. 'I'm wise enough to know that none of us can fight against destiny. Even you can't destroy our love.'

15

'It's a bit spartan, I'm afraid,' Fay said. 'Carl never was one for possessions. You don't mind sharing a bathroom? There's only the one.'

Raphael smiled. 'I can't see any reason why I should mind that.' She was, he thought, rather an endearing character. S. had always complained that clairvoyants interfered with the communication lines, but he couldn't imagine that Fay Calman's romantic dabblings would wreak much havoc. Her red-rimmed eyes, moreover, suggested that she had enough unhappiness in her life already to be getting along with.

'Yours not to reason why, sweetie,' the porter's voice said sharply. 'Get on with it.'

'And the rent?'

'Sixty pounds,' she said. 'In advance. But you get free sheets for that. Electricity's extra and there's a phone-box at the end of the street.'

Not quite so impractical as she looked, then. He took six £10.00 notes out of his wallet and handed them to her.

'You're getting a real bargain,' Fay said. 'And there's a lovely view of the garden. Max, I told you not to come in until I called you. Out.'

Max looked at her severely. 'I've got something to discuss.' He looked at the door. 'Something private.' He pulled at her hand. 'Now.'

'You don't know anything about him,' he hissed when they were safely on the other side of the door. 'He could be a mass murderer, and you'll be alone with him. What's he want to live in Carl's room for if he's so rich? Ask him what he does and then check up on him.' He looked at her despairingly as her face broke into a smile. 'It's not funny. Didn't you read about that man in Muswell Hill and all the people he chopped up?'

Fay laughed. 'He's not the type. I am a clairvoyant, you know. I can tell.'

Max looked at her gloomily. 'Cards are one thing,' he said. 'Life's another.'

Fay was too elated to be troubled by Max's forebodings. Hadn't the clairvoyants all said that Mr Wonderful was a foreigner and that he would come to her door? In this light, even her discovery of Carl's secret reading habits became part of the wonderful workings of fate. If she had never found the magazines, there might have been no room to offer, no reason to bring him to her. Still, it was baffling that he could have known. Was he, too, psychic?

'You don't mind if I do a pendulum on you, do you? Just to be sure.'

Raphael stared at her. 'A pendulum? To be sure of what?'

She smiled evasively. 'Hold your hand out. It won't take a minute.' She took a small silver globe from her pocket and dropped it to hang from a chain over his obediently extended palm. 'Perfect. Keep still. Is this a good house for Raphael Sartis?'

Horrified, he snatched his hand away. 'A very good house indeed. I don't think there's any need to question that.'

'I decide to rent a room. An hour later, you ring on my door and ask if I have a room for rent. And you're foreign,' she added, as though that explained everything.

'You have something against foreigners?' S. could have warned him that he would be dealing with a lunatic.

'*Fiore d'amore*,' Fay warbled and looked at him expectantly. 'You've been to Naples? It needn't,' she added with the evident wish to encourage him, 'have been in this life.'

A cat insinuated itself between his legs and began to rub its body gently against his ankles while another crouched on the table, in leaping distance from his shoulder. The air thrummed with purrs of anticipation.

'Ah,' Raphael said in a faltering voice. 'Reincarnation. How very interesting. And were you Neapolitan in a previous life?'

It was apparent that she had only been waiting for him to ask. 'Sancia, Princess of Naples. That's from three of the best clairvoyants in London. That's why I'm living in this dump. When the man comes, the man from the south, he comes to this house. And here you are.'

'Here I am,' he said firmly. 'On the recommendation of your next-door neighbour. She didn't have a room, so she sent me here. Nothing psychic about it.'

'Ho-ho,' the porter interjected. Did he have nothing better to do with his time than eavesdropping? 'I don't even like pasta,' Raphael said hurriedly, covering the spasmodic twitch which the inner register always prompted. 'And I've never been to Naples.'

'Well, that's that, then.' Fay tried for a smile, and failed. 'More fool me. Forget I ever mentioned it, will you? I'll get you a bath-towel.'

The brusqueness of her tone did not deceive him. Poor friendless woman, he thought. What could S. have to fear from such a harmless eccentric? Some gesture of comfort was required. 'No,' he said. 'Don't go. I'm terribly sorry. I didn't mean to upset you. I may not be the man you're waiting for but I do think you're most – most– '

She had closed her eyes. 'Go on.'

It wasn't his day. He had done no more than put his arms around her shoulders when a shriek from the spirit register was followed by a crash of fists on the front door. A cry rang out that must have echoed down the full length of the street.

'Mummy, you've got to come quick! There's a sex maniac in the kitchen and he's assaulting Mrs Calman!'

'No such luck, eh,' Fay said as she popped a handful of pills into her mouth. 'Can't be too careful,' she added munching vigorously. 'I'm a walking magnet for other people's viruses.'

'But I don't –' She had gone, leaving him to the attentions of the sidling cats.

Lucy was not interested in her friend's new lodger. In her present state of mind, she would not have noticed if Fay had emerged from the kitchen with a knife sticking out of her ribs. She wanted solace. She wanted reassurance. She wanted to be told that Gareth Lloyd-Evans loved her. And, as the clock ticked lugubriously forward to ten o'clock and the cards were spread out for the fifteenth time, it became apparent she was not going to leave until that glaring falsehood had been dragged from Fay's lips. Max, long since overwhelmed by boredom, lay curled in the corner of the room on a heap of cushions. The cats sprawled along the back of the sofa, watching the cards unfold their dismal story with unblinking eyes.

'But he does love me. I know it. I've always known it,' Lucy sobbed. 'If only I hadn't mentioned the letter so soon. Oh God, Fay, I'll kill myself if you can't see something.'

'You won't be the only one if I have to go on doing this for much longer.' Yawning, she shuffled the pack. 'Carl hasn't come to pick up his stuff. He ought to have been here by seven.'

'He won't show up until it's late enough for you to be worried sick and take him in,' Lucy said perceptively. 'There he is. Not Carl,' she added irritably as Fay's eyes flickered to the door. 'Gareth. Look.' Her polished nail tapped the card with obnoxious familiarity. 'Ohh!' squeaked Lucy. 'It's just like an electric current running through me when I touch it. What's he thinking?'

Fay stared down, willing the wretched man to feel a twinge of remorse. It was, she thought, the least he could do, after all the hours she had spent on trying to make Lucy realise the hopelessness of the relationship. But all she could see was Carl, homeless, helpless, alone. Tears filled her eyes.

'Well?'

She blinked the tears back before Lucy could suppose she was shedding them for Gareth. 'Nothing.'

'Nothing?' Lucy's eyes were huge and dreadful in their demand.

'Nothing.'

Groaning, Raphael rolled on to his back, roused into wakefulness by the sound of ungoverned grief. The bed was hard as a board and moonlight streamed through the unguarded windows. Above his head, the ceiling creaked and shuddered in protest against the reverberations of a steady and resolute bounding on the floor above. The kitchen light blazed briefly in his eyes as the door flew open to show a tall blond-headed boy staring in at the bed. 'Oh shit,' the young man said. 'So she did mean it.' Unable to think of an adequate response to this, Raphael did his best to give an impression of a man who was soundly asleep. Through half-closed eyes, he watched the boy come towards him, bend over him and then drop by the bed as if in prayer. Raphael held his breath as he dropped still lower, sliding his thin body under the bed before, after a brief scuffling, he emerged empty-handed, flushed and with tears in his eyes. 'She's fucking done it this time,' he said heavily. Then he rose to his feet, wiped his eyes and walked out of the room. His disappearance was followed by three shrieks.

'Carl!'

'Gareth!'

'Mummy!'

'No peace for the wicked, is there, old chap,' tittered the voice of the spirit register. 'And you haven't even started causing trouble yet.'

Raphael chose not to answer. The weight of so much human misery was crushing. What business had S. with ordering him to add to it?

What if he didn't? Petrified, he waited for the register's response to this piece of blasphemy. None came: it seemed that even the porter was not above an occasional lapse of vigilance.

Well then, what? Wasn't he one of the old originals, the first six who had laid down the laws? S. would have to allow him his right to a personal interview if he demanded it. He wasn't a nobody. He would simply state that he had elected to exercise his powers as a free agent and to take the consequences.

And go straight into the Hundredth System? He shut his eyes. No. Their happiness wasn't worth it. Not at that price. This was his last chance, and he would be crazy not to take it. S. had, in his way, been generous. He hadn't been asked to destroy a city or to spread disease. The evil expected of him would barely amount to a speck on the eternal calendar. Others seemed to find it so easy. The porter would probably have had the whole of Selena Street blown up by anonymous terrorists and been back in the Eighteenth System by now. Raphael clenched his fists.

'Exterminate,' he said hopefully. 'My name is legion. Even as the grass, they shall wither. If you can't be bad, be nothing.' It was no use. S. had offered him the chance to have compassion struck out of his characteristics list, and he had been foolish enough to think he could keep it and control it. And here he lay, struck down by it, a helpless, almost human victim. Keeping compassion had been a fatal error, but he had known that as soon as he kissed Lily Tremain.

Lily! Lily, who was all ready to fall in love with him, if she had not done so already! Lily Tremain was his salvation. One human wish was all that was required by law to break his bondage to S. Lily must wish him to stay with her, condemn him to ordinary human status. It was as simple as that.

16

Harriet, fearful of having her car spotted by the vigilant Miss Press, had parked around the corner before taking up her post. She had, since she intended to do well in her exams, brought along her book on Blake's symbolism, but her attention had been devoted entirely to the drab range of windows behind which Victor toiled devotedly at his book. Poor Victor. The light in his study had burned bright and unflickering since her arrival. Not for a moment, although she had rather hoped he might, had he strolled to the window to refresh his mind with a glance at the dull dark trees of Selena Street. He had, on the other hand, strolled into his kitchen several times and bent over the corner in which she knew the fridge stood. Patiently, Harriet watched his silhouette move across the blind. She was glad that he had not forgotten to eat. She hoped that he had noticed and perhaps partaken of the cake which she had thoughtfully placed there. She felt a bit guilty about the cake. It was one of her mother's home-baked fruit ones, of which she had promised to eat a slice every night to keep up her strength. Large and comely herself, Harriet's mother made no distinction between her daughter's well-nourished limbs and those of an anorexic. Harriet, conscious of the barb in Victor's affectionate tributes to her as his pretty little pudding and Harry the Podge, had for the last two weeks confined herself to a diet of apples and yoghurt from which Harry the Sylph must surely one day emerge.

All was quiet on the southern front of the street as the silhouette showed itself again upon the kitchen blind. It did not bend but faced the window. Harriet trembled with excitement. Should she show herself, proclaim her love, or should she keep to the safe black shadow of the tree? She took one hesitant step forward and shrank back again in a flutter of nervousness as the blind shot up. She heard him open the window. He was leaning out and the branches hid him from her. Drawn to the light like a moth, she leaned forward, and froze. There at the window, naked as Eve and proud as Lucifer, stood Sally-Anne Quinlan, her long red hair flaming like a beacon in the night. Behind her, wrapped in the very same yellow towel in which he had lovingly swaddled Harriet after her bath that morning, stood Victor Grenderlyn. Harriet's eyes misted over, but not before she had registered the final and most bitter detail. Sally-Anne's fine white American teeth were crunching down on a slice of her mother's fruit cake when she made a face and held it away from her face.

'Yuk!' she said. 'It's stale.' And she dropped it over the window sill. 'It's your lucky night, mice,' said Sally-Anne.

'And mine, my pretty,' said Victor and he pulled the window shut.

The stones of Miss Press's garden rockery gleamed whitely. She had only to put a hand over the low wall to take one and hurl it at the treacherous Victor's window and, with any luck, she could knock out one of Sally-Anne's brilliant white teeth. Harriet was a gentle girl who had been known to shed tears at the sight of a dead butterfly, but the sweetness of her disposition had never been more severely tested. She grasped one of the stones, she rolled its smooth weight in her hand, she gazed with longing and hatred at the veiled window of Victor's kitchen. She swung back her arm. And let it drop. What if she hit Victor? Even now, confronted with the inescapable evidence of his treachery, she could not bring herself to take the risk of wounding him. Sadly, she replaced the stone in Miss Press's rockery and sat down on the wall, empty of every feeling except grief and humiliation. She had made a fool of herself. She had set her sights too high. She had dreamed of becoming a professor's wife when she had done no more than join the queue of giggling students who visited the Selena Street house for private tuition. He probably told every one of them how lonely he was and how happy she made him. Only she had been fool enough to believe him and to think that fat, frumpy Harriet Smith, who didn't know an auxesis from an asyndeton, could be the chosen object of his love.

'Looks like there are two of us down on our luck tonight, gorgeous.'

Harriet blanched as she saw the pale young man coming purposefully towards her across the road.

'Aren't you going to say hello?' He sat down beside her and held out a cigarette. 'You shouldn't be doing this, you know,' he said. 'There's no trade on Selena Street. But you're too good for King's Cross, aren't you, darling?'

'You needn't imagine everybody is as disgusting as yourself.' She felt in her pocket for her car keys. She didn't want to move away too suddenly. He did look most peculiar. He might be violent.

'Two lonely people,' Carl said, unperturbed. 'Two lonely, lonely people. Unloved. Unwanted. Rejects of society –'

'Oh, shut up,' Harriet said crossly. She felt better for seeing somebody who was clearly in a far more debased state than her own. 'Speak for yourself. You certainly don't speak for me.' She pulled down her skirt, pushed her hair out of her eyes and stood up. 'I'm going home and so should you.'

'Nowhere to go,' said Carl. 'Unless you don't mind putting me up. I won't bite. I won't even try to screw you unless you want me to. I just don't fancy a night on the pavement.'

She looked at him uncertainly. 'You must have some money.'

'Yeah.' He laughed. 'Only Fay's such a hooping genius she forgot that the bank's closed at night and I don't have a service card. She's thrown me out. Didn't even bother to say why.'

In every fibre of her being, Harriet wanted to walk away and leave him to Fay, whoever she might be. But, without understanding why, she stayed where she was.

'Just one night, then,' she said. 'You can sleep on one of the sofas in the common-room if I let you in. But just this once.'

Carl looked at her with his wonderful shining eyes. 'Gorgeous,' he said, 'you're an angel.'

17

Raphael sighed with pleasure and rolled over on to his side. It had seemed the least he could do to find a bed for the wretched young man whose room he now occupied. It was a good start. He felt better already.

'Wasted energy,' snapped the register. 'Do I need to remind you of the way you're meant to use it?'

'Meant? I'm still a free agent.'

'Up to a point. So long as you're prepared to take the consequences.'

'Of making things worse.'

'Worse for them is better for you, sweetie. When were you born, yesterday?'

He closed his eyes. 'I want to talk to S.'

'He's busy.'

'I'll talk to him later.'

'Permanently busy.'

'I'll talk to Opal, then.'

'Opal's not doing any earth-dealings. He's busy on combustion in the twenty-fifth.' The porter's voice grew suddenly servile. 'The Master's on the internal line. He's sending Fœdora.'

'Thanks,' Raphael said bitterly. 'I feel so much better for hearing that.'

'Joke?' the register said. The line went dead. Connections cut. Raphael got out of bed, pulled on his trousers and a clean shirt, drew the bedcover neatly up over the crumpled sheets and sat down to wait.

An hour passed before Fay Calman knocked at his door. 'Are

you awake, Mr Sartis? There's a lady here for you. I told her you were sleeping, but she just said she'd stay until you woke up.' She dropped her voice. 'I thought you said you wouldn't be bringing friends in. I don't like having strangers in the house. It upsets the atmosphere.'

'I'm terribly sorry about this. She won't be staying long.' He opened the door.

'Raphael, my dear! I had no idea you'd be asleep at this hour. I just wanted to be sure you'd settled in. I've had such trouble finding you, but your kind neighbours were very helpful.'

Raphael took the black-gloved hand which was languidly extended to him. 'Fœdora, you look wonderful.' She did. He couldn't really think that there had been any need for her to assume the appearance of a Russian princess for a simple business visit, but he was bound to admit that it was vastly preferable to most of her disguises.

'What delicious creatures,' Fœdora murmured, bending to trail a glove over Dora's grizzled back and to scratch Colette delicately between her ears. The cats squirmed. 'Dear thing,' said Fœdora, swinging Dora up into the air and neatly avoiding her flailing legs and outstretched claws. 'I do so dote on cats.'

'So you don't mind fleas?' Fay said pleasantly, a remark which won Dora instant release. 'Can I make you some tea, or coffee, Mrs –'

'Oh please, all my friends call me Fœdora. It's so sweet of you, but I never take stimulants. They don't agree with my metabolism. If you did happen to have such a thing as a little vinegar?'

'Sure, if you don't mind having what's left in the pickled onion jar.' Fay tipped out a tumblerful, licked her fingers and held it out. 'Marvellous for the arteries. I'm so glad to see someone else with a good sense of their health.'

If Fœdora had hoped to disconcert, as Raphael suspected from his knowledge of her love of practical jokes, she concealed her disappointment admirably. More to her credit, she drank the vinegar, draining it in a single gulp before she answered. 'Oh, I live on it. I always tell my friends, forget the champagne, don't bother with the oysters. Just be sure to put a big flask of vinegar by my bed. And look at me before you laugh, I tell them.' Fœdora stroked her smooth white cheek. 'Not bad for sixty-five, would you say?'

'Sixty-five!' gasped Fay, who had put her down for a well-kept thirty. 'And all through vinegar!'

'All through vinegar,' Fœdora said gravely. 'Well, Raphael dear, are you ready to show me your room? You don't mind my dropping in, do you?' She flashed a dazzling smile at Fay. 'It will be a very short visit, Mrs Calman. Just a promise I had to keep. I always keep my word, don't I, Raphael dear?'

Glumly, he nodded. 'Always.'

'Well, I'll leave you to it,' Fay said reluctantly. She wanted to know more of the beautiful visitor's cosmetic secrets, but it was apparent that none were to be forthcoming. 'I don't eat breakfast myself, Mr Sartis, but if you want to make yourself some coffee tomorrow, the kettle's on the side and the cups are in the sink. You don't need to put the cup away. There isn't anywhere to put it. Just drop it back on the pile.'

'It's awfully rude of me,' Fœdora murmured, 'but I couldn't help noticing the dearest little white shelf over in the corner. But I'm sure it has some other function.'

'But there isn't – how on earth could I have missed seeing that before?' cried Fay, bewildered. 'My sight isn't that bad. Good God!'

It gave Raphael a moment of spiteful pleasure to see Fœdora's involuntary shudder of pain at the reference to the power who in their world was known only as Him. Serve the stupid creature right, never missing a chance to exhibit her powers. It had, he was ready to admit, been impressively done. She had even had the foresight to arrange a spider's web on the shelf's supporting bracket in order to blend it into the general aspect of neglect.

'Dear Raphael. I knew you'd appreciate it,' Fœdora purred as she coiled herself on his bed with feline grace and let her coat fall back from slender, startlingly white shoulders. 'Well, I couldn't bear to think of you living in such squalor and not even able to keep a cup on a shelf. One must do what one can for one's friends.' She glanced at the grimy window with its curtain of nettles. 'Do you think I might be allowed to –'

'No, I don't,' Raphael said sharply. 'S. didn't send you in to do a home-decorating job. And I'm sure I don't need to remind you of his attitude to frivolous use of powers.'

Fœdora's eyes widened mockingly. 'You're telling me?' She took out a small black cigar and lit it as she propped her back against the cupboard which also served as the bedhead. 'I must say,' she said through a cloud of smoke, 'Sartis is a great improvement on Clegg. S. never told me you were going to be such a pretty boy.' She stretched out a languid hand to touch his arm. 'Good enough to eat. I almost wish this wasn't a business visit.'

Mindful of the fact that he was temporarily dependent on Fœdora's goodwill, Raphael assumed an appropriate look of regret. 'Who couldn't wish it otherwise, with such a ravishing visitor?'

Fœdora sighed as she looked down the length of her body to her elegant legs before she drew them up towards her, allowing him a glimpse of lace and black stocking-tops. 'It's so long since I had any simple pleasures. Not that working with S. isn't enormously exciting,' she added hurriedly. 'It's only that there isn't any time left for myself. It never stops. I had to go to the Hundredth System before I came here, just to check productivity, and, well, you must have heard what it's like. I was only dropping in and I can tell you, my dear, I felt absolutely drained by the time I left.' Her narrow eyes never left his face as she flicked a spiral of ash into the air. 'You do know what you're in for if you disobey us, my sweet? It really isn't fun in the Hundredth System.' She touched his arm again. 'S. has always had a soft spot for you. There's no limit to what he'd give you if you'd only learn to behave sensibly.'

Raphael smiled. 'No limit?'

'Within reason, of course,' Fœdora said gently. 'You've run up a fair-sized debt on your past histories. But S. told me himself that he's prepared to overlook a great deal. And there is another point.'

'Yes?'

'If you don't do the job properly, someone else will.'

'Unlikely. Selena Street's not important.'

'S. doesn't like clairvoyants. They interrupt the schedules.'

'And the others? Can you honestly tell me it makes any difference to S. whether their lives are destroyed or not?'

Her stare was blank. 'Any difference? Raphael, these creatures are the termites of the galaxy. They're the most susceptible to our treatment of all the planets in the Third System.'

'And the most advanced.'

'Technologically. Spiritually, they're in regression.' Fœdora smiled. 'Every little bit of work helps at a time like this. And we all know you can do it. S. has tremendous faith in you.'

'Nevertheless,' he said, 'I'm exercising the right to use my powers as I choose.'

She lay very still. 'And how might you choose to employ them?'

'As my namesake did. For the granting of wishes. The fulfilment of dreams.'

'And you think that will give the termites a chance to get into the A. system?' She grinned. 'Wishes breed avarice, my dear, and we all know how A. feels about greed. Can't bear it. You'll be handing your new friends to us on a plate.'

'I'm not in control of the longer-term issues. I want to do some good here for a change. Perhaps S. even had that in mind. He did mention *La Peau* –'

Fœdora yawned. 'Well? Remember what happened to Raphael de Valentin. If he mentioned it, my dear, he meant it for a warning. Still, I've done my best.' She stood up and drew her coat over her shoulders. 'Such a pity. We really thought you'd started to improve when we saw you taking the flowers from the grave.'

He kissed her ice-cold cheek. 'I'll see you to the door.'

She shuddered. 'That woman's there. The less I see of earth-people the better, thank you very much. It's bad enough being named after one without having to speak to them. Horrid little things.' She pulled the coat tightly around her. 'Any messages?'

He thought. 'Yes. You can tell the porter there's a fault on the register. It's giving me dreadful headaches.'

'That, sweetheart, is going to be the least of your problems,' said Fœdora. 'Don't say I didn't warn you.' She bent her head, folded her arms and recited the messengers' creed of faith with impressive rapidity. The head and body disappeared at once. The feet remained planted on the floor.

'Must have left a word out,' said a voice very close to his ear. 'Would you be a dear and give them a kick?'

Briefly, he toyed with the possibility of keeping them for blackmail purposes. It would, on the other hand, be difficult to explain their presence to Mrs Calman.

'I'll get the porter to turn the register off,' Fœdora said.

'You'll have to do better than that.' He put his shoe on one of the feet and pressed down.

'Bastard!' Fœdora screamed. 'All right. I'll tell S. to give you a month's probation. Now will you do it?'

'Anything for a pretty foot,' he said as he kicked them. They rose neatly into the air, stood on tiptoe – and vanished.

A moment later, Fay tapped at his door. 'I've made some

coffee and tipped out the other pickled-onion jar. I was just wondering if your friend might – oh, she's gone already,' she said sadly as he opened the door. 'I was going to ask if I could take a look at her aura. I just couldn't get it in the kitchen light. I'm very good on auras.' ·

'I'm sure you are,' Raphael said nervously as he saw Fay's eyes probing the air above his head. 'Fœdora particularly asked me to say how sorry she was not to have had time to stay and talk to you.'

'She did?' Fay's eyes brightened. 'Well, I'm always here. Tell her I'll give her a free reading. I'd really like to get a look at her previous lives, if she'd let me. Sixty-five,' she added wonderingly. 'I can't get over it. I'm going to start drinking vinegar tomorrow. What I wouldn't give to look like that!'

Raphael smiled. 'It could be achieved, if that's your dearest wish.'

'Don't make me laugh,' Fay said bitterly.

'I don't want to,' he said. 'Is it? Tell me. I'm curious.'

'So I see,' Fay said. 'My dearest wish? You can laugh if you like. It doesn't bother me. I'd like to spend an evening with Charlie Everest.'

'The television policeman?'

'Well, it's only a wish,' Fay said. 'That's half the fun, isn't it, the wishing?'

'And if it came true?' He looked at her intently. 'You'd be happy?'

'Ecstatic,' Fay said. 'Just ecstatic. And on that pleasant note, I'll go to bed. Mind to shut the door if you don't want Dora on your pillow.'

Spreading happiness on Selena Street would, he thought, be an enjoyable business. And since Lily Tremain's wish would certainly involve him, he could look forward to his fair share of the pleasures in store.

'And after that?' the register hissed. But Raphael was already asleep.

The Granting
of Wishes

1

Sally-Anne had gone and Victor Grenderlyn, spared the necessity of having to offer physical proof of his appreciation of her magnificent body for a third time in nine hours, lay alone in his bed with a familiar mixture of regret and relief. The process of conquest had lost none of its charm; the demonstration of his prowess now frequently overshadowed it. It had occurred to him at some point in the early hours of the morning that a man of his age might very well be killed by too much sexual exertion. Was it time to consider giving Sally-Anne the push in favour of a less demanding girl? In a week or two, perhaps. Not quite yet. She was, after all, so excellent a mate in her brisk unemotional atheleticism and in her refusal to give any value to the declarations of love which were his habitual way of expressing gratitude. He could almost say he did love her, if only for her detachment.

Whereas Harriet – Grenderlyn moaned and buried his head in the pillow as he remembered the round anguished face he had seen gazing up at the window last night. He had done his best. He had almost dragged Sally-Anne away from the window – God only knew what Miss Press would have to say about that exhibition – but he was fearfully conscious that he had been too late and too slow. Poor little Harriet – Grenderlyn dashed a sentimental tear from his eye as he racked his mind for something to comfort her. Could he spare his splendid, second, review copy of Symonowsky's *The Eighteenth-Century World of Poetic Imagery* (cunningly secured by the ancient ruse of claiming that the first copy had failed to arrive and a hint to the publicity department that his review would be most favourable)? A £40 book was worth £15 in the second-hand bookshop, and £15 was more than Grenderlyn considered Harriet's restored happiness to be worth. His eye moved on, to the pile of copies of a paper he had given to the Swedenborg Institute on Blake's prophetic themes. Just the thing, and so much more personal. He seized the top one and wrote above the title in a fine flourishing script: 'With fondest thoughts to my dear little Gretel.' He paused. It was Gretel, wasn't it, who had made the gingerbread house? The tactful allusion to her cake-making abilities must surely appease and suggest, however disingenuously, that he had partaken of and enjoyed her offering before she saw it consigned to the earth.

Ten to eleven. Grenderlyn rose and took himself (his head was carefully lowered as he passed the mirror) into the bathroom. From here, after purging his body with cold water to dash away any lingering memories of the night, he went into his study for the proposed continuation of his book.

Women were, as the wise ones knew, no more than Polyfilla to the gnawing emptiness of Grenderlyn's unrealised dream. What he yearned for, and what had so far cruelly eluded him, lay here and still untapped in the bowels of his new computer-system. All the riches of his knowledge lay ready and waiting to be transformed, miraculously, into a logical and finely articulated sequence. It had lain ready for what was becoming an embarrassing length of time. In the interim, what Grenderlyn seemed to be achieving, far less desirably, was a seedy notoriety of the kind he most dreaded. At one or two of the academic gatherings which he had recently attended, he had sensed that the smiles and kind words which greeted him were less genuine than the laughter which broke out, soft and deadly, behind his back. Expert butterfly of the social world that he was, Grenderlyn had never turned his head to look and to betray himself. He knew all too well that it was directed at him and that nothing is more injurious to a man's reputation than the visible mockery of his peers. His students worshipped him, but only by his book could he hope to attain to the kind of eminence he craved and honestly felt that he deserved.

Grenderlyn was one of that considerable school of ambitious men who, by a deft combination of ruthlessness, administrative skills and industry, succeed in rising to a position for which their brain has not thoroughly equipped them. His parents, a gentle and modest couple of retired music teachers, lived in West Finchley. Having little contact with the university world, they preferred to mix with their old friends and fellow-exiles from Lübeck and Hamburg, and were too proud of his success not to be puzzled by his evident discontent. The time had passed when they could hint hopefully at their desire for a grandchild. Dimly and uncomprehendingly, they understood that Victor's sense of the family and of continuity was not theirs. Things would be better, he always said, when he had finished his book. But when, they asked each other as their son privately asked himself, would that be? The old parents no longer dared to ask after its progress on his rare, and always too brief, visits.

They had, although they were unaware of it, inadvertently strayed dangerously near the truth during their son's last appearance and it was for this reason, although he did not care to admit it, that Grenderlyn had found excuses to stay away from them for longer than the customary month. They had, the father and son, been looking through an album of faded newspaper cuttings kept from the days when Anna Braun, now Mrs Josef Grenderlyn, had enjoyed some renown in her native Lübeck as an interpreter of Chopin.

'Always Chopin brought tears to their eyes when Anna played,' said Josef fondly as his wife came into the room. 'Even now, Mr and Mrs Rejt from downstairs were in tears when Anna played them the *Berçeuse* last Sunday.'

'Only because I had put too much pepper in the stew, Josef,' Anna said. 'You know how Victor hates it when we are sentimental.' She sighed as she looked at her son in his waistcoat and grey flannel suit, so English, so integrated, so indifferent to the past. She snapped the album of cuttings shut. 'You don't want to look at these. Eat some of the cake, Victor. You need to fill your cheeks out.' She clicked her tongue. 'That nice lady lodger of yours should be looking after you better.'

Grenderlyn shuddered. 'The less I have to do with Mrs Calman's cooking, the better. The only time she gave me a cup of coffee, the handle was covered with catfood. But tell me about the Chopin, mother. I'm curious.'

'You see,' Josef said happily. 'I told you the boy was interested.'

'Boy!' said Anna. 'At fifty-three, you call him a boy!' She smiled to soften the blow which had already registered its impact in Grenderlyn's acid smile. 'So why should you be curious?'

It was difficult to speak through a mouthful of chocolate cake, but years of academic dinners had made an expert of Grenderlyn. He chewed briskly, swallowed, and spoke. 'Why didn't you want to spread your wings a bit? Why not Liszt?'

'Liszt!' Anna's plump shoulders shook. 'He wants to know why I didn't play Liszt!'

Josef smiled benignly. 'Well, why didn't you?'

'Because I always understood my own limitations,' Anna said. 'To play Liszt, I would have needed the wings of an angel. I had very good wings, but they were the wings of a seagull, not an angel. My good sense was to know the difference and not to struggle for what I could never achieve.' She had looked at her son with what had seemed to him to be a clear-eyed indication that she recognised their shared predicament. 'So there you are.'

'No further questions,' Grenderlyn had faintly murmured. Shortly afterwards, he had made his excuses and departed, leaving his parents to wonder what they had done to distress him.

The distress had not yet left him. Every time since then, when he sat down to confront the flickering green lines of his indexes and cross-referenced slabs of potentially useful material, he was haunted by the sense of the yawning gap between his aspirations and his ability. The words, when they came, served only to emphasise the chasm's presence. Today, watching the hateful cursor flickering attentively before his eyes, he felt an overwhelming longing to smash the screen to bits. Instead, being the obedient slave to systems of logic, reason and rational behaviour, he sat grimly still, doing his best to ignore the fact that two hours had passed by with no more important fact coming into his mind than a profound longing for the telephone to ring and distract him from the course of duty.

It rang, at last, at 2.30.

'Not, I suppose, that it's of the slightest interest to you,' Miss Press said crisply, 'but there's a very interesting article about St Giles's church in the paper today. I popped it through your door, but I thought I'd let you know before Fay's cats get it. You might let me have it back when you've finished with it.'

'Thank you, Millicent. Very thoughtful of you,' Grenderlyn said meekly.

'Too busy to come in for a drink, I suppose?'

At this hour? Did she never stop? 'Afraid so. The book –'

'Still at it!' Miss Press's tone was rudely incredulous. 'I'm surprised you haven't given it up by now. What you need, my boy, is a bit of fresh air and some stiff exercise. Clean your brain cells out. You've not been looking yourself lately. Too much womanising.'

Impertinent old trout. 'Now, Millicent, you know I'm just a quiet bookish fellow –'

'I've known quieter monkey-houses,' Miss Press responded.

'You should hear what your tenant has to say about the cracks in her ceilings. You're not dropping books on those at three in the morning, I'll be bound. And you'd better tell your young lady-friends that they're not invisible from that kitchen window of yours. They may go in for that kind of thing in Germany, but we don't much care for it in Selena Street.'

'I know. I'm terribly sorry.'

'So you should be. And don't you give me any of that boys-will-be-boys nonsense. You're fifty-five.'

'Three,' he said furiously. 'And only just.'

'Give or take a year. Old enough to stop messing about with girls young enough to be your daughters.' Miss Press paused to soften her voice. She had a very precise sense of the limits to which bluntness could be taken. 'I've got that nice little Harry coming to supper here on Wednesday, so you might do her the favour of having a quiet night for a change. I don't suppose she knows the half of it.'

'And she's not going to,' Grenderlyn wheedled. 'I've known you far too long not to appreciate that you're the soul of tact.'

There was a pause while he waited anxiously for her reply. 'Why we let you get away with it beats me,' Miss Press said crossly. 'It's not your charm, I'll tell you that. And mind you get that hedge of yours cut. It's a disgrace to the street.'

Breathing heavily, Grenderlyn repaired to the bathroom in search of a Paracetamol. He was in the act of swallowing it when the telephone rang again. Blasted woman.

'I'll get the hedge cut first thing tomorrow, Millicent.'

'My goodness, *who* is Millicent? I never heard a man sound more terrified.'

'Hello, Francis,' Grenderlyn muttered. He wiped his forehead. It was all her fault. He could willingly have strangled her. Francis Wainwright was the producer of a lavish new series of programmes for Star Channel, who had been persuaded by a sequence of artfully arranged moves, a hint here, a whisper there and all orchestrated by Grenderlyn, that this was the man who was most ideally suited to chair the first four of them. He was not a man by whom Grenderlyn wished to be seen as a browbeaten cutter of hedges or, worse still, an object of mirth. 'Everything coming along well, is it?'

'Oh, fine, fine.' Francis was still howling with laughter. 'Sorry, what was that? I was just telling Mary. You certainly hide your lights under a bushel. We must get you down here to work on the orchard. Mary's been trying to find a man to prune the apple trees.'

'Really? I'm glad you rang, Francis. I've been drafting out the first three introductions,' Grenderlyn said rapidly. 'And I wanted to let you know that I think I've really caught the note we want. Informative, entertaining, plenty of popular appeal –'

'We won't be using them, Victor.'

He sat down and turned the computer off. 'I'm sorry?'

The director had apparently opted for a different format. A dual chair, male and female. Naturally, his thoughts had turned to couples. 'It's just a shame that you're a bachelor, Victor,' Francis said, but Grenderlyn could detect no shade of regret in his voice. His brain, always agile in a tricky situation, whirred like ticker-tape over the ways in which he might maintain this vital foothold in the world of communications.

'You said that John Sayle was leaving that programme on literary landscapes, didn't you, Francis? I had a few ideas about that the other day. It might be interesting to –'

'It's not going to work, Victor,' Francis said. 'I'm really sorry about this. The test run we did – it was a bit of a problem.'

'Problem?'

'Nothing personal. We just didn't feel you communicated with the camera. It's nothing unusual, but it does present difficulties. We have to attend to the ratings, you see, and, well, we just didn't feel you had the kind of personality that was going to affect them advantageously. OK Mary, I'm coming. I really appreciate all the work you've put into this, Victor. I want you to know that. Bye.'

'Bye – sod!' Grendel said bitterly as he replaced the telephone. 'Shit. Liar.' He pressed his hands tightly together, trying to calm himself. Somewhere out there in the grey corridors of Star Channel, a rejected female had found a way to take her revenge. It was not possible that he had – how had Wainwright put it? – failed to communicate with the camera. He, Grenderlyn, who could hold a lecture-room of students in the palm of his hand? Inconceivable.

Work was no longer possible. Fretfully, he strode up and down the narrow passages, too distracted to care when he knocked over and smashed the red-and-gold William de Morgan plate purchased for him the previous summer by Melitza Hadda, a moist-eyed and unusually determined student from Lebanon whose first lover he had unwittingly become.

Ignorant of the value of his broken gift, Grenderlyn kicked the fragments into a corner with all the contempt that he accorded to Melitza's letters. (She still wrote once a month, although he never answered.)

The bells of St Giles's began to chime, rehearsing for the matutinal concert of which Grenderlyn was in the habit of thankfully depriving himself with ear-plugs and closed windows. Returning to his study, he shut the door, glared at the computer and strode towards the window to close out the maddening sound.

He thought at first it was Harriet who was standing on the far side of his garden wall with her elbows propped on the top. A closer look showed a girl of greater height and slighter build. The hair was sunny blonde and the legs in little white shorts were long and brown. A slow, satisfied smile spread across Grenderlyn's face as he surveyed this delectable potential victim. She glanced up, so swiftly that he only just had time to adjust his face to the noble look of the thinker, drawing inspiration from the high scudding clouds. It was an expression which had a singular effect on impressionable young women. With his eyes studiously turned away from her, he withdrew and plucked from its peg the battered panama hat which, he had been told, gave him the aspect of a rakish poet. He donned it, smirked at the mirror, and turned back to the window.

The scene had changed. A young man, wearing a hat of which his own would look the most wretched parody, had appeared, gliding like a snake out of the Calman nettles. His trousers must be magic or his skin uncommonly thick, Grenderlyn thought, for no spasm of pain crossed his face as he slipped through the vicious jungle towards the wall and, with repulsive familiarity, kissed the girl's hand. He watched anxiously, his desire whetted by the unexpected appearance of a rival. Would she spurn him? Far from it. She leaned forward and clear as the bells of St Giles's, her voice rang up to the window.

'Have you met Grendel yet? The man who owns the house. The lady across the street was warning me about him. Apparently, he's the most terrible old lecher. He was up there a moment ago, leering at me.'

He shrank back into the shadows. Grendel? A terrible old lecher? Was that how Millicent described him behind his back? Was that the image which provoked the disquietingly audible titters at the staff table when he joined them for lunch? Sweat broke out on his forehead. 'A shame that you're a bachelor' . . . 'messing about with girls young enough to be your daughters.' Was this awful mockery the price of his years of freedom and pleasure? Grenderlyn was not a man who accorded any respect to deities or superstitions. He scorned the idea of retribution, but he wondered now, just for a moment, whether he was wrong to do so. Absolutely not, he decided, banishing the sad spectres of the multitude who bobbed before his eyes with Melitza Hadda at their head. It was, on the other hand, true that the taking of a wife would do much to restore his image as a respected pillar of the academic community. If he had a docile and complaisant spouse, Grenderlyn mused as he swept the shattered fragments of Melitza's plate into a piece of newspaper and tipped them into the bin, she would do things like this, the small and mundane tasks he so disliked. She would prepare meals for him in his study. She would deal with all those ex-students who assumed that he was still uniquely theirs by virtue of a two-week liaison. She would decorously grace his side at those vital functions where to be uncompromisingly single, neither widowed nor divorced, could all too easily suggest inadequacy or a dubious morality. Yes. The time had come for him to take a wife.

Harriet.

Grenderlyn started. Had he thought that? Why Harriet? A nice enough little girl and full of affection, but did that equip her for the role of wife to a man who was destined one day, with luck, to become chancellor of the university? *Harriet?*

Why not?

Grenderlyn's head was beginning to ache. It was absurd, and yet, now that the notion had lodged itself in his head, he found it curiously attractive. She could cook. She was malleable and young. She looked, when she was happy, as pretty as a flower-garden and he had no reason to suppose that she would ever look anything but happy when she was married to him. 'Harriet,' he said aloud and felt strangely at peace with the idea. He turned on the computer. His mind was suddenly quickening with the sense of what he had to say. Rapidly and confidently, his hands began to move over the keys.

'What are you smiling at?' Lily asked as Raphael's face suddenly spread into a beam of pleasure. 'Has your headache gone? Poor you, I'm not surprised you had one with all those people coming and going last night.'

'Gone as if it never was as soon as I look at you,' Raphael said happily.

'Oh,' Lily said, pleased. 'That's nice. I do like compliments.'

'Good,' said Raphael. 'Because I intend you to be paid a great many.' He took her hand again. 'But I want you to do one thing for me in return. Will you tell me after dinner tonight what it is that you want most in the world?'

'Why? Don't tell me that you can make dreams come true?' She pulled her hand away and shaded her eyes, staring at him. 'You are the most unusual person, Mr Sartis. I'd almost believe it if you told me you could.'

'Lily, you are so pretty.' He leant forward to kiss her. 'Don't make fun of me. Tell me if you like me.'

She nodded, bright-eyed. 'Very much. Even though I hardly know you . . . Stop it, Raphael. That man's room looks straight down on us.'

Reluctantly, he released her. 'I think Professor Grenderlyn has too much on his mind to think about us any more.'

'How can you possibly know?'

He laughed. 'Let's just say I have a secret source of knowledge. I'll call for you at eight.'

When she had gone, he propped his back against the wall, looking up at the lavender sky of early evening. Unquestionably, he had made the right decision. He was beginning to feel almost human.

2

There was a visitor in Fay's kitchen, a black-haired man with a rollicking laugh and a body which threatened destruction to the small chair on which he was uncomfortably perched. Squeezing past the fridge in the hope of gaining his bedroom door before being detected on his way back from the garden tryst, Raphael realised he was already under surveillance.

'Taking a look at the estate?' the visitor inquired. 'You Mr Surteess, yes?'

'Sartis,' said Fay. 'Raphael, meet Spiro Vathos, a very old friend of mine.'

Raphael's hand was gripped and wrung with a vigour which, while seemingly well-intended, caused him discreetly to flex his fingers and make sure they were still intact.

'French,' said Spiro, looking him in the eye. 'I don't like the French, but I hope I like you.'

'Sure you will, Spiro,' Fay said. 'I did the cards on him last night. He's OK.'

'You did the cards?' said Spiro. 'Fay, you promise me last month you stop all this nonsense.'

'Nonsense to those too dumb to believe in it,' Fay said amiably.

Sprio laughed and tapped the side of his head with a wink at Raphael. 'Crazy. You don't mind living in a madhouse? One crazy lady. Good heart, though.' He pushed a chair back. 'Siddown, Mr Surteess. Drink.' He poured a tumbler of evil-looking black liquid from an unmarked bottle. 'Special-brew wine.'

'If you happen to like brimstone,' said Fay, pouring it back again. 'You want me in the courts for killing my tenant?'

Spiro shrugged his massive shoulders. 'You don't know nothing about wine, Fay. It's good *mavro*. So, you paid her money yet? Sorry to be asking, but our friend here isn't so quick at business.'

Raphael smiled, thankful to have been spared the wine. 'I think Mrs Calman – Fay – has the making of an excellent business woman.'

'Raphael,' said Fay. 'I like you. This man credits all women with the brains of sheep. Eighteen years I've been looking after myself and he still doesn't think I can be trusted to read a gas bill without his help.'

'I don't think it,' said Spiro. 'I know it. I keep telling her she needs to marry me, let me look after the business for her. She don't listen. Me, I learnt about business the hard way.'

'Oh-oh,' sighed Fay. 'He's off.'

'Lemme tell you about myself, Mr Surteess,' said Spiro, leaning towards Raphael with a confiding wink. 'Thirty years ago, I come here from Athens. I no speak the language easy like I do now. I no have nothing, Mr Surtees, nothing but hope. I sleep on the pavements –'

'What about your Aunt Maria?' Fay broke in with a broad smile at Raphael.

'I sleep on the pavements,' Sprio repeated calmly. 'I live on a crust of bread a day, but all the time I am thinking.' He tapped his forehead again. 'Very busy in here. I take job as porter, as cleaner, work, work, all the day, all the night to make money.'

'Spiro, I'm sure Mr Sartis doesn't want –'

'I like him to know how I come to be good businessman,' Spiro said irritably. 'How he going to understand if you keep interrupting? Many years, many many years, I struggle – stuggle – until I have enough money to buy little brokedown building. I do it up nice. Work, work, work. I sell –', he pinched his fingers in the air, 'so. Nice profit. I buy next little brokedown building. Mr Surteess, you know what I planning to buy this week?'

A building seemed a logical guess.

Spiro beamed, showing an impressive mine of gold fillings. 'Bigger than building. I buy property site for two hundred flats, and when I finish, I sell half a million each. But I never forget the crust of bread. And always I try to help my friends.'

'That's true,' said Fay. 'He may look like a bear, but you'll never meet a kinder man.'

Spiro spread his hands. 'She talks like this and when I ask her to marry me, she laughs. You married man, Mr Surteess?'

'It's all right, Spiro,' said Fay. 'It's my next-door neighbour he's chasing, not me. Anyway, you know I've set my heart on Charlie Everest.'

'And you think a film star's going to set his heart on this?' Spiro waved at a row of half-empty catfood tins on the table. 'When you get the house clean, maybe.'

'I'm not joking,' Fay said. 'Am I, Raphael? Didn't I tell you my wish?'

He nodded. It seemed to him that Mr Vathos was well suited to the task of looking after this pleasantly chaotic woman, but his was only the role of the granter of wishes. 'You're sure that's what you want?'

'Is she sure!' Spiro said. 'Five years, and I've never known her miss his programme. She tell you how she went to the Savoy when he came to London and how she wait four hours to see him when he's gone out the back way?'

'Oh, shut up, Spiro,' Fay muttered.

'No,' Raphael said. 'She didn't tell me.' He stood up. 'I have to change my clothes, if you'll excuse me.'

Shutting the door behind him, he sat down on his bed and closed his eyes for a moment, wondering how he could most convincingly bring Mr Everest into her life and why, of all the things she might have chosen to make her happy, she had opted for such an unlikely source of joy. Sighing, he pressed his hands to his forehead. Yes, that was the way she would find most credible. Next door, the telephone rang and Raphael started to strip off his shirt. He had done his good deeds for the day; now he could look forward to Lily and his reward.

Fay went to answer it and Spiro listened, fascinated as he always was by the speed with which she changed from a gentle, easy-going woman who seemed to have nothing more important on her mind than the next cup of coffee, to a tough operator, selling her skills as ruthlessly as a commodities broker.

'Hi. Fine. I told you to get back to me this morning. I wanted to tell you not to let them have more than a day to make their minds up. Otherwise it's going straight to Fidelity.' Her voice changed. 'You what! Yes, you're right. I'm surprised. So he just called you out of the blue five minutes ago? Very interested! You're a clever girl, Mary. Yeah – yeah, keep him on the hook. Friday's good. About four o'clock. No, I can handle it on my own. Just get him round here. We'll talk tomorrow. Bye – shooting sugar balls!' She came back to the table and sat down bolt upright, staring into space. 'Pour me out of some of that brimstone brew of yours, Spiro.'

'That was your agent?' He couldn't work out whether she was pleased or not. 'You got a new deal?' Fay shook her head before she swallowed the dark wine in one gulp. 'Not bad for a lady who says she doesn't drink, Mr Surteess,' he said as Raphael came back into the room. 'Hey, what you looking at him like that for, Fay? You got something against pink shirts? Why you act so funny?'

'Charlie Everest just rang my agent,' she said. 'He called my new script in. And he wants to come and see me to talk about it.'

She did not look as pleased as Raphael had expected. 'Well,' he said. 'What a coincidence.'

'Isn't it?'

Spiro broke what was beginning to be an uncomfortable silence with his big easy laugh. 'So what you going to say now, Fay, now you get to meet this man of your dreams? You want me to come along and tell him how you watch all his programmes?'

'I do not.' She looked round at him with a dazed smile. 'Oh Spiro, you don't know what this means to me.'

'Don't I?' He glanced away.

'Boy, oh boy. Can you imagine! Charlie Everest sitting in here, begging for my script – clothes!'

'Maybe you wear the red shirt and blue jeans I see you in last week,' said Spiro. Fay's mouth twisted with contempt.

'No way.' She bent to scrabble in the cupboard under the sink. 'Where did I put those Dior sandals? Black sandals, blue silk dress with splits up the side – oh hell!' she said with a sudden wail. 'What am I going to do if he doesn't fancy me?'

Spiro put his arms round her, wrapping her close. 'You're beautiful. Any man fancy you.'

'I'm old.'

'In the prime.' He kissed her on top of her head. 'You better go, Mr Surteess, or your lady-friend get angry waiting.'

'I'm going.' Shuffling past them with averted eyes, he felt like a criminal. This was one wish which he was already regretting having granted.

'Your bill, *monsieur*.'

No wonder they hid it away and tried to sweeten it with an offering of chocolates, he thought ruefully as he glanced down at a folded sheet of paper on which the only figure to be presented was a far from insignificant total. It was as he had remembered: arrogance, in this world, had always been thought to be a guarantee of quality.

'Is it awful?' Lily did not look as though she would much mind if it was as she helped herself to the larger of the two chocolates. 'Lovely. Do you want the other one?'

'It's yours.'

A chocolate-fed Lily was a pretty spectacle of contentment. The waiter bent to gather the payment and paused to smile. '*Madame* has enjoyed her meal?'

She shook her head. 'He paid. Ask him.'

'Very satisfactory,' Raphael said coldly. He didn't like the way the waiter was grinning at Lily.

'You do have the funniest expressions,' she said. 'Very satisfactory. I thought it was amazing.' She propped her chin on her hands to gaze at him. 'I like treats. Can we do it again?'

'As often as you like.'

'But you'll be going back to Paris soon. Won't you?' Her mouth kept its smile, but her eyes were anxious.

'It depends.'

'How long will you stay? Here, I mean. Just out of curiosity.'

She had stopped smiling. He was almost sure of her now. 'I said. It depends.'

'On what?'

He leant forward to touch her face. 'Among other things, on you.'

'What other things?' Since the restaurant was only a half-hour's walk away and the night was, unusually, almost tropical in its heat, they were strolling back under Lily's guidance across Camomile Hill. They had come over the crest and the lights of Selena Street lay below them, yellow and kindly. 'Well?' Lily fanned a moth away from her face with a branch of flowering elder. 'What else?'

'Nothing that matters.'

'So if I choose you to stay for my wish, you will?'

He caught her hands in his and pushed away the branch to look at her face. She was laughing. 'I could,' he said earnestly. 'But only if that was your wish.'

She moved restlessly, not wanting to spoil the evening with too much gravity. 'Doesn't grass smell lovely after a hot day! Like hayfields. I do sometimes wish I didn't live in the city, don't you?'

He was irritated by her frivolity. 'That's not what you wish.'

Her eyes gleamed like a pretty witch's in the dark as she narrowed them and tossed her hair back. 'So you want to know what I really, really want?' She put her arms round his neck and pressed her mouth to his. 'There,' she murmured. 'Now can you guess what I'm wishing? And don't you dare do it by reading my mind or I'll wish for something you wouldn't like.'

'Why would you think I could read your mind?'

She leant back in his arms to look at him with a clear, untroubled gaze. 'I'll tell you why. You knew my name before I told you it.'

He smiled. 'Not very difficult when you had all your morning post sitting on the kitchen table.'

'Oh,' Lily said, disappointed. 'That's a shame. I was rather impressed.'

More of a shame still, in Raphael's view, was the fact that she had distracted him at the crucial moment. All that he could see in her thoughts now was the thought of movement of some kind. Still, she had wished as she kissed him. It promised well.

'Race you down the hill and the first one back to Selena Street wins,' cried Lily, flying away down the slope in long coltish bounds. Following, he thought he heard the sharp crackle of

Fœdora's laughter in the soft rush of the wind. But she had wished, surely she had wished, for him to stay. He had nothing to fear.

3

'Oh please, Miss Press, I really couldn't –'

'Rubbish,' Milly said, as she refilled their glasses. 'If I can, you can, and do stop looking at the window, dear. If Grendel wants to see you, he's only got to walk across the street.'

'Sorry.' With an effort, Harriet wrenched her gaze back to the cheerful blue-and-white kitchen which also served as Miss Press's dining-room. 'I suppose you've known quite a lot of them,' she said, pushing aside the overladen plate of cheese and biscuits which had been placed in front of her, despite her feeble remonstrations.

'Of who, dear? Coffee?'

'Please. Just black would be lovely. Of Victor's girl-friends.'

Millicent looked at her thoughtfully. 'Quite a few. I used to call them the Kleenex brigade. All those tissues. Helen, or was it Mary, went through a whole box of them one night when he wouldn't answer the bell. Poor little thing. I put her to sleep in the spare room but she was back over there at dawn, hammering on the door and wearing her voice out. What you all see in him –' She sighed. 'It beats me.'

'You said yourself he was kind,' Harriet said, stung by the scornful note with which Miss Press spoke of her beloved. 'And he's a brilliant teacher.'

'I dare say.' Millicent's tone was sceptical. 'Brilliance is all very fine, but I've no time for a man who can't even change a light bulb without calling in an electrician.'

'Oh, he told us a really good joke about that!' Harriet seized the chance to show off his wit. 'How many surrealists does it take to change a light bulb?'

Millicent shook her head.

'A fish!'

'Oh, no, dear.' Millicent laughed, but not at the joke. 'You've got it wrong. You can't change a light bulb with a fish.'

'Surrealists,' Harriet said hopelessly. 'It's a joke. The fish isn't real.'

'The Tony Hancock jokes. Now they *were* funny.' Millicent pushed back her chair. 'I'll put the kettle on. You go into the sitting-room, Harry. Make yourself at home.'

Left unguarded for a moment, Harriet hurried across the kitchen and towards the sitting-room's prettily curtained windows. She tweaked them apart and gazed up at the bright squares of lights in Victor's home. At least Sally-Anne wasn't there. She had gone down with flu and serve her right, Harriet thought uncharitably, for standing in front of open windows with no clothes on. No silhouette against the lights this evening, however hard she strained her eyes for a glimpse. He must be working.

'Grendel working at night? You must be off your head, girl.' Talking to Carl had been almost as dispiriting as talking to Miss Press. Harriet's gentle face hardened. How cruelly he had repaid her kindness in finding him a place to sleep – she had even given him her own blanket. Not satisfied with telling disgusting stories about Victor which he had probably invented, he had kept her shivering in the common-room until well after midnight while he rambled on about his own hard luck and how nobody loved him. And then, just when she was beginning to feel quite sorry for him, he had told her how he – no, she couldn't even bear to think about it. A kind deed didn't shine like a candle in a naughty world. It just got you into trouble. She had allowed her own good nature to get the better of her common sense once too often; Carl could look after himself in future. She had enough problems of her own. Oh, but she wished, how she wished –

'Enjoying the view?'

She dropped the curtain and cast about for some plausible explanation for her proximity to it.

'I was looking at your photographs.' She snatched one up at random from the window sill. It showed a big smiling man with a handlebar moustache, posing with his hand on the bonnet of a sports car. 'He looks nice.'

'Bobbie?' Millicent's hand trembled a little as she set down the heavy tray of coffee and liqueur bottles. 'Black, you said?' She poured the cup out and settled into her customary chair by the hearth. 'That's Captain Snetherton, my dear. You've heard of him, I suppose? One of the finest racing drivers I ever knew.'

Harriet was startled out of self-engrossment. 'You knew lots of racing drivers, then?'

'I should have,' Millicent said crisply. 'I was the champion of the British Ladies' Racing Club for four years running. Not to mention winning the European Ladies title. But Bobbie Snetherton was in another class altogether. Handsome as Apollo, and didn't he just know it! He'd put on a bit of weight by then,' she added, seeing Harriet's glance at the photograph. 'If he'd handled women as he handled cars – well, he didn't, but it never stopped them falling in love with him. And marrying him. Silly fools.' Millicent sipped her coffee with sedate pleasure. 'He couldn't even remember their names. Beth – that was wife number three, told me he called her Jaguar.'

'Quite a compliment, really.'

'You're so young,' Millicent said wearily. 'I don't suppose you've even heard of a Jaguar SS100. It was his car.'

'And were you in love with him?' Harriet couldn't imagine Miss Press ever having been in love, she looked so cool and self-contained.

'He used to ask me to marry him twice a week,' Millicent said. 'But I always turned him down. I'd seen enough to know better. He wasn't a man who suited marriage.'

'Do you think Victor suits –'

'He died in '48,' Millicent said. 'Went out of control on a corner. They couldn't get him out in time. I was there with wife number five. *She* went to pieces, of course. Quite lucky for me, when I look back. I was so busy taking care of her and getting the funeral sorted out, I never had time to think. I had her here for three weeks, sobbing over Bobbie's letters and saying she'd never marry again. I knew better than that, I may say. I intro-duced her to a very nice pilot and it was wedding-bells before you could say, Jack's your uncle.' She took off her spectacles and polished the lenses on her sleeve. 'I never raced again after Bobbie died, never even went to a meeting. Couldn't bear to watch.'

Harriet was relieved that the telephone rang at this moment. She felt uncomfortable in the presence of Miss Press's tragedy. Beside it, her own seemed suddenly small and foolish.

'Press here,' Millicent said briskly. 'Speak up, will you?' She was shouting herself, in the manner of old-fashioned people who have never quite grown used to speaking to an invisible person. 'Oh, Harry. No, you cannot come round for a drink.

You've had a good few already by the sound of it. Put your head under a cold tap, man, and stop snivelling.' She winked at Harriet. 'You want who's address? Never heard of him. I've told you before, Harry, I don't know any television producers. No. Send them to Francis Wainwright at Star Channel. My neighbour says he's a friendly sort of chap. I'm sure he'll help. No, I don't want to put in a word for you. I'm sure your poems will speak for themselves. That's right. No harm in wishing. 'Night, Harry.'

'Poor old chap,' she said as she uncorked the calvados. 'He's been writing poems for twenty years, and not one of them published.'

'I've seen him up near the bus-stop, haven't I?' Harriet asked. 'A little red-faced man with a bowler hat?'

'That's Harry. Well.' Millicent raised a bottle from the drinks-tray. 'You'll have a spot of this? Lovely stuff, calvados.'

'Isn't it a sort of brandy?' Harriet's head was spinning already, although Miss Press, who had drunk two glasses to her every one, seemed quite unaffected.

'Apple juice,' said Millicent, pouring two liberal glasses. 'An apple a day keeps the doctor at bay and I can't abide doctors.' She dipped her finger in the bottle. 'Bobbie thrives on it.'

'Bobbie? Oh, does he?' Harriet's voice was faint as she envisaged some macabre drinking rite with Captain Snetherton's photograph. Perhaps Miss Press was a little unbalanced. Grief did have a funny effect on people. Still, if he had died forty years ago –

'Not him, silly girl. The budgie. He loves his little drink, don't you, dearie?' She twisted round in her chair to face the birdcage. 'Cheep-cheep.' She pushed her finger through the bars. 'You're very quiet tonight. Cheep-cheep. Drinkie. Most peculiar,' she said. 'I had no idea budgies slept with their feet up. Look, Harry, it's so comic.'

Harriet obligingly bent forward to observe this unnatural sight. The bird was indeed lying on the floor. 'I think he might be dead, Miss Press,' she said.

'Dead!' Millicent looked at her indignantly. 'Of course he's not dead. I only bought him a week ago. He was perfectly well at six o'clock, swigging gin like nobody's business.' She opened the cage door and poked him with her finger. 'Come along now, Bobbie. Stop messing about. You know you like calvados. Oh dear,' she said. 'You're right. I did wonder about giving him gin after whisky.' She closed the door and dropped a newspaper over the cage. 'Still, not a bad way to go.'

Harriet thought this was rather a heartless reaction, but Miss Press was clearly not the sort of person who made a fuss about death. You were alive, and then you weren't. She wished she could be as rational in her love.

'Grendel,' Millicent said briskly. 'I know you're longing to talk about him, so we might as well get it over. No hard feelings if I'm frank?'

Mute and terrified, Harriet shook her head.

'It's all right, dear,' Millicent said. 'I'm not going to eat you. I like you, Harry. You're a pretty girl and you've got a kind heart. Look at the way you were telling me how you fixed that wretched Calman boy up for the night. I'd have had him in here if I'd known. I don't like to think what mightn't have happened to you.'

'Anyway,' Harriet prompted. 'You were going to say something about Victor.'

'You aren't his type,' Millicent said with terrible bluntness. 'You'd better take my word for it. That redhead's more his style. She can give as good as she gets by the look of her. Oh no, dear, what you need is a nice young chap of your own age, someone who's got his life in front of him still. Even if Grendel did take a fancy to you, think what you'd be getting. A fifty-five-year-old man with a bald patch and no prospects.'

'He has got prospects!' Harriet was so angry that her teeth were chattering with rage. 'He's writing a great work –'

'And has been for the last eight years.'

'And he's going on a whole series of television programmes –'

'Seeing's believing, and I've heard that before.'

'And he's kind and good and noble and –'

'And nothing I can say is going to make you see sense,' Millicent said wearily as the doorbell went. 'That'll be old Harry with his poems. You'd better dry your eyes, dear. I didn't mean to upset you. I just want you to face facts.'

Too dizzy to face anything except her present and woeful state, Harriet slumped back in her chair. It was time to go, but her legs were leaden weights and the room was spinning. She tried to remember what she had had to drink and felt worse. Two large whiskies, most of a bottle of claret and a beaker of calvados – not to mention the sherry-soaked trifle of which, forgetful of her resolutions, she had had three helpings to assuage her sorrows.

'Oh, oh, oh!' moaned poor Harriet as she turned and twisted in her chair and groped for a tissue to wipe her streaming eyes. Her fingers stiffened with terror as she heard a low, familiar voice beyond the door. Victor? Here? Now? Staggering to her feet, she looked first in the mirror behind her and then for somewhere to hide the flustered face which stared back at her with the red and glassy eyes of a drunk marmoset. On impulse, she dived for the curtains and shrank into the bay which offered a modicum of shelter.

More than a modicum was required to conceal her presence from the vigilant eye of her hostess as, baffled and displeased by the brusqueness of Grenderlyn's manner, she returned to the room with him striding in her wake.

'No need to go looking for him through the window, dear,' she carolled as she plucked the curtains back. 'You've got a visitor.'

'Hello, Harriet.'

She couldn't even lift her head, she was so overcome with drink and dismay. 'Hello,' she whispered to the carpet. 'I – I was just going.'

'When Victor's come all the way across the street to find you!' Millicent cried with sparkling irony.

'I don't feel very well.' She leant against the wall as the room swooped in on her with a rush of black wings.

'Two aspirins and a glass of water, Milly,' Grenderlyn said, putting an arm round Harriet's shoulder and leading her gently back to a chair.

'Exactly what I was about to get.' Millicent threw him a dark look. 'Quite the little doctor know-it-all, aren't we?'

Grenderlyn sat down opposite Harriet. 'I'm in Millicent's black books for treating you badly,' he said. 'But I'm going to make it up to you, Harriet.'

She looked at him with such sad and puzzled eyes that he, the master of flirtatious eloquence, found himself hunting for unaccustomed phrases of gentle reassurance.

'I've been thinking about you,' he began.

'There we are.' Millicent was back, determined to seize the helm of this ship before it lurched out of her control. Trust old Grendel to turn up and start causing trouble just when she was getting the girl into a sensible frame of mind. She held the glass to Harriet's mouth. 'Drink it up, dear, and just sit quiet for a bit. And don't let him start talking any of his nonsense to you.' She planted herself in front of the hearth, legs sturdily set apart as she glared down at Grenderlyn. 'Drink?' Nobody would ever be able to accuse her of being inhospitable, but she knew how to make a challenge of her invitations.

'Very gracious of you, Milly.' He smiled at her amiably. 'I'll help myself.' Taking a respectably small measure from the calvados bottle, he settled back to enjoy the spectacle of her discomfiture. Knowing the virtue of his own intentions gave him a pleasant sense of moral superiority.

'Given me a good write-up, have you?'

Millicent folded her arms. 'I've said what I've said. Mind your own business.'

Grenderlyn raised his glass to her. 'Since it is my business, I probably have a right to mind it. Lovely calvados.'

'We *were* enjoying it,' Millicent said pointedly. 'We *were* having a very pleasant evening. Weren't we, Harry?' Her eyes pleaded with Harriet to see the sense of joining her in this attempt to unseat an unwelcome guest and send him packing. But Harriet's eyes were fixed firmly on the floor and her unhappiness only betrayed itself in the white knuckles clenched against her glass of water. It seemed, however, that Millicent had triumphed, for Grenderlyn drained his glass suddenly and stood up.

'Going already?' Millicent did not bother to suppress the satisfaction she felt at such an easy victory.

'I'm taking Harriet home.'

Her eyes rose for a moment. 'Oh, but I've got –'

'She's got work to do.' Millicent cut in. 'Unlike someone I could mention.'

'Home across the street,' Grenderlyn said calmly. 'How do you feel? Bit better?'

Harriet's eyes filled with tears again, so astonished was she by this new Victor who smiled at her so kindly and spoke as if he really cared how she felt.

'I really ought to go back.'

'Of course you should.' Millicent was brisk. 'Who let you down this time, Grendel, the redhead or the blonde next door?'

Grenderlyn looked down on her from his considerable height. 'I've often wondered,' he said gently, 'why there wasn't a name for a female peeping Tom. A peeping Milly, perhaps? Come along, Harriet. Old ladies mustn't be kept on their feet too long.'

Harriet looked at Grenderlyn and then at Miss Press. She took the hand which Grenderlyn held out to her. 'Let's go.'

There was nothing for it but to be graceful in defeat. Millicent summoned a pitying smile. 'I'll see you out.' Standing in the arch of light as they went down the path, she fired her last dart. 'And mind you don't get had up for baby-snatching!'

Harriet turned to wave at her. 'I'm nineteen, Miss Press.'

'No more sense than a grasshopper,' Millicent muttered under her breath, but she smiled and waved back. 'Poor silly child.' She closed the door and went back to her sitting-room to deal with the deceased budgerigar. She did this briskly with two sheets of newspaper and a quick trip to the outside dustbin. Dogs deserved the full rites of burial; a bird which couldn't hold its drink was unworthy of any mark of respect. Glancing down the street to make sure that her neighbours were behaving themselves, she drew in her breath as she saw the grave-robber sauntering out of Mrs Tremain's house. She waited the few seconds until he reached the steps down to Fay Calman's basement before she struck.

'Don't think you'll get away with it, young man.'

He turned. 'I'm so sorry – were you speaking to me?'

'I was.' Millicent raised one hand and pointed to the starry heavens. 'You may think it funny to take flowers from those who can't protect themselves, but I'll tell you something, Mr Sartis. You won't get past the big policeman in the sky with crimes like that. He's watching.'

'Really?' Raphael strolled across the street. 'Do tell me about it. I had no idea that things were so advanced. What do they call it? Sky Watch?'

'God is not a funny subject,' Millicent snapped.

'Oh, God,' he said. 'I thought you were talking about a satellite security-system. Well, between you and me, dear lady, I don't suppose God cares much about Sir Hubert Harrowby's flowers. There's many a better man than Sir Hubert whose bones haven't been allowed to lie in consecrated ground.'

'Indeed?' Millicent was trembling with rage. 'And what, sir, gives you the right to judge the dead?'

'I'm not judging anyone,' Raphael said. 'I just thought you should know the facts. Sir Hubert Harrowby married for money, pushed his wife down a stone staircase two years later and then stole his niece's inheritance by a legal trick. He left two hundred pounds in perpetuity to the church to make sure of a decent burial. Why else would they have put such a glowing testimonial to the old villain? But perhaps you like rogues.'

'Have you no shame?' Millicent hissed. 'How dare you stand here and insult the memory of that fine and noble man! If you were a gentleman, sir, I would strike you. As you are not, I wish you goodnight.' She was pleased with this little speech; it should, she thought, put the brute in his place.

'I'm sorry,' Raphael said.

'So you damn well should be. What are you staring at me like that for?' His eyes, she would remember afterwards, had become very bright and strange, quite as if he was trying to hypnotise her.

'I'm sorry about the child,' he said. 'Roberta.'

Millicent felt her heart give a terrible bump. 'Get away from me,' she whispered.

'She calls herself Paula now,' he said. 'Married an American businessman when she was twenty-eight. Divorced him five years ago. Lives on her own. Comes to England quite often. She wants to find you.' He looked directly into her eyes. 'And, if you wish it, she will.' He raised his hat. 'Pleasant dreams, Miss Press.'

Slowly, she retraced her steps to the door. When she had closed, and bolted, it behind her, she sank into her chair and poured herself a stiff drink from the tray at her side. Her hand was shaking so much that she could only hold the glass steady to drink from it by pressing the cold rim hard against her teeth. How could he conceivably have known? Nobody had ever heard about the child except the discreet agency who, when they learned the circumstances, agreed to find two foster-parents.

Roberta had been the result of the only slip-up in a long and merry liaison, which had successfully outlasted Bobbie Snetherton's five marriages. The relationship had always been good-humoured and clearly defined; it had worked because it was based on an uncommon blend of tolerance, selfishness and grace. Bobbie had wanted wives he could walk over and who would look after and indulge him in the way which befitted a champion of the European race-tracks; Millicent, who thought doormats deserved to be shaken and trodden on if they insisted on lying on the floor, had found him two of the most obliging of his spouses and had done everything short of presenting them with the ring. They could have the pleasure of ironing Bobbie's shirts and polishing his silver cups; she had the fun.

And there had been a lot of fun, Millicent thought as she raised her glass to Bobbie's smiling photograph.

'Here's looking at you, kid.' Their shared passwords from their favourite film, the phrase with which they had gleefully greeted each other on the stolen weekends in Paris, Perth, Perugia, wherever and whenever Bobbie could find an excuse to escape. 'Here's looking at you, kid,' he had chuckled as they swaggered in dark glasses, phoney mobsters, down the narrow streets of Positano – they had always chosen places beginning with a P. for pleasure – and into the gloomily carpeted halls of the Prince Albert Hotel, in some town of which she could no longer remember the name. P. for a pleasure which had never waned, a sense of wickedness which had never failed to stimulate. And P. for the precautions which had been forgotten on their last fling, in Penrith. Such a pity it could not have been Paris and that her last romantic assignation should have been overcast by the memory of a steady drizzling rain sliding down the windows behind pale grey curtains from which the cheerful print of cabbage-roses had long since faded.

Penrith had been the setting for Roberta's conception, the misfortune on which neither of them had counted because they were the ones who always got away. Millicent's hands squeezed her glass as she remembered their last conversation, just before the race in which Bobbie had been killed, the conversation in which she had told him with a bright and superficial laugh that she was pregnant and asked him what he wanted to do about it.

'Nothing much I *can* do, so far as I know, kid,' he had said, his eyes looking past her to check that nobody was close enough to hear.

'I could go ahead and have it.'

His eyes had flickered and she had known it was hopeless, silly even to say it.

'I'm a married man, Milly.' He had patted her shoulder. 'You know the ropes. Get it seen to. We don't want any complications.'

That was all Roberta had been to him, a complication, a faulty cog. She had often wondered what she would have done if Bobbie had lived. Probably what she had done anyway, after finding it was too late for an abortion. Discreetly removed herself, and got rid of the poor little thing as quickly as possible. Jackie, the widow who had spent three weeks under Millicent's roof, had never had a clue what was going on. Nor had anybody else.

And Roberta? Millicent felt her face settling into the compressed lines which were the nearest she ever came to tears. It had been the only indulgence she had allowed herself, to give the baby a name as close as possible to her father's. Giving her away had not been easy. Crueller still had been the promise she had been asked to make. Never to get in touch. Never to find her and tell her who she was. The foster parents who had been chosen had asked that and, having no choice, she had agreed.

Roberta. She lay back in her chair, picturing her. A tall, pretty woman with Bobbie's dark hair and her own bright blue eyes. A strong woman she must surely be, with two such parents. A woman old enough to look long and hard at her foster-parents and known that she was not like them. Forty. Old enough to know the truth and even be proud of it, forgiving enough, perhaps, to want to make a friend of her mother –

'Oh, of course I wish it, damn you,' Millicent said aloud.

And shivered as she heard the telephone peal in the hall.

4

Too dazed to feel the joy which she had always supposed would be unqualified at such a moment, Harriet stood in Grenderlyn's bedroom, clutching a pile of shirts in one hand and his gift of a lecture-paper in the other. An unshaded light bulb burnt fiercely down on her aching head.

'There!' He gestured triumphantly towards the open cupboard. 'Two shelves and six hangers. And you can have the top shelf of the bathroom cupboard for your toothbrush.'

'Thank you,' she said with dismay. Perhaps she could pack up her other things in a case for her parents to keep and just bring the bare essentials to Selena Street? Living in a small space was going to be very good for her self-discipline, she told herself.

Life with Victor sounded altogether as though it was going to be a fairly disciplinary experience. She was amazed by the care with which he had planned it all out. A chart above the oven showed the times at which he liked to eat, how many minutes to boil his breakfast egg, and the hours at which he wanted to be brought a cup of coffee in his study. A second chart by the telephone presented her with a list of the local shops and the days on which she should visit the butcher, the fishmonger and the supermarket with her allowance of twenty pounds. Looking at the list of Victor's requirements, she had wondered how far she could make twenty pounds go and blanched when he said that she must be sure to keep the change to spend on herself.

'Well, there we are.' He beamed at her. 'All settled.'

She handed him his shirts, dimly wondering why he thought it fair that she should have six hangers to his twenty-five. 'If you're sure.'

'Sure?' He looked irritated. 'Of course I'm sure. You'll be a splendid wife. I've been on my own for far too long.' He put his arm around her. 'My own little wifelet.'

Harriet hung her head. 'Why not Sally-Anne? Why me?'

Why indeed, he wondered, looking at the big blonde child who fate had proclaimed should be Mrs Grenderlyn? 'The heart has its reasons of which reason has no understanding,' he said grandiloquently. 'Pascal, as I'm sure you know.'

She did. Still it was good to be reminded of how much she would learn when she lived in the company of such an erudite man. Her education would be her reward; it was simply petty to mind about things like coat hangers and shopping allowances. Emboldened by her new role, she put her arms around his neck and kissed him warmly. 'Oh Victor, I do so want to make you happy.'

'And so you shall.' He disengaged himself. 'Time for bed. I've booked the registry office for ten o'clock.'

'Already! But you hadn't even asked me! What about my parents?' She was almost in tears. 'I can't get married without telling them. And St Thomas's is so beautiful. They always wanted me to get married there. It wouldn't be any trouble for you, Victor, I promise. They'll arrange it all.'

'Now, Harriet.' His face was so grave that she stopped in mid-wail. 'Are you telling me that your parents' wishes matter more than your future husband's happiness?'

'But I don't see why –'

'I'm a busy man, Harriet. I don't have time for all that silly rigmarole. If you want your parents there, you can ring them first thing in the morning and tell them where to come. And if they can't make it, we'll ask them to come to lunch sometime. So long as it doesn't last for more than an hour. I've never allowed family occasions to interrupt my schedule.'

'Yes, Victor. I mean, no, Victor.'

He was gracious in victory. 'You have the bathroom first. There's a spare toothbrush on the window-ledge. You can use that.' He glanced at his watch. 'I'll be along in five minutes.'

Harriet looked at him from the door with an uncertain smile. 'I don't suppose there'll be time for a honeymoon? I always thought I'd like to go to Venice.'

'Go away?' He stiffened with horror at her insensitivity. 'Harriet, you know I'm working on a very important book. I can't go off gallivanting. And what about your revision? I don't want to be responsible for ruining your chance of getting a decent degree.'

She was instantly appalled by her own thoughtlessness. 'I'm really sorry. I should have remembered the book. Is it going well, Victor?'

It was. Ever since he had been seized by the extraordinary notion of marrying Harriet, it had been as if he was possessed by some supernatural intellect. He had written six chapters in five days and he knew exactly what was to follow. The whole work lay there in his mind, clear as a map, ready to be fed into the machine.

'Not bad,' he said, 'I'll tell you what, Harriet. Dinner tomorrow night at our favourite Indian, and it's on me. How about that?'

She was speechless.

5

'Maximilian Medway, attention, please!'

Max jumped. 'Sorry, Miss Roth, is it my turn?'

'Do you know, Max, I rather think it might be.' The young teacher's frown concealed her anxiety. It wasn't like Max to sit day-dreaming in the free creation class; he was usually on his feet as soon as she looked at him, eager to show off one of his tiny, intricately detailed drawings of animals. Today, he sat slumped at his desk, poking a pencil into the ink-stained holes and seeming not to hear until she called his name for the third time and the children started giggling.

Miss Roth, being a person of principle, had always done her best to disguise the tenderness she felt for this thin, grave-faced child, who neither sought friends nor made enemies and who only ever seemed genuinely happy when he was drawing or playing elaborate mathematical games against himself. She knew little of his background. The headmistress had told her that he was an only child and that the mother was a difficult woman, whatever that might mean. From Max himself, she had elicited only that their house had a nice garden and that he spent a lot of time on his own. Wanting to know more, she felt intuitively that it was wiser not to ask. A forced confidence could cause more discomfort than the guarding of a secret grief.

'Well, Max?' Her voice was gentler than his vagueness merited. 'And what have you got to show us today? Hold them up so we can all see.'

Instead of doing as she asked, the boy came up the classroom to her desk, the sheets of drawing-paper rolled tightly in his hand. 'These,' he said, and laid them on the desk.

'But Max, you know better than to come up –' She stopped and bit her lip as she looked down at his offerings. One was an angry scrawl, a heavy pencil dragged again and again across the page in long defacing lines. The other showed a small creature – it might have been intended for a monkey or a baby – trapped in a mesh of squares and spikes, caged as brutally as the child's imagination could devise. Discreetly, under her lashes, she glanced at the little boy's face. He was staring past her at the blackboard with determined indifference, daring her to make any observation. Behind him, the children had fallen silent, sensing that something was wrong, hoping, no doubt, for a bit of drama to enliven the lesson.

'Very nice, dear,' she said. 'You can leave them with me.' She nodded to him to return to his desk. 'Now, Samantha, what about you? What have you got for us?' Sammy could always be relied on to entertain them.

' "What a wonderful bird the frog are," ' the child began, and the tension dissolved into giggles. God bless Ogden Nash.

She signalled to Max to stay behind when the bell clanged for the morning break. He came to stand by her desk, polite and reserved, while the children pushed through the door and scattered out into the concrete yard.

'Yes, Miss Roth?' He didn't look at her. She pushed the drawings towards him.

'Why?'

He feigned innocence. 'Don't you like them?'

'Do you think I should?'

'You're the teacher.' It was said without rudeness. He didn't want to be drawn into a discussion.

'Max.' Knowing she shouldn't, that there were barriers which a teacher should never try to cross, she still reached out to rumple his hair and pull his skinny little body towards hers. 'I wish you'd tell me what it is that's upsetting you.'

'Nothing. Please, Miss Roth, can I go now?'

Embarrassed, she relinquished him. 'Of course. I'm sorry. I only wanted to help.'

He turned at the door. 'Nothing's wrong. I don't need help.' His voice was shrill with humiliation. She should not have interfered. She turned away to watch through the window as, head high, he walked through the clusters of children, walking quite fast, never stopping until he reached the brick wall at the far end of the playground.

Max scrambled up on to the low parapet and drew his knees up under his chin. Head down, he shut out the bright sunshine and took himself out of the unreal refuge of school, back into the grown-up world where children were irrelevant.

It had been really bad ever since Daddy left for his holiday. He had known she was desperate to ring up Gareth last night from the way she kept hurrying him up and yelling at him when he asked if he could stay up and watch television with her. (So much for her promises of all the things they were going to do together while Daddy was away; all she had done so far was to pack him off to Mrs Calman's for a day.) She must have had some idea that Gareth was going to visit her; she'd soaked herself in scent and put on that rhinestone-studded mini-skirt which made her bottom look so big. Of course, he hadn't come. He never did. And then she'd telephoned. You could tell when she was talking to Gareth because her voice got so stupid, high and fluttery, as if she was pretending to be a little girl. He'd heard the au pair sniggering in the galley. It was awful, knowing other people laughed at her like that. Not that Mummy noticed. She didn't notice anything nowadays. Later, he'd heard her crying. He had heard her step coming up the stairs, heavy and sad, and had prayed that she wouldn't come into his cabin and start telling him about it. He had pulled the sheet right up, over his eyes, and turned his face to the wall, feigning sleep while she bent over him and whispered his name. Later still, he had lain very still in the darkness, listening to the harsh cries of her private grief. Never, never as long as he lived, was he going to let himself fall in love and go through all that. He had seen far beyond the soppy poems Miss Roth made him learn, and he knew better.

The bell rang, calling them back to the classrooms. Max shut his eyes and lifted his face towards the sun. 'Oh God,' he said. 'Oh anybody, stop her being so miserable. Let something happen to make Mummy happy, please.'

6

Carl and Harry Carpenter were sitting on a sunny bench outside the Three-Legged Rabbit, puffing their cigarettes and getting down to the meaning of life over their second pint of bitter.

'Get a leg over her, did you?' asked Harry, whose sex life was impurely vicarious.

'Not a chance. She'd knotted herself up tighter than a mailbag – I've got to have it, Harry. Christ, I hate myself.' Carl stared into his glass with moody eyes. 'I've got a devil's mind.'

'Nothing a few drinks with a friend can't cure, lad.' Harry flicked his fingers at the barmaid who, with only two customers left to tend, was sunning her legs on the doorstep. 'Off yer bum and get us two more halves, Maisie. I'll tell you what your trouble is, Carl – negative thinking. You've got to decide what you want from life and go for it. Look at me, writing poems for twenty years and nothing to show for it but a pile of rejection slips big enough to set St Paul's on fire again. Do I give up?' He thumped the table. 'Like hell, I do. Why not? Because I know what I want and I keep after it like an old dog after a bone. It's the challenge that keeps me going, if you follow me. Sent them off to some bloke on the culture programmes last night. And who's to say it won't be the break I've been waiting for? You think about it, lad. What do you want, really want out of life?'

'Sex,' said Carl. 'Every day, all day.'

'Other than sex.'

Peace, thought Carl. 'Home,' he said. 'I told you she kicked me out.'

Harry sighed. 'You did, lad, you did.'

'Cow,' said Carl. 'I never got in her way, never did her any harm. All I asked was to be left alone. I went round this morning. She wouldn't even let me in. She's put some hopping frog in my room. How does she think I'm going to live on three hundred quid while she's cashing in on my room? I've spent fifty already.'

'You shouldn't have chucked that job in, Carl. It was good money.'

'Yeah. For sitting in front of some sodding board all day, designing bathroom units for Vathos Properties.' He shook his head. 'Spiro's a good bloke, but it's just not my world. I've got some self-respect.'

'Money helps. Thanks, Maisie.' Harry's leer was a dentist's dream in potential repair work. 'You're looking very lovely today, my dear.'

'I always am when you've had a couple of pints. Time in ten minutes.'

'What about the new laws?'

The girl grinned. 'You think we're going to stay open just so you and your friend can get plastered? Ever heard of cost-efficiency?'

'Smart girl, Maisie,' Harry said, watching her move away. 'What about your parents?'

'Forget it.' Carl was bored. He was fond of old Harry and grateful for somewhere to stay, but Harry was no use as a solver of life's problems. No point in telling him how he felt about his parents.

He'd only seen his father once that he could remember. His mother had taken him to a film in the West End when he was twelve and when they came out, it was pouring with rain and there were no taxis. And then, just as they'd flagged one down, a tall man came running down the road with a little red-haired woman scampering after him, and he'd shoved straight past them, pushed the little woman in, jumped in after her and slammed the black door. As they drove off, he'd twisted round in his seat to stare at them. That was all he could remember of his father, a narrow angry face scowling through a strip of glass. His mother hadn't even tried to laugh it off; she'd just burst into tears. He'd never seen her cry before. It was as if a dam had burst. Cried all the way back on the bus – he could still remember the hot embarrassment he'd felt when he saw people turning to stare and whisper and her not even having the sense to hide her face in a hanky. She hadn't explained then what it was that had upset her. But when he was fifteen, old enough to feel outraged that his father had never asked to see him, his mother had sat him down in the drab front room, like a stranger, and given him, such as they were, the facts. How his father was a bad man, a gambler who had gone off and left them when Carl was two, gone on a promise of working some system which was going to make them rich. He had never come back, had never been traced. She hadn't set eyes on him until that night in the rain, hadn't even known he was in England. It was a couple of weeks after then that his mother put her head in a supermarket bag and tied a string round it to keep the air out. He'd found her in the unremarkable light of a November afternoon, lying stretched out on her bedroom floor, past saving, beyond grief. He had panicked. Lit out and never stopped running until he met the river boys. Never went back. Never wanted to. Nobody knew what the story was, not even Fay. He had no parents. It was easier that way.

'You're quiet,' Harry said.

'Just thinking.' He leant back against the wall, drinking in a feast of tanned legs and bouncing bosoms as a gang of girls loped past them towards the local tennis-court. Maybe he'd go along and watch them later, soak up a bit of sun and enjoy the view. They passed on, leaving him with nothing better to contemplate than a couple standing at the bus-stop on the far side of the road, a rangy, straggling-haired man and a plump little blonde with her hair pinned up in a bun. Turning to flag down the bus, she caught his eye and waved to him before it lumbered to a halt and hid her from sight. When it moved on, the rangy man had gone and she was running in and out of the traffic towards him. Carl blinked.

'I know her. It's the girl who put me up for the night.'

Harry squinted into the sun. 'Nice-looking kid. Cheerful.' He nudged Carl's elbow. 'You could do worse.'

Pink and breathless, Harriet beamed down at them. 'Hello, Carl. I thought it was you. Victor had to hurry – he's got his work to do – but I said I'd just be a few minutes.'

Carl did the introductions. 'Harry, Harriet.'

'Two many Harrys.' The old man got to his feet. 'Thanks for the drinks, mate. Look after yourself.'

'He didn't have to go.' Harriet sat down and kicked her shoes off. 'That's better. It's so hot! I thought I was going to pass out in the registry office.'

Carl slid a hand behind her and patted her plump bottom. 'He could see I fancied you. What's it going to be – gin, vodka, glass of champagne?'

Harriet widened her eyes in mock-astonishment. 'My, we are lavish!' She waved at Maisie. 'Vodka and tonic, please, with lots of ice. I thought you were broke.'

'I've been to the bank.' He looked at her with approval as she crossed her legs, causing her white skirt to slide up to enticing brevity. 'I like the gear. Suits you.'

Harriet blushed. 'I had to get it in the most awful hurry this morning. I hadn't got anything white except a pair of jeans and a tee-shirt. Oh, thanks – that looks lovely.'

'That'll be £12.50, and no last orders,' said Maisie. 'And no cheques.'

'Charming.' Carl fished in his pocket. 'No cheques and no change. Settle for £10.00?'

'Only if you fancy a bit of washing-up.'

'It's all right.' Harriet took out her purse. '£2.50.'

Carl looked at her with increased warmth. She really was a nice girl. 'So what were you doing at a registry office?'

Harriet giggled. 'What do you think? What people usually do – getting married.'

'Married!' He almost dropped his glass as he found a face for her companion at the bus-stop. She was looking at him with such a pleased and excited face that he swallowed back his sense of outrage. 'Mrs Victor Grenderlyn, eh? That was quick. I thought he had someone else up there a couple of nights ago.'

Harriet looked at her toes. 'That was something quite different. Victor doesn't like to waste time when he's made his mind up.'

'So I see. Well, I'm glad you got what you wanted.' He drained his glass and almost choked as the enormity of what he had just seen was borne in on him. 'You mean to say the swine couldn't even pay for a taxi to bring you home!'

Harriet kept her head down, but he could see a dark flush of colour spreading down to her low-cut neck. 'I like buses. And Victor thought it would be nice to get a bit of fresh air.'

'I'll bet he did. It saved him spending an extra three quid.'

'Be quiet.' She looked up at him. 'I'm not going to stay here and listen to you insulting my husband.' Her voice wobbled suddenly. 'Tissue.'

He gave her his handkerchief. Poor kid, she was really keyed-up, probably didn't know what had hit her yet. 'Get the vodka down,' he said. 'It'll do you good.'

Sniffing, she sipped it. 'Sorry. It's just I had Miss Press going on at me about him last night and now you again and it's all a bit much. I wish everyone didn't have to be so horrid about him. He's so kind and good. He is, honestly.'

'Yeah.' He couldn't keep the sarcasm out of his voice. 'That's the trouble with people as modest as Grendel – they can't bear to let you know it. No, I'm only joking. I don't know him that well. I did think he might have chosen someone a bit older, though. You'll be pushing him round in a wheelchair by the time you're thirty-five.'

'No, I will not. He's very athletic. On his bicycle, I mean,' poor Harriet said, blushing again. 'Did you find somewhere to stay?'

'Kind of. I'm dossing down on old Harry's sofa for the moment, just until I get myself together.' He didn't like her pitying glance. 'I'll probably go and stay with this bloke I know called Father Gerard in the country. Out near Radlett. He runs a kind of a retreat for artists. It's great. Lots of fresh food, clean air, no hassle, none of this muck.' He waved his hand at the traffic steaming up the hill in a haze of acrid smoke. 'I might go out there today or tomorrow.'

'How funny,' Harriet said, staring at him. 'That's where my parents live, Radlett. I didn't think of you liking things like that. Fresh food.'

'Yeah. Well. I do. I never eat things out of tins. I always made Fay go down to the market and get fresh vegetables – she'd have eaten the catfood so long as her precious pendulum said it was safe.'

'Pendulum?'

'Her spiritual thermometer.' He looked at her anxiously. 'Whatever you do, don't let her get you into all that stuff now you're in the same house. It's nuts. You don't want to believe it.' She wouldn't want to, he thought, not if Fay let herself go on the subject of Grenderlyn. 'So where's he taking you for the honeymoon?'

The change of subject was so sudden that Harriet was caught off guard. 'He – well – there didn't – we thought we'd take a late honeymoon,' she said lamely. 'Selena Street's so peaceful in July. God, I almost forgot – I promised to buy the lunch! He'll be waiting for me to come back and cook it.'

'Harriet.' He put his hand over hers. 'It's OK. I'm not going to rape you. You mean you're just going to sit there and cook for him on your wedding day?'

She glared at him. 'Why shouldn't I? I like cooking.'

'He's got his precious book. He won't even notice if you're not there.' It excited him to feel her hand fluttering like a trapped bird under his. He pressed it down and squeezed her fingers. 'We could catch the 2.20 bus and be in Radlett by 4.00. You could come and see Father Gerard with me. You'd like him. And we'd go for a walk in the woods, have a drink in the pub and be back in time for your dinner. I know it's not much, but it'd be a bit more like a celebration. You can't just go back there and start frying sausages.'

'Victor doesn't like fried food.' She looked at him wistfully. 'That's such a kind idea. But I can't do it, Carl. He'd be so upset. I mean, he only married me two hours ago.' She stood up and pulled down her skirt. 'Give my love to Radlett, won't you.' She looked at him earnestly. 'I really am happy,' she said. 'It's what I wanted, you see.'

He wondered who she was persuading, him or herself?

7

'More fool you,' said Raphael who, ever since he had tuned in on the proceedings, had been thinking that Carl and Harriet made a far more likely couple than Grenderlyn and Harriet. Why was it that none of these humans could see what was good for them? The promotion of happiness was turning out to be a more complicated business than blithely he had supposed.

Raphael was eating a discreet lunch of smoked-haddock sandwiches in the rustling light-splashed woods which fringed the northern edges of Camomile Hill. He had chosen them as the best place in which to conceal himself until the hour that he might be supposed to have finished work for the day.

He had wondered at the time why S. had been so insistent that he should seem to have a job; now that he had spent a night under Fay's roof, he knew. It had been just before eight in the morning when he had been shocked from slumber by the sound of pipes, whistles, low grunts and loud rhythmic cries. When it became apparent that neither a protective mound of blankets nor two pairs of ear-plugs were going to decrease his pain, he crawled out of bed and opened the door to remonstrate.

'I do think –' The words died on his lips. A tape recorder stood on the floor in a sea of newspaper. Under the table, the cats were savaging the reddened bones of last night's take-away tandoori chicken. In the middle of the chaos, her eyes closed, her hands clasped, clad only in a pair of purple bikini pants and a plain cotton bra, stood his landlady. At least, he presumed it must be she. Identification was a dangerous business when every centimetre of her face was smothered in a thick white layer which gave her the look of a Japanese dancer.

'Hi-ah-ooh-aagh!' Her eyes opened. 'You interrupted my mantras.'

It had not until now occurred to Raphael to compare her to Medusa. Nervously, he backed away into his room.

'So sorry.' Stepping backwards, he struck the iron bedframe and let out an involuntary cry of pain.

'Oh, shit!' She turned the recorder off and glared at him. 'Now look what you've done. You've just gone and wrecked my inner rhythm.'

'I'll go back to bed,' he said humbly. 'Er, how long will you be doing the mantras for?'

She shrugged. 'Couple of hours? It's spiritually healing.' She looked at him thoughtfully. 'I can show you some if you like. We could do them together.' She raised her arms and drew them slowly down the sides of her body. 'They make you feel so good. Very calm – Dora, get your snout out of my muesli bowl! – and serene.'

Raphael was not listening. The prospect of another two hours of oriental shrieking filled him with horror.

'There isn't another room you could use?'

Fay looked at him coldly. 'I thought you said you had a job to go to. This is mine. Putting my inner self together. And I do it right here, in my kitchen.'

'I don't always go out to work. I was planning on doing some of it at home.'

Fay folded her arms. 'Then you can't stay here. I'm sorry, Raphael. I'm used to my privacy. You go to work, or you go. It's that simple.'

So here he was, skulking in the woods when he could have

been sitting in Lily's garden. Lily was there now, her golden head bent over her notebook, too intent to notice that the thieving Dora had wriggled through a hole in the wall and was lunching off the plate of ham which lay so invitingly on the grass. Lovely Lily, her hair like a shining bell. He tuned in to the level of her shoulder to see what she was writing and smiled as he saw that she was engaged on nothing more ambitious than the old game of pairing names to spell out the secrets of their feelings. 'R-A-P-H-L-S-A-S and I'm adored!' She tipped her head up to the sun with such a dazzling smile of pleasure that Grenderlyn briefly forgot his masterpiece and leant with longing eyes towards the window.

A reassuring-enough vision to satisfy an anxious lover, one would have thought, but Raphael only sighed and shook his head. Again and again, he had peered into her thoughts. He knew now that she had a great many secret wishes and that many of them were astonishingly frivolous. An hour since, for example, she had been wishing she had a Ferrari when she hadn't even passed her driving test. But never did her thoughts turn in a direction which told him all he wished to know, what she had asked for on Camomile Hill.

8

It was the first time Millicent had ever neglected Sir Hubert's grave on a Tuesday afternoon, but she had more important matters to attend to than the Harrowby monuments today. Roberta – she must try to get used to calling her Paula now, although it was not a name she had ever cared for – would be here at midday tomorrow. The house must be cleaned, the food prepared, the bed made up.

She was engaged at present on arranging the books by Paula-Roberta's bed, a slow business since she was concerned to let them give a good impression of her own character. Books, so her own mother had always told her, were the first thing to look at in a new friend's house; nothing so clearly betrayed an empty mind as a bookcase which held nothing but popular novels and a few *Reader's Digest* magazines. Armed with this nugget of wisdom, Millicent had already exchanged a battered collection of crime-fiction paperbacks for Harold Nicolson's diaries and an Iris Murdoch which she had never managed to finish – so exhausting trying to work out who was having an affair with who, when they would keep chopping and changing like a warren of rabbits. To these, she now added a history of the area which included a charming acknowledgement by the author to 'Miss Millicent Press, who so graciously allowed me to share her memories of the pre-war years', a history of British motor-racing which included several flattering references to her professional achievements, and a short account of St Giles's church which had inexcusably omitted to mention her name in connection with the Harrowby monuments. Gazing on the assembled pile with quiet approval, Millicent allowed her thoughts to run forward to the delightful prospect of the two of them, mother and daughter, strolling up to St Giles's together. How pleasant it would be to see the vicar's startled stare when she made the introductions – 'I don't believe you know my daughter, Mrs –'

Mrs what? Millicent's smile withered away with horror. She didn't even know her name. Didn't know a thing about her except that she had a very strong American accent. She had been so astonished that she had simply accepted the woman's claims as gospel truth. What if she was an impostor, a criminal who was planning to weasel her way into the house under false pretences and then rob her, even perhaps murder her? Millicent was so appalled that she had to sit down on the bed and take ten deep breaths.

A calm approach was what was required. What exactly *had* the woman said when she rang up? That she had moved to England quite recently and that she had felt it was time to do a bit of excavation work. That was the phrase. She hadn't liked it. It had made her sound like a corpse that was being unearthed for inspection. Nor had the rest of the conversation been much more to her taste. There had been an aggressive note in the crackling voice which had made her feel quite tempted to tell her to go and do her excavating elsewhere. It hadn't been the way a daughter should speak to a long-lost mother. Too bossy by half, it had seemed to Millicent, who was used to giving orders, not receiving them.

She hadn't liked it, but she had known where her duty lay, had told the woman to look on Millicent's home as her own while she was in London. A glow of satisfaction had warmed her as she replaced the receiver. She had behaved beautifully, no doubt about it. No questions, no excuses, no mention of the bridge afternoon she would have to postpone, just a generous, open-hearted response.

Too generous, too damned trusting for her own good. 'Milly, my girl,' she said to herself, 'you'd best watch out.' Perhaps she'd have a word with Sergeant Fairweather, ask him to drop in for a spot of sherry after lunch tomorrow. But would any hardened criminal be intimidated by the sergeant's pink and faintly porcine face? Somehow, she doubted it. The telephone downstairs rang sharply, urging her into the uncomfortable limping stride which was the nearest she could get to a run without having to lie up on a sofa for the rest of the day.

'Hi,' said a faintly American voice.

'Paula?'

'Fay. I wondered if you'd heard the news about Grendel.'

'Dead?' She couldn't get her mind off the subject.

'Married.' Fay was exuberant. 'And you know what? I saw it in the cards last week. Dark man, blonde girl. I couldn't figure it out, but of course it must have been old Grendel and this woman.'

Panting, Millicent sat down to rally her thoughts. 'And you say it was all there in your cards before it happened? You really saw it?'

'Sure,' Fay said, surprised by the earnestness of the question. She had only said it by way of a preface to an apology for Dora's latest attack on her neighbour's dustbin, scattering its contents half-way down the street and lifting a cloud of orange feathers into the rose-bushes. 'Look, I'm sorry about the cat, Millicent. It won't happen again. She got out before I could stop her –'

'No need to apologise, my dear. You can't be everywhere at once and we all know how hard you work.' Millicent allowed the honeyed grace of her forgiveness to sink in before seeking her reward. 'I've been wondering if I haven't sometimes been a little unkind about your psychic powers, Fay.'

'You told me to set myself up in a gypsy tent on Brighton pier last time we talked about it,' Fay said dryly. 'I don't have time to quarrel about clairvoyancy today. You to your view, me to mine. I don't like arguments. They upset my hormone levels.'

'I'm not arguing, I'm asking,' Millicent said with unwonted meekness. 'I'd like your advice. You don't see – well, I'm not quite sure how to put it – any violence around me, do you?' She waited anxiously.

'What kind of violence?'

'Murder,' Millicent whispered.

'I can see you cooking up some roast beef,' Fay said after a pause. 'I don't like meat myself, but murder seems a bit of a strong term.'

'But you don't see anything physical, nothing like an attack?'

Fay's laugh was loud and unfeeling. 'Some of us should be so lucky – no, I'm sorry, Millicent. I don't see too much of that kind of thing in store for you this week.'

Idiotic woman. 'I didn't mean –'

'Sorry – someone at the door. I've got to go.'

Unsolaced and fearful, Millicent stared at the whirring telephone.

9

Grenderlyn's dining-room had an uncherished appearance. Dusty prints of angry-looking old gentlemen in wigs glowered down from the brown walls on two rows of hard brown chairs and a long brown table, on the middle of which stood a squat yellow buddha on a glass mat. An upright piano sulked in a corner under a heavy red cloth with dusty fringes. On the mantelpiece, wedged between two piles of leather books, stood a large photograph of a younger but still easily recognisable Grenderlyn in cap and gown, shaking the hand of a small, mournful-faced man. It was not a room which led Harriet to think that Victor had been deceiving her when he said that he liked going to parties better than giving them. Here, she felt, was the room which she could safely transform without causing him displeasure. He clearly never used it. She would surprise him.

She had done her best. She had polished and put out the silver candlesticks which had been hidden away behind the soup tins in a kitchen cupboard and replaced the buddha with a big bunch of pink and white flowers in a jug; there didn't seem to be any flower vases. The ugly mustard-coloured curtains had been drawn back and the french windows opened. All that remained now was for her to lay out the plates of real pâté de foie gras with truffles, the hot toast; the two spoons of caviare and the chilled bottle of Pouilly-Fuissé. It had been alarmingly expensive, but this was their wedding-lunch. Bringing in the iced white cake which the patisserie had let her have cheap because it was two days old, she hoped that he wouldn't make fun of her. How could anyone feel properly married if there wasn't a cake?

Pleased, Harried surveyed her handiwork and found it good. So was the foie gras. Licking her fingers, she went into the sitting-room and looked through the alphabetically ordered row of records until she came to Handel. She eyed the Wedding March, shook her head wisely – too obvious – and put on the *Water Music* instead. Happily, she sat down to wait.

Not for long. 'Turn it down, can't you?' Victor shouted. 'I'm trying to work.'

'But it's past lunch-time, Victor. I've got it all ready.'

Silence. Harriet bit her lip. She had clearly interrupted him at some crucial moment. Thank goodness she hadn't tried making something which had to be eaten straight away. The record ran to its end before she saw him slinking past the open door with a tray in his hand.

'Oh, don't –' She hurried after him to watch, anxious-eyed, as he stared about the room.

'I don't like pink,' he said, looking at the flowers. 'Still, very decent of you to get all this.' He put one of the plates on his tray and poured out a glass of wine. 'Good idea. Something I can pick at while I'm working.'

'But I wanted us to have lunch together.' Her voice trembled. 'Mightn't we?'

Grenderlyn's smile was all benevolence. 'I thought we agreed that I was going to take you out to dinner.'

'I don't see what that's got to do with lunch. All you've got to do is sit down and eat it.'

He shook his head. 'Lunch or dinner, Harriet. Never, ever, lunch and dinner. And I'd rather you kept the window shut. It lets all the dust in.'

'But I dusted everything!' She was almost in tears. 'I thought you'd be so pleased. Now where are you going?'

He turned in the door with a pained smile. 'To have lunch peacefully, in my study. Why don't you have a couple of aspirins and lie down for a while? You seem a bit edgy. No?' His face brightened. 'I know what's bothering you – I haven't given you anywhere to do your work.' He took her by the elbow and led her back into the sitting-room. 'Now – oh my God, I don't believe it. Damn.' Loping towards the record-player, he picked up the disc and held it towards the light. 'Finger-marks all over the grooves. Ruined. How many more did you take out?'

'Only that one. I'm sure it isn't ruined. I'll clean it for you – oh, Victor, please don't look at me like that,' cried poor Harriet. 'I can't seem to do anything without annoying you.'

'I'm not annoyed, Harriet,' he said. 'I'm sure you meant well. I'll see you at seven, after I've had my bath.' Tray in hand, he turned at the door. 'You might take those flowers down to Mrs Calman downstairs. Tell her to keep those wretched cats out of the garden while you're at it.'

'Yes, Victor.' Yes Victor. No, Victor. Why had nobody warned her what marriage to a great man was going to be like?

10

Fay already had a visitor. Grateful though she was to have been saved from having to waste her valuable psychic energies on Millicent Press, she was becoming increasingly angry about the way Lucy kept dropping in on her for free readings on the pretext that she was just passing by. The way from Lucy's office to Lucy's home could not conceivably pass Selena Street without a twenty-minute detour. Who, at three o'clock in the afternoon, did the woman think she was fooling? The only unusual thing about this afternoon's visit was that, so far, Lucy had not mentioned the cards.

'No work today?' she inquired, pointedly, as Lucy held out her hand for a third cup of coffee. 'Doesn't that secretary of yours get tired of holding the fort?'

Lucy's smile was that of a superior being. 'I've always told you, darling, delegation's a great art. There's nothing Jan loves more than thinking she's indispensable – just a drop more cream. Besides, I'd hardly be going to work on the day when –' She checked herself. 'Your psychic powers don't seem to be working very well. I was sure you'd have guessed by now.'

'I'm too old for guessing games.' Stifling a yawn, Fay sat down. She really didn't like the company of women like Lucy, rich, lazy, monumentally egocentric, the kind of women who drifted from the clairvoyants' cards to the psychiatrists' couches in a permanent state of expensive dissatisfaction. No wonder that poor little kid looked so depressed and that John Medway had gone off on a sailing holiday by himself.

'Well?' Lucy's smile shifted from the enigmatic to the playful. 'Aren't you even going to try?'

Fay folded her arms. 'Surprise me. Gareth's run off with a belly-dancer. God, I don't know,' she said hurriedly as Lucy's mouth dropped with horror. 'You told me to guess. You won the pools. John – it's John, isn't it? Stop messing about and tell me what's happened.'

'I did warn him,' Lucy said defiantly. 'I told him I'd been having dreams about shipwrecks. He could have listened. I had a call this morning. They found the yacht, what was left of it, washed up near the Portorosa marina. They think he must have been hit on the head by the spray rail just before it turned over.' She lowered her face, but Fay saw her peeping at her through her eyelashes before she pulled out her handkerchief and started dabbing at her cheeks. As a performance of grief, it would not have collected many awards.

Fay shut her eyes. 'What about Max?'

'Thank God he's got me. I'll have to go and pick him up soon. I can't say I'm looking forward to telling him, but he's a very resilient child. He doesn't feel things as much as I do. Never cries.' Lucy put away her handkerchief and renewed her lipstick, frowning into her pocket-mirror. 'I'm not sure about this red. It's a bit bright. They've discontinued that Chanel one you liked so much.' She snapped her bag shut and put it back on the table, out of reach of the cats. 'Fay, you know why I'm here.'

'No,' she said bleakly. 'To tell you the truth, I don't. You ought to be driving down to that school and working out the best way to tell Max that his father's dead. I'm the one you visit to look at the future. You're in the present now, and it's pretty terrible.'

'Oh, it's awful, absolutely awful,' Lucy said hurriedly, 'but I don't need to go for five minutes. You know how I rely on you. Should I do it subtly? I could just send him an invitation to the memorial service. That's quite discreet.'

'Lucy, he's your son!'

'Not Max,' Lucy said. 'Gareth. He won't stay with Felicity for five minutes when he knows I'm free.'

'You never give up, do you?'

'And haven't I been proved right!' Abandoning all pretence of grief, Lucy lifted a radiant face towards her. 'Say what you like – I don't care. You've never understood the bond between Gareth and me. We're like twin souls. I've always known that fate would bring us together in the end. It's destiny.' Her eyes rolled up to the ceiling, as if destiny was a map laid out in its cracked surface.

Did one admire or deplore passion when it became as ruthless as this, Fay wondered? Never in her blackest imaginings had she envisaged a situation in which Lucy would invite her to see God's hand at work in bringing about John Medway's death. What kind of a God would drown poor harmless John and leave that small, sad-eyed child at the mercy of such a mother?

Still, something must be said; Lucy was looking at her expectantly.

'You must admit it, Fay. It's no good pretending.'

'Pretending what?'

'You saw it in the cards.'

She hadn't, but it wasn't worth arguing. 'I do think you ought to go and pick up Max.'

'He's not going to disappear.' But Lucy glanced at her gold watch and stood up. 'Well, I can see you're in a bad mood today. You never did understand our love.' She smiled kindly. 'It's not your fault. It's something rather special.'

'Oh, it's that!' Fay took a deep breath and smiled back. 'I'd be a lot less worried if I didn't understand it, dear. Give my love to Max. And Lucy?' She followed her down the passage to the door. 'Don't go telling him Gareth's going to be his step-father, not yet. Wait a bit.'

'What do you think I am – mad?'

'Just go easy,' Fay said and, thankfully, shut the door. Back in the kitchen, she wished that she had offered to go with Lucy. It was no good just feeling sorry for the child. She ought to do something, keep him away from the sight of his mother's shameless joy. And how long would that last? For as long as it took her to get on the telephone to Mr Lloyd-Evans. Perhaps she should offer to have Max to stay for a few days, put him up on the sofa, maybe? Silly idea; he'd been desperate to get away on that last visit. Carl would have known what to do. Carl, for all his idiocy, was good with children.

Angrily, she stabbed at the keys of her typewriter. No, she

was not missing him. She was not. If her eyes happened to be smarting, it was only because of the lingering fumes of Lucy's cigarette. Never let it be admitted, even to herself, that she ached to have him back. She had unmade his bed and now Raphael Sartis was in it and she was sixty quid a week to the good. Better for her. Probably better for Carl, wherever he was. Wherever – so long as – if he could just ring. Just let her know. 'Oh, damn!' Fay's hands dropped from the keys as the cracked doorbell whimpered into life. All she needed now was another dose of Lucy. Wiping her eyes on the back of her hand, she went to the door.

'Am I interrupting you?'

'If you are, you have,' said Fay. 'And if you have, there's not much point in asking. Or apologising.'

'I'm so sorry,' said Harriet, bewildered. She wished Victor had warned her. Mrs Calman was nothing like the friendly neighbour she had hopefully envisaged from his vague description. She held out the flowers at arm's length. 'My husband said you might like these.'

Fay stared at her. 'Do I know your husband?'

'Victor.' She felt herself starting to blush. 'Professor Grenderlyn.'

'Oh, you're the bride!' Fay stared at her and shook her head. 'Funny. I always saw him marrying an older woman in the end.'

'Victor let you read his cards?' Harriet was shocked.

'Good God, no,' Fay said. 'Much too scared of what I'd find out. I did suggest it once. He was off up to his rooms like a scalded cat. Dora! Come back here, you old bitch! Just because I said "cat" –'

'It's all right,' Harriet said, breathlessly. 'I've got her. Oh, isn't she a darling!' She scratched Dora between the ears, a caress which usually resulted in paroxysms of fury and much parading of teeth. Now, rather to Fay's chagrin, she responded with a thrum of purrs, patting her paws on the girl's soft cheek to indicate her pleasure. 'Carl was telling me about her,' Harriet said. 'I think he misses her.'

'Takes one to know one,' Fay said crossly. 'You'd – Carl? You've seen him?'

'About two hours ago. He was at the pub on the hill. With a friend. A poet, I think he lives around here.'

'Harry Carpenter.' Fay's mouth tightened. 'And he didn't happen to mention why he's chucked his job in, I suppose?'

'He said he wanted to find himself,' said Harriet. 'He seemed quite sensible about it. I mean, an artist isn't ever going to get much fulfilment out of drawing bathroom units.'

'More than he'll get out of hanging around pubs with drunks like old Harry,' Fay said crisply. 'Well, since you've brought the flowers and rescued the cat, you'd better come in.'

It wasn't the most gracious of invitations, but a warm yellow light gave the kitchen a welcoming appearance, and anything was better than sitting alone in Victor's dark grey sitting-room.

'Honestly, Mrs Calman, I'm sure he'll be all right.' An hour had passed and they were still on the subject of Carl. It had not taken Harriet long to realise that her new neighbour's bark was a good deal worse than her bite. Within ten minutes of telling her that Carl was a lout and a layabout and warning her to have nothing more to do with him, she had been asking how he looked and whether he seemed to be eating enough and if he might, by any chance, have said anything about wanting to come back.

'I'm sure he does,' said Harriet, although she could not remember Carl having said anything about it. 'He's really fond of you. I think he just needs to sort himself out a bit. He did say something about going to see a Father Gerald –'

'Father Gerard? He'll be lucky. Fifty quid every time you put your nose round his door. Still, Carl wouldn't know. He wasn't paying.' Why couldn't he settle for a nice girl like this, Fay thought, a girl who actually seemed both to be sensible and fond of him? Wasted on Grendel.

'That was a quick marriage,' she said affably. 'First I knew about it was when your husband came waltzing back from the registry office this morning. I've never seen the man look so pleased with himself. I thought he must have finished that famous book at last. Casaubon's Last Crusade, we all call it.'

'He has, well, nearly.' Harried beamed. 'He said it was all my doing. Ever since he decided to marry me, it's been going like magic.'

'That must be fun for you,' said Fay. 'Marry me, marry my word processor. Mind you, I'm delighted he's got married. I'll be able to –' She stopped herself on the brink of saying that she wouldn't need to worry about the threats to her ceiling any more. 'I'll be able to stop worrying about his lonely old age.' Then she added to make up for this burst of untruth, 'To be honest, I always thought Gren – Victor was married to his ambition.'

'You mean, you saw it?' Harriet had gone quite pale. That was the trouble with being a clairvoyant. You only had to make a harmless surmise for it to be taken as a direct message from the other side.

'No, dear, not like that. I told you I hadn't done his cards. I'm sure you'll make him very happy.'

'I do hope so.' Harriet's face seemed to have shrunk to the size of an elf's with worry. 'I do want to. It was what I wanted, more than anything in the world, to marry Victor – and now, of course it was silly of me to imagine, only everything I do is wrong.' She was very low on self-esteem. Perhaps she wouldn't have done for Carl after all. 'I bought lunch and that was wrong. I put on a record and that was wrong. And now I'm sitting telling you about it and that's bound to be wrong.'

'Don't be silly. Everybody needs to talk.' Fay said it automatically. She wasn't interested in hearing about Grendel's un-husbandly behaviour. 'So you're another one whose wish came true? Here, stop sniffing.' She held out a piece of kitchen paper. 'Blow your nose.' It was an invitation to a new host of germs to come dancing into the kitchen in search of their natural victim, but Fay had something more disturbing than a virus on her mind. 'Better?'

'A bit. Sorry.' Harriet sat still, waiting to be told what to do. She sensed authority in Mrs Calman's manner; if she listened carefully, she might learn the secret.

'You really wished it? Wished it out loud?'

'I don't know. I think so. Does it matter?'

A girl wished for marriage to a confirmed bachelor and here she was, married to him. A frantic wife wished for her husband's death, and there was poor John Medway buried in the briny deep. A woman made a wish that she could meet a television star and there he was, all set to visit her. The coincidences of life, as she was always telling her clients, were far stranger than those of fiction, but three? And how many more had she not heard about? Old Millicent had sounded pretty odd on the telephone, now she came to think about it. Something was up. But what?

'Well?' Harriet looked at her anxiously. '*Does* it matter? Wishing it couldn't make Victor want to marry me. Although it did almost seem like that. He just walked into Miss Press's house when I was having supper with her and said he wanted to get married. Do you think, I mean, you are a clairvoyant – does he really love me?'

'Why else would he have married you?' No point in telling her the brutal truth, that no woman who was truly loved ever needed the confirmation of a clairvoyant to know it. She filled up Harriet's cup and patted her downcast head. 'Best thing that ever happened to him.'

'Maybe,' said Harriet, but she sounded unconvinced.

11

'I'll tell you something odd about yourself,' said Lily, stretched out on her bed with Raphael at her side. She twisted round to look down at him. 'Do you want to hear what it is?'

He stroked the silky golden hair which made him think of cornfields. 'Go on.'

'You're always worrying about other people being happy, but you never look happy yourself. Not even now.' She kissed the corners of his mouth. 'Why not? Is something wrong? I wish you'd tell me things you think about. You never do. It makes me feel as though I only know a little bit of you.'

He looked up at her. 'I thought about you so many times today. I thought about your smile and about your beautiful eyes and the way you tilt your head back when you laugh. And I thought about being like this, about lying beside you and looking at you. This is the closest thing to happiness I've ever known. So now you know what I think about.' He pulled her down to lie on him, her face against his. 'And it can go on, Lily. It can.'

She pulled away again. 'There you go again. You sound so solemn! Why worry so much? Of course it's going to go on. Why shouldn't it?'

'Tell me what you wished on Camomile Hill,' he said. 'Please, Lily.'

'That again?' Laughing, she slid down to the end of the bed. 'I'll tell you. But not yet.' Her face was turned away from him now as she leant forward and started brushing her hair. The evening light struck through the half-drawn curtains, burnishing her cheek and shoulders and kindling flames of red in the strands of gold.

'I'll tell you something,' he said. Her face was transparent in its eagerness as she turned towards him.

'Yes?'

'I'm in love with you.'

'I love you, too,' she said, but he saw the shadow of disappointment cross her face. She wanted more than he dared to give, the knowledge of who he was.

When Dreams Come True

1

At six o'clock in the morning, the sky glows pink as a washed oyster-shell over the winking lights and the sleeping houses of Selena Street. Deep in a dream about Charlie Everest, Fay lies snuggled under the red blanket in which, when she feels insecure, she wraps herself like a small Father Christmas for the whole day. It's a good dream. She sighs and murmurs and stretches her mouth in a beatific smile while the cats assemble at her feet, sensing that the time of quiet watchfulness is almost over and that a round of purrs will rouse their mistress to her principal duty in life of feeding them.

Across the street, Millicent is at peace at last, free from a hideous nightmare in which a smiling child came to her door and was instantly transformed into a bloodhound with great red eyes and teeth like yellow daggers. The terror of her limping flight is fading now. Slowly, Millicent's hand slips down from the fold of blanket which had seemed to be her walking-stick and drops, open and easy, by the side of the bed.

Lily, curled in the warm hollow left by Raphael's body before he crept away, is dreaming, as always, about Lily as she will one day be, envied by Sarah, admired by all. This one is of her arrival at a party which consists only of extremely famous people. As she walks through the door, the conversation stops. Astonished, they gaze. (Who can she be, this mysterious and beautiful young woman? Oh, haven't you heard about her? That's Lily Tremain. Isn't she magnificent?) Raphael plays no part in this agreeable spectacle.

Out of my dreams and into your arms – it doesn't seem strange that Gareth should have elected to wear a cowboy hat, cuban boots and a vividly checked red and green shirt as he strides towards Lucy over a plain of rippling wheat, or that he should be singing her favourite song from *Oklahoma*. Nor does it seem odd that a great circle of cowboys and fresh-faced girls in swirling skirts should be leaping and pirouetting around them as Gareth sweeps her up into his arms and proclaims his undying love. 'And I love yoo-oo', Lucy sings back at him in a voice as sweet and clear as a silver bell. 'My dream's come troo-oo.'

But these were only dreams. For Victor Grenderlyn, the only person in Selena Street who had been awake for – he looked at his watch – 22¾ hours, the dream had already become reality. He poised his hands over the keys and let them fall on to the words which seemed to him, at this moment, more beautiful than any line of poetry: THE END.

'Victor, aren't you ever coming to bed?'

The end. Eight chapters of flawless argument, pursued to a conclusion which had all the majesty and sweep (he could see the reviews already) of a Beethoven sonata. So he failed to communicate with the camera, did he? Let the Wainwrights of the world read this and see if he was or was not one of the great communicators, a man who might still, if they showed a proper respect for his worth, be persuaded to appear on their miserable little programmes.

'Victor, you must get some sleep.'

All that remained to be done now was the slow pedestrian haul of footnotes and revision, a last trudge before he was seized by the eagle's talons and swept aloft into the hall of fame. Immortality! The prospect so stirred him that he actually left his chair and threw open the window to gaze up at a sky from which the delicate colours of dawn were just drawing back to reveal the still, deep blue of a mountain lake, untroubled by a single shadow. So would his fortune be, a glorious and unending summer of honours well-deserved.

'Why won't you answer?'

'Answer what? I didn't hear you.' Smiling, he turned towards her: large, willing, simple Harriet, so utterly unsuited to him. Marrying her, he thought sadly, had been the only irrational thing he had ever done. But he would be magnanimous. Never let it be said that Victor Grenderlyn was a selfish man. He would allow her to share in his moment of glory. 'Harriet,' he said solemnly. 'Come to me.'

He took her hand and led her towards the machine, pushed a switch to illuminate the last lines of the text. 'You see what it says there? I've finished it.'

This was easier to respond to than most of Victor's statements. Admiration was all that was required, and Harriet gave it unstintingly. 'So now we can go on our honeymoon,' she added timidly. 'You did say –'

He had, indeed. No escaping from that. But she noticed that his smile was wan.

'Venice,' she said quickly, before he could change his mind. 'Oh please, Victor, you did –'

'Venice it is,' he cut in. He couldn't bear pleading voices. They reminded him of Melitza Hadda, sobbing out stories of her ruined life. 'Still, we don't want to start throwing away money. I seem to remember reading about a very reasonable hotel near the station. There won't be the views of course, but it seems to me that you get a much more authentic sense of a city if you stay away from the tourist spots. How about it?'

Was ever a man more thoughtful and kind-hearted? 'Oh, Victor!' she said.

2

A few streets away, Carl was beginning to understand why the simple act of snoring could drive people to violent remedies. He had been startled a few weeks before to read of a hostel murder in which an elderly pensioner had been brutally attacked by the young man who had been obliged, by shortage of beds, to share his room for a month. He had, he said, been driven to it by the pensioner's snores; when asked if he didn't feel that murder was an excessive response to the problem, he had said that it might have been a bit drastic, but that he didn't see what else he could have done.

Not that he wanted to murder Harry, but the old man's bedsit was not designed for two people when one of them couldn't sleep without sounding like a volcano on the brink of eruption.

The sooner he got himself somewhere else to stay, the better. Even his cardboard box had been a bower of bliss by comparison.

'Hew-aha-acha-acha,' Harry rumbled into his pillow. 'Acha-eugh-eugh.'

Sighing, Carl pushed back the blanket and slid his feet down on to the cold linoleum. Buttoning his shirt neatly down to the bottom (Carl, for all his obsession with sex, was neurotically modest and he didn't want the old chap squinting at his privates), he felt his way through the grey darkness towards the stove. He lit the gas for Harry's pre-war tin kettle, before sitting cautiously (Harry's furniture had been assembled from local skips over the years and tended to be missing a vital limb) on one of the two chairs.

Harry's home was a dump, a squalid pirate's den of curiosities. Its owner liked to describe himself as a collector, but it would have been a hard job for anyone to guess what logic lay behind his choices. The mantelpiece of leering Toby jugs was not, for example, easily linked to a dusty pile of gas masks in the corner. The telephone, which Harry claimed had come from Sir Winston Churchill's home at Chartwell, looked venerable enough to have been Mr Bell's first attempt at telegraphic communication. The bath (one of the portable tin variety in which the bather can only crouch with his knees pressed to his chest) was alleged to have been used by Queen Victoria. And never since, from the dusty appearance of its interior. The only object about which Carl had found it easy to enthuse (for Harry was like a child among his treasurers, yearning to show them off and have them admired) was the old chap's bed: an empress's folly, or so it seemed, a mahogany swan whose head dipped decorously over the pillows, whose wings could be snapped shut to hold the sleeper in a snug wooden cradle, and whose webbed feet could be pulled out on iron struts to provide a dignified method of descent.

But there was no doubt that the bed was the one comfortable object in the place, and Harry was in it. Carl, too long-legged to lie with any ease on the broken leatherette sofa and too warm-blooded to be comforted by the single and very thin blanket Harry had managed to unearth from one of his sacks of stolen trophies, had spent a miserable night. The common-room sofa on which Harriet had laid him to rest under her own flower-sprigged duvet, bless her heart, had been a king's couch by comparison and he was more homesick than he cared to admit for his clean, hard little bed in Selena Street. No good thinking about that; the Frenchman was in it and, from the few gloomy hints thrown out by Spiro when he rang him last night, the Frenchman was there to stay. Poor old Spiro. What with the Frenchman and Charlie Everest, he didn't sound to be getting much joy out of Fay. Silly woman, mooning over film stars when she had a man as decent as Spiro eating his heart out for her.

He lit a cigarette off the gas before returning to his perch. So, what next? He hadn't wanted to take up Spiro's offer of his spare bedroom. Accepting it would have been half-way to putting himself back at the drawing-board for Vathos Properties and if there was one thing Carl was sure about, it was that he was not going to go on designing bathroom units. Pity about Harriet and Grendel; a few more nights on the common-room sofa wouldn't have done him any harm and she really was a nice little thing, not bad-looking, either. No, it looked as though Radlett was the best option. With any luck, there would be a call from Father Gerard this morning. 'Not that I wouldn't want to tell you to come straight along now,' Father Gerard had said when he rang him last night, 'But you know how it is at the Retreat. Ten visitors here at the moment and none of them easy. And how's the dear lady herself? Writing those screenplays, is she?'

He had sounded a bit odd, come to think of it. There had been a noticeable pause, after he'd explained that he wasn't being sent to the Retreat this time.

'It's just that I've always remembered how happy I was there,' he said. 'It felt good, you know.'

'That's what we're here for, lad,' Father Gerard had said. 'You know our motto. "Free our souls, and we will find our selves." So it's just a friendly visit you're thinking of making? Well, that's a fine idea, and I'm sure we can sort something out. I'm a bit busy now, Carl, but I'll ring you tomorrow and we'll see what we can do. Maybe you should have a word with Mrs Calman about it first. And you be sure to give her my best wishes.'

Carl drew the acrid smoke deep into his lungs and doubled up in a spasm of coughs as he stubbed out the long butt. Bloody fags. No, he didn't think he'd go round to Selena Street with Father Gerard's greeting. It was one of the things which irritated him about Fay, the way she never seemed to understand what a great man Father Gerard was. He hadn't forgotten what she'd done with the photograph they all got given when they left the Retreat. She didn't have to have it framed and put up for everyone to look at, but neither did she have to use it as a scoop for the cat litter. He had felt it like a physical pain when he thought of the good father's face being subjected to such an indignity. It had taken him half an evening to scrape off all the shit before he took it back into his own room. And she hadn't even tried to apologise. He'd known what it was all about, of course. She was jealous of Father Gerard's spiritual powers.

'Don't do it, Mum!'

Appalled, Carl turned to see Harry, bolt upright and wild-haired, staring at him over the splendid fan of the swan's mahogany tail.

'I'm not your mum, Harry. Lay off it, will you.'

'Sorry, mate.' Harry blinked and rubbed his eyes. 'Bad dream. You're up early.'

'It's past ten.'

'Like I said, early.' Yawning, Harry emerged from the swan. 'Got the kettle on, have you – I'm never alive until I've had my morning cuppa.'

Carl glanced at him as he shuffled towards the stove and held his hands towards the flame. 'Do you ever get out of those clothes, Harry? I'm surprised you don't stink the place out.'

'Ah, that's science, that is.' Harry dropped a tea-bag into a cup and stirred it with his finger. 'When you're over the first month or two, the dirt settles down to a pretty steady level, see? Builds up to a nice thick layer on the skin and there you are – free heating. Baths, now. You see, what they do is activate the bacteria, get them all perked up and ready for action. Leave them alone and they're no trouble at all. Right now.' He rubbed his hands. 'Get some clothes on. We've got work to do.'

'Work?' Carl's face sharpened with apprehension. 'You're not thinking of getting me to go out busking for you?'

'Frightened your friends might see you? Nah. I told you I never do recitals on Fridays. Fridays are skip-days.'

Carl stared. The things people did – who in their wildest dreams could have supposed that Harry was a closet exercise freak? 'Where do you do it? There's not room to swing a rope in here.'

'Skips, lad, skips.' Harry drained his tea. 'I saw them bringing in one a couple of days back. Outside one of those foreigners' mansions in Pope's Road. If there isn't some good stuff to be found in there by now, my name's not Harry Carpenter. Amazing what they throw away. I had a leg of lamb last week from one of their bins. Barely touched, just a slice off the end and out it goes. Something to do with religious practices, I suppose.'

Carl felt his stomach beginning to churn. 'That cold chicken we had last night –'

'Nothing wrong with it, was there?' Harry looked concerned. 'I gave it a good wash down under the tap. You said you liked it.'

'You said it was fresh.'

'I gave it a good sniff, Carl. Can't have been in the bin for more than a day and I never take stuff that hasn't got a bit of paper round it. You can't be too careful.' He rubbed his hands. 'Well, we can't sit here talking all morning. Two hours on the skips and then we'll pop down to the Rabbit.'

Carl had never thought of himself as snobbish, and he preferred now to tell himself that it was the idea of theft, not the embarrassment of being seen as a particularly degraded kind of local tramp (and seen he would surely be; he could think of at least three of Fay's friends who lived in Pope's Road) which was so distasteful. Perhaps he could lay claim to a stomach bug? If he hadn't got one now, he soon would have – chicken in the bag had acquired a whole new meaning in the last minute. But a stomach bug condemned him to spending the day in Harry's room, and there weren't even his magazines here to while away the time. Harry hadn't got any. He'd already checked and found nothing more appetising than a faded photograph of Harry's mother, large, windswept and plain, on Blackpool Pier. An urgent appointment?

'It'll be cutting things a bit fine if I'm catching the bus to Radlett for lunch, Harry.'

Harry reached across the table and gave his arm a friendly pat. 'I wouldn't be in too much of a hurry, Carl. It didn't sound to me as though your Father Gerard was all that keen on the idea of you dropping in, to be honest. Bit of a fair-weather friend, he sounded to me. They're all very nice and welcoming when you're paying the bills in those places –'

'Oh no.' Carl shook his head. 'You've got him wrong. Father Gerard's the kind of man who'd give you the shirt off his back. Money doesn't mean a thing to him.'

'Is that so?' Harry looked at him doubtfully. 'Well, a man like that's not going to worry what time you get there. You come and give old Harry a hand, eh?'

It was a considerable relief to Carl to hear a distant hammering on the front door. 'You've got visitors.' He pulled his trousers on. 'I'll go.' And, with any luck, be gone, he thought as he tried to ease himself round the back of Harry's chair. 'Move over.'

Harry shook his head. 'Not on your life. I don't like callers. I had one last week asking why I wasn't on the electoral register. They won't catch old Harry like that. You stay here and let him hammer. Or her.'

'Think what you're missing. You could have won the pools.' He managed to push his way past and out of the room, on to the dingy flight of stone steps where crates of old beer bottles and sagging piles of newspapers marked the passage of time.

'I don't do the pools,' Harry bellowed from below. 'Don't you open that door. I don't care if it's the royal family and a court chamberlain. You tell them there's no Carpenter here.'

'Sorry about keeping you waiting.' He had managed to wrench back the bolts – from the way Harry locked himself in, you would have thought he was guarding an overflow from the Bank of England – and drag the black door back on its creaking hinges.

'Mr Carpenter!' The man held out his hand with the eager readiness of an insurance salesman. 'I was beginning to be afraid I must have missed you. I'm Francis Wainwright. May I come in?'

Carl looked at him. Small, pink, going a bit thin on top. Wrong clothes for a salesman, but he was carrying a black briefcase which vaguely hinted at items for sale. Briefly, he drifted into a fantasy of stripper-style underwear, lovely little wisps of lace and satin ribbon. Fay had had a woman coming round with stuff like that once for randy housewives. Or so she said. You never could tell with her.

'Mr Carpenter's not buying anything today,' he said. 'But I don't mind taking a look. What have you got, then?'

The man stared at him. 'I don't seem to have made myself clear,' he said. 'This is a business visit. Now, if you'd be kind enough to let Mr Carpenter know I'm here, I'd be most grateful.' The glance at his watch was pointed and almost rude. 'I don't have a great deal of time to waste, Mr –?'

'Just Carl.'

'Mr Carpenter's friend, I take it?'

'Who asked you to take anything?' Carl demanded, glowering. What did the man think he was, a pervert? 'I'll give you bloody –'

'Oh, I don't think you will.' Mr Wainwright gave a smile as small and fast as if he had interest to pay on every tooth he exposed to the light. 'Not when you have the goodness to let me explain myself. Mr Carpenter was kind enough to send me some of his poems.'

Wainwright. Of course. The man at Star Channel. Here, asking to see Harry? It had to be some kind of a joke. 'I'll tell him you called,' he said, preparing to close the door.

'But you don't understand: I liked them. I want to use them.'

Carl stared. He looked serious enough. His face was pink and positively glowing with sincerity. 'I want,' Wainwright said in the loud and careful voice of the Englishman in a foreign country, 'to use his poems. I want to speak to him about it. But my time is – very – limited. Here is my card. Give it to him and tell him that I am here. Do you understand?'

He took the card and looked it over. 'Yeah,' he said. 'I understand. Give us a minute.' He tore back down the steps, taking them four at a time, kicking the old crates and newspapers out of the way as he went. 'Harry! Harry?' He could see no sign of movement in the cluttered room. 'You can come out. It's only me.' Silence. 'Don't you want to hear how much they like your poems?'

Harry's head poked out from under the bed. 'Who's they?'

He threw the card towards him. 'Only the telly bloke. He wants you to go on Star Channel. You're going to be famous.'

Harry groped for the card, peered at it and shook his head. 'He ought to have written. You go back upstairs and tell him to send me a letter.'

'Harry, he's waiting. He's come all this way to find you –'

'I didn't ask him, did I? I'm not having television people spying in my home. First it's them and their cameras and then you've got every burglar in London on your tail.'

'He hasn't got a camera.'

Harry gave him a withering look. 'Not one you can see. Don't you know anything about modern technology? I've got good stuff in here, mate, and they'll be a sight quicker than you to spot it. That telephone – it's worth thousands.'

Carl pulled a cover across the rumpled sheets of the swan and kicked the gas masks into the corner. 'The only thing Mr Wainwright is going to notice about your telephone is that it hasn't been dusted for twenty years. Now, sit down on the sofa and get a smile on your face. For God's sake, Harry, it's what you've spent twenty years hoping would happen.'

Glaring, Harry sat. 'Well, they're not getting me for nothing, I'll tell you that. And since you're here, you'd best make yourself useful. I'll have you for my agent. Nothing to it. Talk the price up and keep an eye on those bits of Dresden on the mantel.'

'That's the spirit.' Carl patted him on the shoulder, wondering if Star Channel knew what they were letting themselves in for. 'Come on down, Mr Wainwright.'

3

The Englishman's home has always been his castle, as Dickens knew when he sent Pip down to visit Wemmick, the solicitor's clerk, in his miniature fortress by the river. John Medway, like Wemmick and many another nonfictional character, had understood that fantasy, in however absurd a form, offers a merciful antidote for the quotidian poison of a world governed by the false and heartless religion of statistics. His home, had it been the pleasant folly of an aristocrat, would have been judged delightful, imaginative, charming. Standing as it did in the tree-lined street of an impeccably middle-class suburb, it was viewed as a monstrosity, an embarrassment and a disgrace to the neighbourhood. Snobbishness never disappears: it simply takes a new name.

Ocean Spray, on the chrome-railed bridge of which a black flag now fluttered a decorous signal of grief, was a striking testimony to its late owner's love of the sea. No flower grew in its garden that was not blue. The gangplank of varnished boards rose to the front door from a sea of forget-me-nots. The portholes of the galley kitchen overlooked a back yard in which an exact model construction of the Battle of Trafalgar was laid out on blue oilcloth. Inside, a brass-railed spiral staircase led up to the Master Cabin, complete with folding double berth, ship's lantern and walls curtained with canvas. A fan had been placed to the left of the door for the purpose of blowing a steady jet of air at the canvas, thus producing a very convincing imitation of the sound of a ship with a light wind puffing out its sails. The one uncurtained wall had, despite angry protests from Lucy, been ornamented with two cartwheels of oiled rope, also a compass backed in velvet and set in a square teak frame. Max's room was genially labelled on the door as 'Midshipman Medway'. The spare bedrooms were identified by handsome brass plaques as cabins three and four. But Mr Medway's finest achievement had, in his own view, been his conversion of the roof into the bridge and awesomely technological control room of *Ocean Spray*. It was here that he retired at the end of the day's work, either to spend a tranquil hour perusing his yachting magazines or to experiment with his newest gadgets, a wheel with an inbuilt computerised compass, a fold-up bathing platform, a retractable mast.

It was the bridge of *Ocean Spray* which had been the principal source of discomfort to the Medways' neighbours. They did not like it when their guests arrived with noisy accounts of a man in full white naval uniform who stood on his roof and shouted obscure commands to observe rights of way at startled pedestrians. They were not amused by the sight of a large anchor being winched down into the forget-me-not bed as Mr Medway berthed his boat for the night. They spoke in whispers of the time when Mrs Medway had been seen dancing a hornpipe by the rich light of a full moon, wearing, it was rumoured, nothing but a small yachting cap. But where eccentricity is known to exist, rumour and exaggeration must always follow.

Lucy had always detested *Ocean Spray*. The first thing she had done after telling the local estate agent to put it on the market was to take down the rope wheels, the canvas curtains and the ship's lantern and deposit them at the local rubbish tip. The yachting cap, together with the various naval uniforms which John bestowed upon his wife over the years, now lay in a large plastic bag in the kitchen, destined for the Help the Sailors Fund.

Lucy had just telephoned Gareth at Flite Holdings, his small but highly successful pensions and insurance business. Even the fact that she had been obliged to leave a message with his secretary and to endure being told that he would try (try!) to get back to her, had failed to lower her spirits. He would call. Destiny was on her side. Smiling, Lucy lay back in her chair and admired her freshly painted fingernails. The strains of *Music for Lovers* rang pleasantly through the room and a large vase of lilies – the least she could do for poor John – scented the air. In the long mirror at the far end of the room, she saw herself flatteringly reflected, and wondered why it had taken her so long to realise how good she looked in black.

The phone rang. Lucy's mouth went into a pout of irritation as she picked up the receiver.

'Oh, Miss Roth. How terribly sweet of you – yes, absolutely devasted. Poor little boy – they were so devoted. No, I should have rung to explain – I sent him to stay with his grandmother for the day. I just didn't feel it was good for him to be here. It's a house of grief, Miss Roth. I'm so glad you understand. Now, I've got rather an important call coming in – thank you. Yes, I'll give him your love.'

Trembling with annoyance, she slammed down the telephone. Blasted woman. Now she'd probably gone and missed Gareth's call. No. It was ringing again. She snatched it up.

'Gareth: Listen, I wondered if I could tempt you to come and have a quick lunch at my home today. Something rather extraordinary has happened. No, just you and me. You *can*?'

He was coming! What was more, he had positively jumped at the opportunity. Fay would have to hear about this. She rang her at once. Not a good idea. She had forgotten that this was the day when Charlie Everest was coming round. It was a long ten minutes before she was given the chance to deliver her news and Fay's response was, to say the least of it, unsatisfactory. She hadn't spent all that time listening to what Fay might or might not be wearing for his benefit, only to be told that it would be 'nice' to have lunch with her beloved.

'Nice! Fay, this is the moment we've all been waiting for.'

'You've been waiting for. I was wondering about the green chiffon – do you think it's a bit much for an afternoon visit?'

'You always look good in green – but Fay, do you think I should tell him straight away? I can't decide.'

'Whenever seems best. I was thinking of wearing the open-toe sandals, you know, the designer ones.'

'Doorbell,' Lucy said inventively. 'Sorry, darling, I've got to go.' Really, Fay was ridiculous. The trouble with clairvoyants, Lucy thought as she looked for the number of the local delicatessen, was that they were completely out of touch with reality.

4

Harriet was bored. Victor had gone to work, leaving her with strict instructions not to touch the computer. There had been no answer to her hopeful tap on Mrs Calman's door. The French windows leading down to the garden were locked. It was strange, Harriet thought with her nose against the pane, that a man of such brilliance should care so little for flowers as to plant marigolds in rows, interspersed with orange and scarlet gladioli. Perhaps the garden was where she should stake her claim: it had begun to dawn on her that she would never be allowed to aspire to more than changing the position of a soap-dish in the house.

Miss Press would be a good person to consult. She might even be persuaded to part with a few cuttings.

Millicent was deadheading a few roses to take her mind off the imminence of Roberta-Paula's arrival.

'Well!' She straightened her back. 'If it isn't the bride! Enjoying married life?'

'Goodness, yes.'

Millicent's lip curled. 'Glad to hear it.' She nipped off a dead bud with delicate precision.

'I've been looking at the garden,' Harriet began. 'I was wondering – you've got such lovely plants.'

'Wrong time of year for cuttings,' Millicent said quickly. 'They've got some very nice things down the hill at the garden centre. You could pick up some seeds for me while you're at it. And how's the famous book?'

Over and out, thought Harriet, impressed against her will by the speed with which Miss Press had turned the tables to her advantage. She bent to sniff a rose. 'Actually, he's finished it.'

'In a week!' Millicent stared. 'Can't be much good. Seen it, have you?'

How was it that Miss Press always managed to put her at a disadvantage? 'It's still in the computer. I promised not to touch it.'

'A big girl like you.' Millicent shook her head. 'You ought to be ashamed of yourself, Harry, letting him bully you like that. You want to show him what's what, my girl. Promised not to touch it, indeed. I wouldn't stand for it.'

Harriet's mood softened. Wasn't this exactly what she had been longing for someone to say? 'You really think I should –'

'I know you should. Stands to reason. You're his wife, aren't you. Share and share alike. And talking of sharing, I don't suppose you're so busy today that you can't come and have a spot of lunch. My daughter –'

'Your daughter? But I thought –'

Millicent looked evasive. 'I was just getting round to telling you about her when old Grendel came crashing in. Whoops – Victor. Good gracious, Harriet, there's no need to look so shocked. I wasn't born in the Dark Ages, you know.'

It was anger, rather than shock, which was reddening Harriet's cheeks. How dare she talk about him like that? 'Not shocked,' she said coldly. 'Just surprised. I'm afraid I shall be busy. Another time, perhaps.'

Millicent, who had settled on Harriet as a sturdy girl, quite capable of protecting her from any violence, was reduced to pleading. 'You wouldn't have to stay long, Harry dear. And I've got a lovely little joint.'

'I really can't,' she said unforgivingly. 'And, actually, it's Harriet. Nobody calls me Harry.'

'Glad to set a precedent,' Millicent said crossly and slammed the door.

Dreamily, Harriet wandered back up the stairs and into the flat. Miss Press, for all her nasty remarks, was right. She would make the bed and hoover the floors and clean all the windows until they sparkled, but first she would take a cup of coffee into Victor's study and unlock the key to the hidden splendours of his book. How impressed he would be when he came back to find that she was ready to discuss his work.

5

'Right, then.' Harry squared his shoulders and fixed Mr Wainwright with a stern and unfaltering stare of the kind he reserved for particularly reluctant benefactors outside the supermarket. 'Here we go.

> Cleave, wanton rose, to the womb of the night.
> Bend your bright eye from the sun's yellow light.
> Rose, let me gaze on your silky gold petals.
> They shine with the glow of the fresh-burnished kettles
> That stand on the hob in my own true love's kitchen
> And reflect all the love that my heart is so rich in.'

Silence fell. Carl dared a glance at their visitor and saw to his amazement that he was apparently wiping a tear from his eye. 'You liked it, then?'

'Course he liked it.' Harry glared at him. 'Frank here's a man of taste.'

'Most affecting,' Mr Wainwright said, but his voice was not quite so confident as Harry could have wished. 'You haven't written anything a little more – forceful?'

Harry thought. 'There's "Walls". About this bloke in prison who can't stand the sight of brick walls after he comes out.'

'Excellent.' Wainwright looked at his watch as Harry cleared his throat in preparation. 'I look forward to hearing it. Now, I don't want to rush you, but I said I'd be in the studio by twelve. The car's outside.'

'That's as maybe.' Harry leaned back with a nonchalant smile. 'And who said I was coming? We've business to discuss, me and my agent here. And you and I aren't going nowhere until we've got a deal. Money, Frankie.'

Mr Wainwright gave a small, irritated cough. 'Naturally, we'll pay all your expenses –'

'Expenses! Thought you'd get me for the price of a ham sandwich, did you?' Harry leaned forward and tapped the side of his nose with a significant smile. 'Well, I've got news for you. Five hundred quid's what it's going to cost you.'

'I see.' Mr Wainwright closed his eyes. This hadn't been a good idea. He'd had his doubts when he first drew up in the street and they hadn't decreased when he was picking his way through the litter on that disgusting stairwell. Now, imprisoned in a basement full of filthy old broken furniture, he found it hard to remember what could conceivably have made him think that this would be a wise departure from his normal morning routine. 'But you always have your toast and cereal first, dear,' Mary had said as he strode towards the door. 'You know it settles your stomach.' How right she had been. How right she always was.

'A cup of tea'll do you good,' Harry said considerately. 'You look a bit under the weather. Put kettle on, Carl.'

Mr Wainwright glanced at the row of grimy cups and shuddered. 'Very kind, but I think I'll wait.'

Why? What on earth had possessed him? He could still, just, remember that it had been as though some powerful outer force was controlling him from the moment he lifted that filthy dog-eared sheaf of poems from his desk with the intention of flinging them into the 'reject' tray, ready to be returned with the standard thank-you-but-not-for-us letter. His hand had been suspended in mid-motion and something – he clung forlornly to the hope that it was good instinct – had said: Stop. He had looked, and he had seen that they were dreadful and yet the instinct, or whatever it was, had spoken again and said: Do it. And he had, from that moment until he reached this horrible dump, been like a robot in the grip of a calm and absolute certainty that he was doing the right thing. He must forget the idea of appealing to the miserable two per cent who represented Star Channel's literary and intellectual following and turn to the masses. Harry Carpenter, not an exponent of literary excellence, was going to be the saving of their flagging audience ratings.

He had thought. But £500 for ten minutes of undiluted trash? And he had not even dared to think of the reactions of his colleagues.

'Five hundred,' Harry said, failing to read his mind. 'Take it or leave it, but you'd be better off taking it. Wouldn't you say, Carl?'

'I would.' He had been so transfixed by Harry's demand that he had forgotten what his role was meant to be until a stony look recalled him to his duties. 'I'd say five hundred's pretty cheap for a poet of Harry's quality,' he said. 'Nobody watches the kind of junk you put on nowadays, Mr Wainwright. You're making the right decision. Harry's what they'll want to watch, and I'm speaking as your average viewer.'

It was almost midday. Francis Wainwright swallowed a groan and came up with a sigh. 'It's not going to be easy, but I can promise my best endeavours.'

Harry spat neatly across the floor, to land a gob in the nearest gas mask. 'Best endeavours be buggered. You won't get me on my feet for that.'

'What he means,' Carl said hurriedly, 'is that it's not solid enough. You wouldn't catch Shakespeare writing a play if all you offered were best endeavours. Now, Harry Carpenter's name may not mean much yet on Star Channel, but we could tell you about places where Carpenter is a name to reckon with.' Like the Three-Legged Rabbit, he thought but felt it unhelpful to add.

Wainwright tugged at his tie and scribbled something in his memo pad. 'Three hundred, and expenses. That's my last offer.'

'Artists can't be choosers.' Harry's tone was grudging, but he gave a little bounce on the sofa and winked at Carl. 'Lead on, Frankie, and make it snappy.' He gave Carl a sharp dig in the ribs as they went up the stairs. 'See how I managed him? Putty in my hands. You weren't so bad yourself, neither. Hey, what do you reckon my autograph's going to be good for in the Rabbit after this?'

'Nothing if you don't get going.' Harry was capering up and

down on the steps like a frisky old goat. He gave him a push towards the car where Wainwright was already sitting in the driver's seat, chattering into a telephone while the engine idled over.

'And for God's sake try to stay sober until you've done the programme.'

Harry grinned. 'Sober? They've enough drink to float the navy in those telly buildings. And didn't you hear him saying they want me just as I am? You needn't look so worried. Tell you what. I'm feeling generous. I'll let you off the rent.'

'Thanks, Harry. You're a pal.' But Carl was still uneasy as he watched the car sweep Harry off to fame and glory. Three hundred quid for poetry they wouldn't give 10p for outside the supermarket? And a prime-time spot on Star Channel? It just didn't figure.

6

'I think we made another tiny little error in judgement, darling, don't you? Harry Carpenter isn't going to last ten seconds out there.'

Raphael started. 'What did you say?'

The shop-girl stared at him. 'I asked if you wanted to pay with a credit card.'

He must have been dreaming. 'Credit? No. I'll pay in cash.'

'That'll be fine.' Her eyes returned to the present he had chosen for Lily, a braided coat in deep yellow wool which he had picked because the model had reminded him of her, wide-eyed, with a long, slightly sly smile. 'It's gorgeous,' the girl said. 'You certainly made a good choice.'

'I hope so.' He allowed himself a cautious glance behind him, but the Bond Street shop was as empty as only expensive shops can be without looking unsuccessful. 'Can you have it delivered this afternoon? Mrs Tremain, 8, Selena Street.'

'Now you see me, now you don't.' It was the voice again, and it was one which he had no difficulty in recognising this time. It had issued, if he was not much mistaken, from the lips of the model. He began to feel distinctly unwell as, turning to stare at it, he saw its mouth broaden in a knowing grin.

'No problem, if you don't mind the extra charge,' the girl said. 'I'll get some wrapping paper. You look awfully pale. Are you all right?'

'Me?' He tried to smile. 'Oh, I'm fine, absolutely fine.' Anxiously, he watched her climb the shop's circular white staircase and move out of sight before he tiptoed across the floor to the model's side. 'Now I see you,' he hissed. 'What do you want this time?'

Fœdora fluttered a spectacular row of black fur eyelashes in a wink. 'Want, darling? I don't want anything you won't enjoy, too. S. gave me some time off so I thought I'd come earth-spotting and see how you were. Liven things up a bit.' She yawned. 'I thought you might be ready to give up a virtuous life by now.'

Raphael glared at her. 'I don't need any help from you. I'm very –'

'Would you like yellow paper with a blue ribbon or blue paper with a yellow ribbon?' The shop girl leant over the upper gallery.

'Nice legs,' Fœdora said.

'Blue paper,' Raphael said hurriedly. 'Please.' He bent over a basket of silk monogrammed squares and picked one out. 'I thought I'd just try one of these on the coat, round the neck.'

'Feel free.' The girl disappeared again.

'It's not a bit of use doing that,' Fœdora said calmly as he twisted it into a noose. 'You can't throttle plastic. But just you wait until she takes the coat off me. That's when the fun starts.'

'That's what you think. I'm terribly sorry,' he smiled as the girl came back down the stairs with the ribbon and paper. 'I've just changed my mind. I'm going to have the brown leather coat on that rail instead.'

'In fact, darling, I'll take the whole rail,' Fœdora said in an impeccable imitation of his voice.

The girl faltered in her stride. 'That's forty leather coats, sir. Are they all to go to the same address?'

'Sure,' Fœdora said swiftly. 'It's for the late-night customers. They love the girls in leather.'

'Just the one,' Raphael shouted. 'One leather coat.'

'And the one on the model,' Fœdora cut in. 'Just strip it off her, will you, darling? Give us a thrill.'

'Please get this straight,' Raphael said, leaning on the counter and staring at the girl with beseeching eyes. 'I do not want the coat on the model. Above all, I do not feel any wish to see you take that coat off her – what are you doing?'

The girl didn't even raise her head to look at him. 'I'm calling the police if you don't leave now sir,' she said. 'And if I were you, I'd call up a doctor. You need psychological help, not coats.'

Stumbling out of the shop in a daze of mortification, he walked straight into Fay Calman.

'Working?' asked Fay.

'It's my lunch-hour.' He seized her arm. 'I wouldn't bother going into that shop if I were you. Awful rubbish. Waste of time.'

'Of yours, maybe. It's my favourite shop.' Fay peered through the glass doors. 'How can you say a thing like that? Look at the coat on the model – it's perfect! And it isn't every day I get to meet Charlie Everest.'

'It's an outdoor coat.'

'So? I'll say I've just been out walking. Or maybe I can take him up on the hill. Hey, I've just realised who the model's face reminds me of. Your friend, the vinegar queen.'

'Fœdora? I hadn't noticed.' He looked at her earnestly. 'I really don't think yellow's your colour. But I did see a dress in that Italian shop on the corner that would look absolutely marvellous on you. I've got a few minutes. Why don't we walk down there together and see what you think?'

'Maybe I'll come and find you there. But there's no way I'm not going to try this one first. Let go of my arm, Raphael. I'm allowed out on my own, you know. I'm a grown woman.' She looked at him with kindly appraisal. 'I'm going to have to do a pendulum on your health. You don't look at all well. I'll call Madame Marakova and see if she can't fit you in for a course of light treatment, maybe the white lights. Buck you up a bit.' She patted his hand. 'And we'll get your aura checked.'

'Fay, I already have a doctor.'

'It's not a physical check-up you need, my dear,' she said. 'Think karma. That's the heart of it all. I'll be seeing you.'

How could he think about karma when Fœdora was smirking at him behind the plate glass and all too evidently intent on causing further mischief? He moved away, but only to the opposite side of the street, from where he could observe Fay as she walked the breadth of the shop to speak to the girl. She pointed to the coat. The girl nodded. Together, they went towards it. The girl reached up to start undoing the buttons.

'Don't do it to me, Fœdora,' he whispered. 'Don't you dare.' But the deed was done. The girl was slipping the sleeves away from the shoulders, pulling the coat free. There was nothing more incriminating on show than the anorexic and primly asexual form of a beige-limbed plastic model. Thankfully, he closed his eyes. Perhaps, after all, he had overestimated Fœdora's vindictiveness. She had been planning only to give him a fright in a new demonstration of the incurable frivolity which S. alone seemed always to find amusing. Still, she had done Lily out of a very pretty coat – no chance of getting it now with Fay's arms firmly thrust into its sleeves – and he had resolved not to go home without finding some suitably splendid object to bestow on her. Money might not be able to buy you love, but gifts, in his experience, always helped and today he was particularly anxious to make some material show of his affection. Lily had asked him to go and have tea with her at her father's house and he had been made aware that this would be an occasion on which he would come under a shrewd and dispassionate scrutiny. A handsome present would go some way towards dispelling any notion that he was a fortune-hunter in the mould of her ex-husband. He glanced at his watch. Plenty of time. He didn't need to be back in Selena Street until three and, at the worst, he had her father's address neatly inscribed in his diary. A present could still be found.

7

Harriet was pleased with herself. She had managed to get the machine to work and was now skimming confidently through the lines of green print. She hadn't, as yet, entirely grasped the argument but that, she felt, had more to do with the bad lighting in Victor's study than anything else. A stained-glass lantern overhead was tiresomely reflected on the screen in a way which made it difficult to focus on the words, but the switch at the door seemed only to operate the lights in the outside passage. The solution, she realised, must lie in the cluster of power-plugs under the desk. Kneeling on the floor, she reached forward to pull them out and, as the lights were extinguished, she heard a faint, ominous click from the desk.

'Oh, my God,' she whispered. 'No. It isn't. It can't be.'

She pushed the socket back again, but she must, in her haste, have dislodged one of the plugs from the adapter. The machine had ceased to operate.

'Calm. Cool, calm and collected,' Harriet said to herself. She went into the kitchen, made herself a cup of coffee and read three pages of *The Bachelor's Cookbook* without taking in a single word. She went back into the study and tried the machine again. Nothing. Then she took all the plugs out of the adapter and, very carefully, tried them one by one until, with a relief which no words could adequately convey, she heard a responsive click from above her had. Trembling, she returned to Victor's chair and pushed the button marked ENTER. Nothing appeared. The cursor appeared, jigging its flag on a sea of green. And nothing else. She pushed one button, then another, until none remained untried, and still the screen was blank.

She looked up the number of the company who made the machine and rang it. A brittle voice responded and inquired what her problem was, as though she had called a psychiatrist.

'Don't you have the instruction manual there?'

'I can't find one,' Harriet stammered. 'The thing is, I pulled the plug out of the wall while I was reading the screen.'

'No problems there,' the voice said cheerily. 'Not so long as you reconnected it.'

Harriet's heart leapt. 'Oh, I did! So it's going to be all right?'

'Straight away? You did connect it straight away?'

'Well, no.' She tried to remember. 'I think I did it after about twenty minutes.'

'There's the answer.' The voice sounded as blithe as though she had just been awarded a prize. 'You cancelled. Disconnect the machine from the main power-system for a space of ten minutes and you engage the erasing faculty.'

'The erasing faculty? You mean I've rubbed it out?'

'Got it in a nutshell.' The voice grew still more cheery. 'Perhaps I could recommend you to take advantage of our special Comp-Train offer this month. I can arrange for one of our reps to call if we fix an appointment for you – say, Tuesday morning?'

By Tuesday morning she would probably be dead. He would never forgive her.

'There's absolutely nothing I can do?'

'Not in this particular case you're specifying.'

'Thanks.' She put down the receiver and hid her face in her hands. People said that the way to comfort yourself was to think that life could always get worse. How could it?

8

At 12.45 precisely, Millicent Press heard the trump of doom, a single firm rap on the front door. Tiptoeing up the stairs, she pressed her face to the bedroom window and looked down, cursing the rambling rose which obscured both the porch and the figure below it. Better be safe than sorry, she thought and drew back to wait for the retreat which must surely follow when no answer came. Unfortunately, in her haste to conceal herself, she knocked a little glass bowl off the sill. It fell to the ground with a clatter and, a moment later, her visitor came into view, scanning the windows with a keen and persevering glance. Millicent edged behind the curtains, but not quite quickly enough to escape detection.

'Mom, is that you?'

Mom? Wincing, Millicent thrust up the sash. 'Paula dear, how punctual: I was just tidying some things. Down in a minute.'

She sounded harmless enough, but Millicent still paused to take her brass knuckleduster from beside the bed before she hobbled down the stairs to open the door. One couldn't be too careful. She bent her head to the spyhole in the door and found herself staring straight into a moon-sized close-up of the woman's face.

'Hi there,' Paula said playfully. 'I bet you're taking a peek at me right now. That's fine, Mom. You look all you want. I've nothing to hide.'

Opening the door, she feigned innocence. 'Did you say something, Paula? I'm afraid I didn't quite catch it.'

'Nobody calls me Paula, Mom. Just plain old Pat will do fine.' The woman pushed her way in and dropped her jacket over the banisters before staring around with a displeasingly pro-prietorial air. 'Well, isn't this so dear! Will you look at these little rooms! You know, I think I could fit your whole house into my last apartment.'

'Could you?' Millicent fought down a surge of dislike. 'Well now, won't you come through?' She didn't like the way Paula was already eyeing her possessions. She didn't, come to that, like anything about her.

'First things first,' the woman said and, pinioning Millicent against the wall, she enveloped her in a disagreeably intimate embrace, bosom to bosom. 'Let the anger pulse out,' she said. 'I'm going to hold you tight and let it come. We're not going to let any negative feelings into this relationship, OK?'

Millicent endured it for a minute. Grappled in hoops of steel, she didn't feel she had much choice. 'Very nice,' she said. 'Very affectionate. But I don't see any reason for you to think I'm angry with you.'

Paula, or Pat, as she must now be known, dropped her arms. 'Your anger isn't with me, Mom. It's in yourself. Rejection's a much harder thing for the doer to handle than the done-to. But don't let it bother you. We're going to work this thing through together. You just have to remember that I can't help if you close me out.'

'I thought you'd already come in,' Millicent said coldly. She returned with an effort to the role of the gracious hostess as she led the way into her sitting-room, a room which was not, in her view, to be dismissed as either dear or little. 'Do make yourself at home, Pat. Have one of the chairs by the fire. Whisky? Sherry? Or would you like a cocktail?' Americans always drank cocktails, she remembered. Peculiar ones with names like Between the Sheets.

'How's your tap?' Pat, firmly ensconced in Millicent's chair, thrust her legs out on the carpet as she stared about the room. 'You know, good old tap.'

'Dance?'

'Water.' She looked with unconcealed disapproval at the tumbler of whisky which Millicent had poured out for herself and was raising thankfully to her lips. 'You really shouldn't, Mom. It's very dehydrating. Drink doesn't solve anything.' Her eyes flickered away to the bowl of fruit which stood on a table by the window. 'Oh my God, that's terrible!' Striding towards it, she picked up the pretty cluster of black grapes and held them out at arm's length. 'Don't tell me you eat these, Mom? Haven't you read the reports? Toxic sprays. Exploitation of female labour. Women have died for these grapes, Mom.'

'Female labour?' Millicent looked at her sharply. 'You're not a feminist, are you?'

Past smiled. 'That's not a term we use any more. Womanwise is the phrase we employ in my communication group. We don't see ourselves as victims of any kind of male supremacy. I mean, just using those words brings a very negative force to the front. The way we see it is that we can empower ourselves –'

'Empower isn't a word.'

'I'm not talking words, Mom. I'm talking concepts. When we start to conceptualise ourselves –'

'And are you going to be in England long?' Millicent found herself glancing at Bobbie's photograph for his approval of this brusque approach. 'Keep it up, kid,' his eyes seemed to say. 'You let her know what's what.' What on earth would Bobbie have found to say to a daughter who talked about being womanwise and conceptualising? Whoever would have thought that such a passionate union as theirs could have resulted in such a loud and lumpish creature?

'. . . not going back until we've worked this thing through,' Pat was saying in the droning voice of the committed psycho-babbler. 'But I'm having problems figuring out the way you English handle relationships. You think people are going to be so warm and friendly, the way they are in Dickens's novels, I guess. And then you get over here and it's worse than New York. They're all so busy running to catch up, they just don't seem to have a moment free to explore being. Still, Mabel – she's the one who started Womanwise – put me in touch with some friends who are setting up a circle in London. That's going to be a very humanising experience. You should join it, Mom. It could be a wonderful way to start exploring the dimensions of our relationship.'

Millicent took a deep breath. Duty, she reminded herself, must be done. 'I don't think Womanwise is quite my style, dear,' she said firmly as she poured herself a second and much larger glass of whisky. 'I'm afraid you'll find I'm rather settled in my habits. I've made a room ready for you and you're welcome to stay for as long as you like, but you'll have to understand that this is my house and that I like doing things my way. I'll tell you what I can about your father. I don't propose to ask you about your life, but I'm prepared to listen to anything you want to tell me. But there isn't a bit of use in try to get me interested in empowering or conceptualising. I don't like it and I don't want it.'

'Right,' Pat said after a long pause. Millicent felt a twinge of remorse. The girl had gone to some trouble to seek her out, after all, and she clearly wanted to be friendly. It wasn't her fault if she had got caught up in that feminist nonsense. Millicent had read her papers and she knew that it all came from women not having enough to do with their lives. They didn't mean any harm. Limping to the window, she took the photograph of Bobbie Snetherton from the sill and put it in her daughter's lap.

'There you are,' she said. 'That's your father. I don't suppose you know much about cars. No? I didn't think so. Well, you've come to the right place to learn about them. Your father was a very fine racing driver and I – although I'm not one for boasting –won the European Ladies' Championship before you were born.'

'I'm impressed,' said Pat, but her eyes had flickered away to the mantelpiece. 'That's a lovely bit of Meissen china. You've got some nice things here, Mom. Very nice indeed.' She smiled. 'Go on telling me about the racing. I want to hear everything about you and Dad. Tell me about the Championships.'

This was better, but the roast beef was waiting to be carved. 'Over lunch, dear. Come along. They were all terribly jealous of me, of course. I don't like to sound pleased with myself, but Bobbie Snetherton wasn't the only man who said I was a real beauty –'

'I'll bet.' Walking meekly at her heels, Pat paused to glance at her reflection in the hall. The smile she gave it was so brief as to be almost imperceptible. 'Go on. I'm so interested.'

9

The table in the dining-room alcove looked all set to win the How-to-Present-a-Perfect-Meal prize of the year, which was hardly surprising, since it was from Sarah Franklin's *How to Present a Perfect Meal* that Lucy had constructed her arrangement. Roses in a silver petal-shaped bowl sprayed out over the best Italian plates on which she had placed napkins in the sculpted forms of fans with a rose nestling in the base. Mindful of Gareth's love of good food – further proof, if any was required, that he was a man of sensual appetites – she had ignored Miss Franklin's advice to put quality before quantity and had lavishly heaped a good two pounds of smoked salmon on to a flat silver salver before surrounding it, as instructed, with frail cornets of buttered brown bread, crisp clusters of watercress and twisted slices of lemon. Nothing too elaborate to follow, she had decided after wondering where to get the pomegranates, persimmons and white peaches which Sarah Franklin proposed for a macédoine on account of their low cholesterol content. There must be simpler ways of lowering one's cholesterol intake, and the local delicatessen had turned out to do an excellent Black Forest cake with plenty of whipped cream and cognac which Gareth was more likely to appreciate.

Clothes had been a larger source of anxiety. The red dress had gone, disgraced, to the back of the cupboard after the disastrous tea of last week. The white track suit seemed to have shrunk and Max had told her that the pink silk dress made her look motherly, which she translated correctly as fat. She had ended on a compromise: keeping on the black dress which so bewitchingly diminished her curves, but adding the hidden treat of a lace bra with the prettiest little pink ribbon threaded through the cleavage, and some very fetching lace camiknickers which might, if the fates were kind, be a helpful heightener of Gareth's desire. Sarah Franklin would probably not have approved, but this was an area in which Lucy felt that she could teach that young lady how to do a thing or two. Her last wise act had been to take the telephone off the hook. Nothing could be less conducive to an afternoon of vibrant passion than another call from Max's teacher or from one of John's grieving relations.

Nothing, but nothing, was going to be allowed to go wrong.

The doorbell pealed. Lucy paused only to squirt the room with her best French scent before she hastened to the door. She took a deep breath, perfected her smile, and flung it open.

'Gare – oh my God. What on earth are you doing here?' She bent to prise open his jaws. 'Take that disgusting gum out of your mouth.'

To look at the child's face, you would have thought the loss of a stick of gum was a greater tragedy than the loss of a father. 'There's nothing wrong with it,' he said. 'It's sugar-free. And I paid for it myself.'

'Never mind the gum,' Lucy snapped. 'Why aren't you with Granny?'

Max chewed slowly, blew a pink bubble, and sucked it in again. 'Granny said she didn't think it was good for you to be all on your own,' he said after an interminable pause. 'She said I was to be sure to ask you to call her and let her know if you wanted her to come over for the afternoon. And have you remembered to ring Aunt Julia and cousin Sheila because they'll be pestering her for details if you don't?' He slipped under her arm and into the house. 'Look at this! Smoked salmon! Who've you got coming?'

Seething, she hurried after him to see a line of muddy footprints stretching down the hall and all the way to the lunch table. There were times when – no, of course she didn't think that. Everyone knew she was a wonderful mother.

'I do wish you'd remember to wipe your shoes, darling. Now come away from that table. I know you're terribly upset, but that's no reason to be naughty.'

Max turned towards her with bulging cheeks. 'You didn't give me any breakfast. And you know I don't like Granny's cooking.'

Lucy counted to ten, smiled sweetly and walked across the room to remove his hand from the plate. 'That's enough. Now listen to me, darling. Mr Lloyd-Evans –'

'He's not coming here!' Max looked at her with horror. 'I thought you weren't ever going to speak to him again.'

'I had to, Max. Grown-ups can't always choose what they want to do, I'm afraid.' His stare was full of cynicism. Inspiration came. 'He's an executor, you see. He's coming here to help with all the money arrangements now that poor Daddy –'

'And you're all dressed up and giving him smoked salmon just because he's an executioner,' Max interrupted scornfully. 'I don't believe you. You sent me to Granny so you could be alone with him.'

'So you wouldn't be bored, darling,' Lucy said cunningly. 'It was you I was thinking about. You don't imagine I want to be on my own with him, do you?'

'You're not going to be.' Max gave her a reassuring smile. 'I'm not leaving you.'

Lucy took a deep breath. 'That's so lovely of you. But it wouldn't be appropriate to have you here, my angel, not for a business discussion. Why don't you – I'll tell you what. Get the keys from the drawer by my bed and I'll let you go in the control room on the bridge. Just this once. There's some cold chicken in the fridge. Take it up there and you can have a lovely picnic. Nice idea?'

Max nodded. 'Super-nice. Don't worry, I'll stay out of the way.' Heading towards the kitchen with obliging speed, he turned just as she was spraying more scent on her throat. 'I do think you're brave, Mummy. You must feel so awful.'

'Awful?' She blushed as he stared at her. 'Oh, awful!' And she did, for a fleeting moment, feel bereft. Then the bell clanged again and she felt nothing but relief as Max scuttled out of sight.

'Gareth! You're here!'

Gareth was looking hot, red and angry. 'Bloody stupid idea having a gangplank,' he said. 'I nearly missed my footing down there. If this was America, I'd be suing your husband for a thing like that.' He stared up the side of the house. 'Puts a different light on him, seeing all this,' he said. 'I'd no idea the man was a nutter. You ought to tell him not to make such an ass of himself.'

The martyr's role always had its appeal for Lucy. 'Oh, my dear,' she sighed, 'you don't know the half of it. The things I've had to endure. Never mind that. Come in and see what I've got ready for you.' She stroked his cheek. 'Bloody Marys, just the way you like them.'

'Not in the middle of the day, Lucy. I'm a working man. The salmon looks good. Why don't we just get going on that?' He moved towards the table with a purposeful smile.

'No little drinkies?' Lucy faltered. 'Not even sherry?'

'Perhaps a glass with the meal.' He looked at his watch. 'I hate to hurry you, but I've only got twenty minutes. Appointment with the lawyers at 2.30.' He smiled at her as he reached for the salmon. 'You look good, Lucy. Black suits you.'

She sank gracefully on to her chair before bringing out her handkerchief for a discreet dab. 'Oh Gareth, you can't think I'd wear it just for vanity? I didn't want to tell you over the telephone.'

He laid down his knife and fork. 'Out with it. What's up?'

'I'll tell you in a moment.' She leant towards him. 'You said you were going to the lawyers? Nothing wrong, I hope?'

'Depends on how you look at it, I suppose.' He resumed his attack on the salmon. 'I'm divorcing Felicity. Things haven't been going well for a long time and there's no point in calling a sow's ear a silk purse any more.' He looked at her reproachfully. 'You aren't eating.'

His precious Felicity demoted to a sow's ear? She could hardly contain her elation. 'Perhaps I will have just a scrap.'

'Go on,' he said kindly. 'That's more like it. That's the Lucy I know.'

It was no use. She couldn't keep it to herself any longer. Glowing-eyed, she gazed upon her love as he licked a morsel from the corner of his lips. 'Oh Gareth, it really is destiny. I always knew it would bring us together in the end. You see, I asked you here to tell you something rather – well, I suppose it's dreadful, really. John –'

Gareth started. 'I thought you promised to be sensible. My God, woman, if you've dragged me all the way here to tell me you've poisoned your husband –'

'He went on holiday five days ago,' Lucy said. 'And I'd like you to know that he left in good health.'

Gareth resumed his attack on the salmon. 'Well, that's all right, then.'

'It is and it isn't. You didn't see the black flag outside?'

His eyes grew wary. 'No. You'd better explain what's going on. And Lucy – do try not to dramatise things.'

'He went sailing. He had an accident. And he's dead. It is difficult not to sound dramatic when something like this happens,' Lucy said plaintively. 'Now do you realise what I've been trying to make you understand for all these years? It was fated. It always has been. Don't you see? Your divorce – John's death – our love –'

His eyes had glazed over. She reminded herself not to sound too emotional; it always made him uneasy. 'I think I'm going to change my mind about that Bloody Mary you were kind enough to suggest,' he said. 'Lemon, salt, and plenty of vodka.'

'I'll get some ice.'

Max was in the kitchen, skulking behind the fridge and trying, unsuccessfully, to become invisible as she approached. She took him by the ear and yanked him out. 'I thought you were going to stay upstairs. Eavesdropping is a very nasty habit.'

'So's telling fibs,' he said in a furious whisper. '"Our love"? *Our* love? To that creep?'

'Is there something I can do?' Gareth called.

'I'll be with you in a moment.' She took her fury out on the ice, hammering it out of its rubbery casing. 'Upstairs, Max. This minute or I'll – I'll –'

'I'm going,' he said. 'No need for threats. You couldn't think up anything worse than this in a million years.'

Nothing so disfigures the face as stress, Lucy told herself as she smoothed a smile into place and sailed through the door. 'I was just trying to comfort poor little Max. It's so hard for him to accept. A child needs a father – more cake, Gareth?'

'Just the drink, thank you.' The rapidity with which he downed it suggested that his inner turmoil was quite as great as her own. 'Oh, darling,' she said impulsively, 'I do know how you're feeling. It scares me, too, after all this time. But life's going to be so wonderful from now on – isn't it? Why are you looking at me like that?'

Gareth coughed and dabbed a drop of tomato juice off his chin. 'Time we got a few things straightened out, Lucy. I'm certainly sorry to hear about your husband. Tragic, absolutely tragic. Terrible for the boy. But you're a strong woman, Lucy. I've always admired you for your strength of character. And you're still young. I'm not a betting man, but I'd be very surprised if you couldn't find yourself somebody –'

'Somebody!' She felt as though she had been dropped in a river of ice. 'The divorce – you said you were going to the lawyers – we always said –'

'You said.' He shook his head. 'The trouble with you, old girl, is that you're so busy saying what you want that you can't hear what you're being told, not even when it's being shouted in your face.'

Trembling, Lucy leant back in her chair. 'Go on. Shout it.'

His tongue flickered nervously round his lips. 'You can't blame me. I never said we had a future. I didn't ask you to go to those idiotic clairvoyants. They only tell you what you want to hear, Lucy. That's their job.'

'Get on with it,' she said tonelessly. 'Say whatever it is that you have to say.'

'Right.' He squared his shoulders. 'I'm marrying Melissa, my secretary. That's what I came here to tell you. I didn't want you hearing about it from some stranger. Naturally, I felt it would be better if you and I could end on a friendly note. I hoped that was how you would see it. I – er – I really am terribly sorry about your husband. Wish I could help. I'll see myself out.'

The devil himself could hardly have made a faster exit. He had managed to get his coat on while he was still talking and his hand was on the door latch while he was expressing his wish to help. Looking through the window, she saw him hurrying down the gang plank and out of the gate. A moment later, she heard the screech of his departing car.

Gareth was going to marry Melissa. She took off her shoes. Slowly, with the gait of a somnambulist, she started to clear away the meal. She washed each spoon, fork, glass and plate, polished the knife blades. She put them tidily away in their allotted places. She mopped out the sink and hung the cloth up to dry. She rang Max's granny and did what she could to appease her for having failed to discuss the arrangements. And then there was nothing left to do and she wished she could feel angry or unhappy or anything that would tell her that nothing had changed. There was no height of rage or depth of grief over which she hadn't ranged in the years of pursuit and yet, now that it was over (she did understand that this part of it was over), she felt almost peaceful, as though she had been exorcised and freed of some tormenting spirit. She was, at last, in the situation which she had fought to deny with all of her considerable energy, and she knew for the first time exactly what the end should be. Looking out of the window, she felt pleased that, on this particular day, the sky should be so blue and that the trees should look so pretty with the afternoon light shimmering in their leaves. Leaving his wife after fifteen years to run off with a secretary less than half his age – how could the poor, silly man ever have imagined he was going to get away with it?

Smiling, Lucy went to the study and unlocked the third drawer down in poor John's desk. Back in the hall, she paused to call up the stairs.

'I've got to go out for a bit, Max. Back soon, OK?'

Standing by the window, Max watched her as she walked briskly down the path and towards her car. Pressing his nose to the glass, he saw her take something out of her pocket, wrap it carefully in a scarf and put it in her handbag. But she had started the engine and driven the car away before he realised just what it was that he had seen in her hand.

His mouth open in a soundless scream of panic, Max tumbled down the stairs and fled down the road.

'Mummy! Mummy!'

Too late. He had wished for her happiness and Daddy had died and now she was going to shoot Gareth and they would put her in prison.

People often said that Max was remarkably mature for his seven years. Now, having dried his eyes on his sleeve, he applied himself to the problem of thwarting his mother's plan of action. The first thing he must do, without a doubt, was to find Gareth and warn him. Armed with a bottle of Coke and a lavish slice of Black Forest cake, he sat down in the kitchen to work his

way through the thirty-five Lloyd-Evanses who lived in the
London area.

10

But would Lucy Medway ever have the nerve to carry revenge so
far, Raphael wondered as he strolled across the mosaic foyer of
the National Gallery where, having previously found a very
pretty turquoise bracelet to bestow on Lily, he had decided to
while away his last half-hour. On the whole, he was inclined to
hope that she would. He hadn't liked what he had seen of Mr
Lloyd-Evans. No, all in all, he was well pleased with Lucy's
positive response. The child would be far better off in the care of
his grandmother – or perhaps that nice little schoolteacher could
be persuaded to do something?

His thoughts turned to the drama which was drawing near,
the scene of his greatest triumph, the gift of Charlie Everest to
his landlady. That, surely, must come to a happy conclusion for
her, if not for poor Vathos. He felt guilty about Spiro. Perhaps a
meeting with Carl would cheer up him? They seemed to get on
well. Maybe if Spiro could do something useful for Carl, Fay
would come to her senses and make the right choice.

Twenty minutes left, and then he must think about a taxi to
Selena Street. There were too many schoolchildren in this room
and he had never much cared for Constables. He smiled
benevolently at the elderly female in uniform who skulked
behind him in a corner.

'I wonder if you could be kind enough to direct me. I'm
looking for the Bouchers.' Self-indulgent, perhaps, but those
plump and opalescent bodies were an exquisite reminder of his
pretty Vicomtesse. Lily, with all of her grace and charm, had
little of Madeleine's sensuality.

The woman looked at him for a long time without speaking.
Then, very slowly, she bared her teeth in a narrow, vulpine grin.
'Not your lucky day, Clegg,' Fœdora said. 'Help! Murder! He's
armed!'

'I don't believe it,' Raphael moaned as the schoolchildren
pounded across the floor towards him and, screaming with

excitement (looking at Constables was no competition for the thrill of chasing armed criminals), bore him to the ground. With one strapping child astride his legs and another attempting to grind his head into the floor, there was no point in even trying to fight back. 'And he looked such a nice young man,' he heard Fœdora say. 'Do bear that in mind when you're taking his evidence, officer. He was very polite. Such a shock –'

Raphael looked wearily up a yard of blue leg to the policeman's blunt-nosed automatic. 'That woman,' he said, 'is not who she seems. Ask them to check her name. She shouldn't be here.'

'Up you get, sir,' the policeman said. 'I'm afraid I'm going to have to ask you to accompany me. Anything you say will be taken down in evidence and you will be free to make a call to your solicitor from the station, should you so wish.'

'I don't have a solicitor.'

'That, sir, is your problem, not ours. If you'd just hold your wrists out.'

'I only asked her for directions. I never laid a finger on her.'

'No, sir. And that's only a water-pistol in your pocket,' the policeman said. 'Out of the way now, kiddies.'

'Bitch,' Raphael said out of the side of his mouth as he was led past Fœdora. She smiled.

'You poor, poor man. I hope you'll be lenient, officer. If there's anything I can do –'

'There certainly is, Miss. I'm afraid you'll have to come down the station with us.'

It afforded Raphael a moment of satisfaction to see the expression of dismay on Fœdora's face.

11

The sight of a leggy oriental girl in spindle-heeled black boots and a short black skirt had caused Carl to drop his quest for spiritual peace and break into a loping run along the pavements when a hand dropped heavily on his shoulder.

'So where you go in such hurry? You get new job with the mail service?'

Regretfully, Carl watched the girl swing out of sight. 'Just trying to catch a bus. I'm going to see Father Gerard at the Retreat. I thought I might stay there for a bit and sort myself out.'

Spiro looked at him with owlish solemnity. 'You have to sort it, Carl, nobody else do it for you. You have to choose.' He patted him on the back. 'You too thin. We go to the Bacchus and feed you up and then you go to Retreat, OK?'

'No hard feelings about the job, then?'

Spiro shrugged. 'Why I going to have hard feelings? I tell you something true, Carl. It not so bad you leave. People not like the way you make the bathroom units. They want a nice colour, soft light, carpet. You make them too technology, like hospital. I wasn't going to say, but now you stop, I make this confusion.'

'Confession.' Carl shook his head. 'How come you can make money faster than Fay makes predictions and yet you still can't talk English?'

'I don't make money with reading grammar books,' Spiro said. 'I not talk so bad. You going to tell me you can speak Greek?'

It wasn't until they were on their second bottle of wine in the restaurant that it became apparent why Spiro had been so eager for a meeting.

'This Frenchman,' he said. 'I don't like him. He there in the morning, looking at Fay when she walking about in little bit clothes doing her exercises. She tell me he not bothered with her, he chasing girl next door. How he going to do that when he see Fay in little bits?'

'Underclothes, Spiro, not little bits. You make it sound as though she's been chopped up.'

'Ha ha!' Spiro shouted, spotting a joke. 'Chopped up. Very good. I like this. Funny. But you not answering what I tell you. Fay, she very attractive – what happen when he alone with her every morning, every night?'

Carl thought. 'You shouldn't worry. Fay wouldn't let him do anything. She'd be much too scared of catching some special virus from Paris. She's a prude, anyway. Look how she was about finding a few magazines.'

'Prune? I don't understand this word. Fay, she a very sexy woman,' Spiro said. 'I don't think she let a few germs worry her when she feel something for a man.'

'Come on. What's worrying you? You're the only man she's ever stuck with.'

'I like Dora,' Spiro said gloomily.

'So do I.' Carl sighed. 'I hope Fay's feeding her properly.'

'No, she see me like Dora. Like pet of house. Not like the Frenchman. How she going to fancy man with Mr Majestic trousers and hair going after that? And now this Everest.'

Carl decided it was time to get some more wine. 'You're not worried about him? She can't make love to a telly, for God's sake.'

'Not telly, him.' Spiro's hand clenched over a bread roll. 'He come to her home today and she tell me not to call. He want to talk movie scripts with her.'

'So?' Carl shrugged. 'They'll talk business. He's not going to sweep her off her feet.'

'But Charlie Everest, Carl! He her big passion. She see him in the cards.'

Carl rolled his eyes. 'Tell me something she hasn't seen in the cards. Remember how I was going to be a great designer and how we had to talk her out of getting Terence Conran round to look at those pillars I did for her. Remember the alien forces who were going to invade Selena Street? It isn't two weeks since she was ringing all those science journalists asking how to recognise a UFO.'

'Maybe Fay see more than you think,' Spiro said. 'This Frenchman – how you going to explain the way he just turn up on the doorstep?'

'Does that make him a Martian?'

'I don't know what it make him.' Spiro was no longer in the mood for jokes. 'I remember how he come in the kitchen and say all nice and friendly, what she want for her big wish? And then Charlie Everest rings to say he wants to see her. You going to tell me it's just coincidence it happen like this?'

'Gotta be.' Carl found himself thinking about the way Wainwright had showed up at Harry's door and of how Grendel had suddenly decided to marry Harriet. Too bad nothing had happened to him except to be thrown out of his room.

'What you thinking?' Spiro demanded. 'Maybe I go in and take care of this Everest. Maybe I punch his face in. We go together.' He signalled for the bill.

Carl, no slouch at removing himself when there was money to be produced, stood up. 'I've got to get to Radlett. Don't let this Everest business get you down. It's all dreams with Fay.'

Spiro looked at him gloomily. 'And now the dreams come true.'

12

'I always fry the potatoes after they come out of the pan,' Millicent said. 'That's the secret. Sure you won't have another helping?'

Pat clasped her hands over her stomach. 'I really couldn't. This is ruining my self-discipline. And the beef was just gorgeous. So much flavour. Go on about when you and Dad were in Pisa. I envy you all that travelling, you know. I always wanted to go to Italy.'

One shouldn't prejudge people, Millicent thought. It was a pity that Pat had let her figure go and she didn't have a clue about making the best of herself with that ghastly haircut which made her look like Friar Tuck, but she was very agreeable and anxious to be friendly. And it was only a few days ago that she had been leafing through a travel brochure called 'On the trail of Tuscan wines', which had given her quite a little pang of nostalgia. A trip would be a good chance to brush up her rusty Italian – Bobbie had always let her do the talking and she had never had any trouble in making her wishes clear at hotels and restaurants. 'How beautifully the signora speaks the language,' she had often heard it said and had seen no reason to think her prowess was being overpraised.

'*Lei vorrei andare in Italia con me, forse?*' She threw it out with a fine rolling of the r's which had always impressed Bobbie.

'*Ah si, mi piacerebbe molto, mamma,*' Pat said and then went on to jabber something quite incomprehensible. It ended on an interrogative note which Millicent could well have done without.

'I, of course, only know the Tuscan dialect,' was the best she could do in the circumstances. 'I thought you said you hadn't been there.'

'I studied Italian and German in high school,' Pat said. 'But I didn't really get into languages until later. Serbo-Croat was the one I enjoyed most.'

'Gracious.' Millicent took a moment to rally. 'Time for coffee, I think.'

'Oh, but that's a great idea, Mom!' Pat was glowing with excitement. 'We could go to all the places you visited with Dad. It'd mean so much more if you were telling it all right there where it happened.'

Telling what, Millicent wondered? This is where your father and I had a very nice night at the Pellegrina and made love under the grand piano in the ballroom? It surely wasn't about that kind of thing that she wished to hear? And, if you took away the meals, which she could still recall down to the last pistachio ice-cream in Parma, there wasn't much left to describe. And she wasn't so sure that she wanted a companion whose Italian would win all the admiration.

'We could go to Siena and Assisi,' Pat was saying.

'Your father and I never went there.'

'How about Florence?'

'Just Perugia, Pisa and Positano.' A knock at the door saved her from the awkwardness of having to explain about P. for pleasure. She wasn't sure that Pat would appreciate the joke.

'I thought you were too busy to come to lunch,' she said, seeing Harriet on the doorstep and remembering only that she had been most unnecessarily rude. 'I do happen to be entertaining a guest.'

'I'm sorry, Miss Press. I really didn't mean to disturb you, but I've done the most terrible thing and I don't know what Victor's going to say and Mrs Calman's out and –'

'What did you do – burn a hole in one of his shirts?'

'Worse,' Harriet said miserably. 'Much, much worse.'

Millicent brightened. Disasters were always interesting. She peered over Harriet's shoulder. 'Well, the house is still standing. We were just having coffee but it sounds to me as though a spot of calvados wouldn't come amiss. I'll have some myself, just to keep you company. Pull that chair up, Pat. We seem to have a drama on our hands. Pat, Harry, Harry, Pat. Well then.' She poured out the drinks with her usual liberal hand. 'What's the problem?'

Harriet swallowed the fiery liquid in one go and choked. 'It's the book,' she said between coughs. 'It was on the computer and I did something to the plugs and it disappeared. And I can't get it back. He's going to kill me, Miss Press. He told me not to look at it.'

'Slow up,' Pat said. 'I'm not getting this. We're talking about your husband, right?'

Millicent saw a chance to impress. 'Harry's husband is a very eminent professor, dear. Victor Grenderlyn. I dare say you may have heard of him. He lives just across the street. I've known him for years –'

'Mom, I don't give a fuck how eminent he is,' Pat said. Harriet jumped. Millicent only pursed her lips and resolved to maintain a lenient attitude. It wasn't Pat's fault that she had been brought up in an uncouth country.

'I want to understand what you're saying,' Pat said. 'Your husband told you not to look at his work? What kind of junk is this? You mean to say you let him hand out orders like that to you and you're his wife?'

'If you'd just listened to what the girl was saying, she told us that she did look at it,' Millicent said. 'And I really don't see any need to –'

'No need?' Pat screwed up her eyes. 'I find this truly horrifying. How old are you, Harry?'

'Nineteen, but I don't –'

'Don't you think you're old enough to take control of your life?' Pat leant forward in her chair. 'If this husband of yours needs to assert himself like this, it's because he has a very real problem about his own inadequacy. I want you to focus on that. He's making his problem into yours. Now, the first thing you're going to do is to challenge that position. You're going to square up to him and say, "Vic, your inadequacy is not mine." '

'Victor,' Harriet said. 'Not that it matters. Not when I've lost the whole of his book. I don't see how I can tell him that it's because of his inadequacy.'

'Listen, dear,' Pat said. 'An adequate husband wouldn't be such a dummy as to leave his precious book unstored. Is it your fault if he goofed?'

'Victor goofed?' The very idea seemed shocking.

'Do try to talk English, Paula,' Millicent said. 'The only goof we know about here is that revolting duck. You mean that he did something wrong?'

Pat reminded herself that these were people who still dwelt in the Dark Ages before the micro-chip. 'When you work on a computer, Harry, you store the material so as not to run the risk of something like this happening. It's his problem if he didn't do it, not yours. Now, let's get back to basics. Why do you let Victor assert himself like this? Don't you value yourself? Aren't you, too, a person?'

'Well, yes,' Harriet said weakly.

'Not "Well, yes." Yes! Affirm it! Be it!'

No wonder Pat was divorced, Millicent thought as she stumped towards the kitchen. Imagine having to go through this sort of nonsense every day. Perfectly ridiculous. As if people didn't have enough to think about. Sensible people had better things to do, thought Millicent as she started scouring out the roasting tin.

The telephone rang.

'Miss Millicent Press?' She knew what that meant. Somebody trying to sell her something. 'Thank you, but no,' she said briskly and put it down.

It rang again. 'I thought I'd made myself quite clear –'

'I have a call for you,' the voice cheeped. 'Just a moment.' There was a pause, a click and then a voice said 'shit' very loudly.

'To whom do I have the pleasure of speaking?' She put on her best head-of-the-neighbourhood-protection-league voice.

'It's me, Milly. Harry. Good old Harry. Sorry about what I said just then. Tripped over something.'

'A bottle, perhaps? You're not in trouble again, are you? Because if you think I'm going all the way up to the police station for the second time in a month –'

'Nothing like. I'm not in trouble, Milly.' He sounded aggrieved. 'I'm about to become a celebrity. I thought you'd like to know. I've arrived!'

Millicent felt one of her headaches coming on. 'Arrived where? Do try to speak clearly.'

'Star Channel,' Harry bellowed. 'That bloke you told me about, Wainwright. He's putting me on telly tonight. Want to hear a joke? What do you call a toadstool in a bar when he starts buying everyone drinks? Fungi. Fun-guy.' An explosive sound pierced her left ear-drum.

'Harry Carpenter,' she said, 'you're as drunk as a stoat.'

'That's as may be,' Harry responded. 'Nothing to worry about. I'll sober up before they get going on me. Programme doesn't go out until six. You still there, Milly?'

'Go and get yourself a glass of water and liver salts and then see if you can't sleep it off,' she counselled.

'You don't believe me, do you.' She heard him shouting to

someone called Shirley to 'come and 'ave a word with a friend'
and flinched. ' "Come on then," he bellowed. ' "She won't bite
yer." '

A series of titters announced Shirley's arrival at the telephone. 'Miss Press? Yes, I can confirm that Mr Carpenter's
talking to you from Star Channel and that he's scheduled for
18.05. He's a real turn, isn't he? Had us all in stitches over
lunch. Is he always like this?' Another girlish shriek was
followed by an entreaty to somebody, presumably Harry, to
get their hands off her leg.

Millicent felt it was a suitable moment to put down the
telephone. Shaking her head, she went back into her sitting-
room and stopped as she saw Harriet, her arms stretched high
above her head, reciting some extraordinary gibberish about
being and becoming.

'The I that hinders the I that I am becoming is being washed
away. I make the I that is I,' Harriet announced, and dropped
her arms. 'Goodness. I hope I'm going to remember it all. And
you really think it's going to work?'

Pat smiled. 'Think? Sweetheart, I know. Just turn the anger
back on him. Let him see you know where the problem lies. In
him.' She widened her beam to include Millicent. 'Harry's
feeling good, Mom. She's going to go back there and take
control. And he's going to respect her for it.'

'Especially when he hears how she managed to lose his book,'
said Millicent who was feeling thoroughly put out by life.

'There was no call for you to say that, Mom,' Pat said as the
new Harriet strode out of the house. 'I'd told her how to handle
the situation.'

'By telling him it was his fault?' Millicent could smile at such
naivety. 'My dear, you don't know Victor Grenderlyn. Well
now, ready for a little gardening?'

Pat sighed and shut her eyes. 'It really takes it out of me when
I'm giving myself like that, you know. I think I'll just rest here for
a while and gather my energies.'

Energies? She hadn't done anything except eat and talk her
head off. But Millicent was not to be deflected from her
determination to behave well, at whatever cost.

'Just as you please,' she said. 'Still, I'm sure you don't want to
be idle. I'm helping raise funds for a new hospital wing. Why
don't you keep yourself busy with the envelope-stuffing?' It
gave her a small stab of satisfaction to see Pat's look of dismay as

she dropped 200-odd envelopes on her lap. 'There you are, dear. It shouldn't take more than an hour.'

'Thanks,' Pat said faintly. 'I really appreciate being involved.'

Millicent's smile was serenely gracious. 'Think nothing of it.'

13

'And then, of course, we must not forget Bulgakov. One of the few writers who had the grace to appreciate that I might have a sense of humour. Some of the jokes are a little crude for my taste but, nevertheless –'

Raphael sneaked a glance at the clock over the door. Two hours had passed and S. hadn't drawn breath. Lily had already left Selena Street by the time the sergeant at the desk had finished inscribing the details of the incident – the non-incident – in a slow, crabbed hand. A second, more frantic call to directories for her father's number had produced the daunting news that Mr Franklin's number was a private one and not to be released. So much for good intentions: a fine impression he would make when it looked as if he couldn't even be bothered to explain his absence.

'Master, I –'

'All in good time. It's so long since we had a civilised conversation. Raji.' S. sighed. 'I miss you. We used to have so many good talks together. Do you talk like this when you are with your little earthling?'

'You should know,' Raphael said sulkily. 'You only have to turn on the register. Or ask Fœdora, since she doesn't seem to have anything better to do than mess things up for me.'

'Are you criticising us, Raji?'

'Of course not, Master. You know how I respect your judgement. But you know what Fœdora's like when she hasn't got a mission to work on –'

'And who is to say that she isn't acting on my orders? Hmm?' The playful hum, which he had mistaken foolishly for amusement, rose to a note of imperial wrath which almost pierced his ear-drums before the line went dead. Whimpering with pain,

Raphael sank forward over the desk where he had been left to muse on his misdeeds.

'Please, Master. Don't leave me now. I'm sorry I –'

'Mr Sartis?'

Mortified, he looked up to see a plump-faced man in a grey suit surveying him from the door.

'I gather you had a complaint about the tea?'

A reference, presumably, to the paper carton of tepid Nile water which had been presented to him when he was confined to his cell. He gathered his wits. Rule one. Never suggest that S. was in any way at fault. Rule two. Never insult policemen, or even men who might be policemen, when you are at their mercy. They also bash your brains out who only stand and wait, or something like that, wasn't it? He couldn't think clearly. His head was still throbbing from the roar of S.'s anger.

'Not at all. The tea was excellent.'

The man came towards him and stared into the untouched carton. 'You didn't drink it.'

'No.'

'But you said it was excellent.'

'Yes.' What was he meant to do – fall on his knees and give thanks for police hospitality? 'It was a kind thought. Very hospitable.'

The man shot him a sharp look, evidently assessing the likely ironic content of this observation. Then he smiled.

'So you like a bit of attention? Well, why not?' The man seated himself on a corner of the table and started cleaning his fingernails with the metal pin of his watch-strap. 'You're a foreigner, aren't you, Mr Sartis?'

'French.'

The man deposited the residue from one of his nails in a notch on the desk. 'Travel a lot, do you?'

'A fair amount.'

'Worrying business, travelling nowadays,' the man said. 'Can't get into a car nowadays without wondering if someone's strapped a bomb under the chassis. Sad world, Mr Sartis. A sad sad world.'

'Very sad,' Raphael agreed, wondering what he had to be sad about. He hadn't been arrested. He was sitting there in his pinstripe, picking at his nails, a free man.

'You don't feel safe walking about unarmed, these days, do you?' the man said pleasantly. 'Never know when they're going to get you.'

'Look,' Raphael said. 'That gun was planted on me. I've never carried an illegal weapon in my life. I don't like guns. I wouldn't want to shoot a rabbit, let alone a person.'

'I was just generalising, Mr Sartis.' He smiled. 'Nothing personal. I quite like a bit of rabbit-shooting myself. Nice stroll in the country on a sunny morning, get a bit of exercise, dynamite a few bunnies and home for lunch – very pleasant. You a country man, Mr Sartis?'

'No,' Raphael said.

'Pity,' the man said. 'There's nothing so civilising as a bit of communication with nature. Pantheism had a lot going for it, in my view. I'm reading *Walden* at the moment.'

'Always a good thing to read around your work.'

The man looked at him sadly. 'Not warden. *Walden*. Thoreau. Now, there's a man who understood nature. Art now, I've never really understood the point of it. What's the use of imitating what's always going to be better than anything you can do with a brush? You tell me. You're someone who appreciates painting.'

'You'd better ask the woman I'm meant to have attacked,' Raphael said sullenly. 'She's the one who stands there all day looking at pictures, isn't she?' Let Fœdora try and get round that. She wouldn't know a Claude from a de Chirico.

'An attendant?' The man grinned. 'It's like the women who work in sweet-shops. They end up hating chocolates. I shouldn't think Miss Wattle knows whether she's looking at a Constable or a Christmas card. She'd probably prefer the Christmas card on balance.'

'Listen to me,' Raphael said. 'That woman is not Miss Wattle. She's a very dangerous person. It's her who ought to be sitting here, not me.'

The man was fastening his watch again. 'What kind of dangerous are we talking about, Mr Sartis?'

He tried to keep his voice even and calm. 'I told you. Very dangerous. I know that's not how she looks at the moment, but that's where she's so clever.'

'I've had a chat with Miss Wattle,' the man said, 'and we've done a bit of checking up on her, as well as you. Spinster, not very well off, sister died two years ago. Lives with her mother in a ground-floor flat in Acton. Not the sort of person I'd expect to interest you, Mr Sartis, to be honest. You're a bit more of a – well, a high-flier. Apartment in Paris, dinners in a nice class of restaurant, pretty girl-friend – it's not easy to see what your motive could be for wanting to attack Miss Wattle with all that going for you. You ever taken any kind of stimulants, Mr Sartis?'

'Absolutely not.' He looked at the man beseechingly. 'Just ask yourself, I do I look like a murderer?'

The man laughed. 'Funny you should say that. They never do. Nothing you want to tell me, then?'

His eyes were blue and kind. For one mad moment, Raphael contemplated blurting the whole thing out, S.'s plans, his own attempts to improve a few people's lives, the dastardly behaviour of Fœdora, the whole truth and nothing but.

'I –,' he said. The man kept on smiling.

'Take your time, Mr Sartis. No hurry.'

He shook his head. What good would explanations do? They'd have him put away in a psychiatric unit if he started trying to explain about S., study him as an interesting case of religious mania. 'Nothing that would help.'

'Pity.' The man stood up, moved towards the door. 'Well, nice talking to you, Mr Sartis. It's not often I get a chance to have a decent conversation here.'

Raphael's smile was brief and bitter. 'Any time, officer. Any time.'

14

The Retreat had altered so much that Carl wondered for a moment if he had come to the wrong place. The weedy laurel-bordered drive had been replaced by a grand sweep of biscuit-coloured gravel flanked by neat grass borders. At the front of the house, a little to the left of a row of large and gleamingly expensive cars, including a sleek black ultra-stretch limousine of the kind he'd only seen on American glamour programmes, was a handsome new brick pavilion trying to look like a Georgian orangery. Through its windows shone the flat blue of an Olympic-sized swimming-pool, surrounded by long wooden chairs draped in white and pink towels. On the lawn beyond it, two chubby young men in blue track suits were running heavily on the spot under the supervision of a luscious-looking girl in a white leotard. Watching her spring up and down with robotic efficiency, Carl felt his spirits lift. This was a new departure of which he approved entirely. Odd, though. Father Gerard had always flatly opposed any suggestion that women should be allowed into the Retreat.

Even the motto over the doorway had altered. 'Free the spirit' had become 'Free the body', suggesting some more fiercely physical scheme of self-improvement which he didn't altogether relish.

Puzzling, Carl pushed his way through the swing-doors – they, too, were new, all chrome and glass – which led into the large and shabby hall which had acted as cloakroom, snooker-room and, illicitly, as the beer-drinking and dirty-jokes room in the old days.

Not any more. Gone were the scruffy green linoleum tiles, the billiard-table and the walls which Carl had helped to paint in the gentle blue which Father Gerard described as the colour of inner peace. The floor had become a plateau of thick sand-coloured carpet guaranteed to stifle every footfall in its obsequious tufts, while the billiard-table had been replaced by a thick slab of pale green marble, long enough to flatten a full-grown crocodile, and supported by disturbingly frail gilt legs. The blue walls, too, had been effaced by an expensive-looking striped paper in shaded pinks, the dusty tones he associated with Fay's squirrelled stores of cosmetic blushers. It was the kind of setting which instantly drew your eyes down to check if your shoes were muddy.

He looked and, naturally, they were, since he had walked through the wooded paths from the coach station, and, naturally, they had already left a black trail across the carpet. For a moment, he was attempted to turn tail and run for it. By the next, he had reminded himself that Father Gerard had never been bothered by anything so trivial as a bit of mud. He started to walk purposefully forward.

A discreet cough stopped him in his tracks. Turning, he saw another vision on which to feast his eyes. This one was even better that the one in the white leotard. She had just the kind of soft honey-blonde hair and big blue eyes he always fancied and she was dressed in a little pink tunic which just skimmed the tops of her long tanned legs. Not all changes were for the worse, not by a long chalk.

'Hi,' he said, sidling backwards to disguise his muddy tracks. 'I'm Carl.'

She opened her soft pink mouth half a centimetre. 'You should have gone round the back. Didn't anyone tell you it's patients only through the front entrance?'

Patients? That was new. They'd never been called that in the old days. It had always been 'the boys' and 'the new boys', a bit like school.

'My fault,' he said, since he fancied her and didn't want to get off on the wrong foot. 'I'm not actually booked in. I just –'

'Didn't you hear what I said?' Weird voice. Didn-yew-hyeer-wut-ey-zed. It heated up twenty degrees as the swing-doors opened again. 'Mrs Duvallier! How lovely to have you back with us!'

A quivering ball of sable rolled across the floor to the desk of Miss Pink Tunic and deposited an expensive-looking leather case on the carpet. 'Well, Herbie's in Nassau doing business and I thought I'd just drop in for a refresher before I flew over. I should've booked, I know, but I thought maybe you could overlook the formalities for a regular.'

'Don't worry about a thing, Mrs Duvallier. It'll be a pleasure. I'll have someone prepare the Floral Suite for you.' Pink Tunic pinged a bell and spoke into a white handset in a tone of hushed reverence. 'Have the Floral Suite made up right away, Laurel. Flowers and fruit. It's for Mrs – absolutely. That's fine, Mrs Duvallier.' A warm white smile that went all the way round to her molars came out and stayed there. 'You can go up straight away. Shall I have Dino come up to arrange your schedule in twenty minutes?'

'Love it.' Mrs Duvallier's head poked up out of the sable collar and her eyes swivelled round to where Carl was lurking behind the marble slab. She gave him the kind of look which suggested that he could just as well have been lying on it with a card through his nose saying: catfish, 20p a pound.

'Is *he* going to take my case up?'

Pink Tunic's smile went away. She looked at Carl. Then she leant forward and said something he couldn't hear.

'Oh,' said Mrs Duvallier. It sounded like a moan of disgust. 'Eugh, I see. Fine. Well, I'll leave it to you.' And she waddled on up the stairs which, Carl now noticed, had also been refurbished in thick petal-pink carpet.

Cautiously, walking on tiptoe so as not to do any further damage, he advanced to the desk. 'I came to see Father Gerard, Miss –?'

Her mouth had gone back into a little clamp. 'He's expecting you?'

Thank God for that. For a moment, he had thought she was going to say she didn't know anyone of that name. If Father Gerard was here, then all was well. He could learn to like pink wallpaper. He could even learn to like fish-slab tables.

'Just tell him it's Carl,' he said 'He'll know.'

She raised her eyebrows, but she also picked up the handset again and spoke into it. Distantly, he heard the sweet Irish accents of the good father, warm and calm as always. Even Pink Tunic felt the force of his benevolence. She was smiling again and nodding her head.

'OK Carl, that's fine. Through the door there and down to the end of the passage. He's through the door at the end. You're to go straight in.'

'Great.' He beamed at her. 'You been working here long? It's quite a change, having beautiful girls around.'

She looked past him at the carpet. 'You can leave your shoes here. I'll have them labelled and put here under the desk ready for when you leave.'

'I'm staying,' he said, handing them over.

'Ah,' she said, like 'Uh'.

'Maybe we could get together a bit later on. There's a nice little pub just beyond Radlett by the river –'

'Down the passage, door at the end.' She bent her head and started leafing through the pages of a fashion magazine.

Rebuffed but not downhearted – she surely wasn't going to spend her evenings playing whist with Mrs Duvallier – he went through the door and down a long beige-carpeted passage until, as directed, he came to a door. 'G. D. O'Halloran. Administration', it read. Rather timidly, he knocked.

'Come in.'

Entering, Carl blinked. Still more changes. White walls, white carpet, a desk on which he counted four telephones and an answering-machine. Flowers – not any old flowers, but hotel-type bouquets of lilies, orchids and roses – cascaded elegantly from white marble plinths in each of the corners facing him and he saw, when he glanced back, what looked like a pair of genuine Chippendale mirrors reflecting his awestruck stare.

'Carl, dear boy, it's such a pleasure to see you, and looking so well.' Father Gerard had risen from his chair to greet him and was leaning forward across the desk to take his hands. He was

pinker in the face and a bit broader in the body but otherwise
unchanged in physical appearance. His clothes were a different
matter. A suit? With a rose in the buttonhole? And a gold tie-pin
the size of a small chocolate bar? Pulled forward by the fervour of
Father Gerard's greeting, Carl caught a whiff of gardenia
cologne.

'The girl asked me to take my shoes off,' he said as he saw
Father Gerard glancing at his feet. 'Bit muddy – I think she was
worried about the carpet.'

'Carpet,' Father Gerard said and chuckled softly as if to
suggest that he and Carl knew there was more to life than that.
'Well, well, I'm sorry, Carl. But she's a good girl. She does her
job well.'

'I'm sure.' A silence fell. 'Nice room,' Carl said.

'Oh, the room.' Father Gerard chuckled again. 'Well, it's
pleasant. I don't care for possessions, as you know, but they
seemed to think that this was appropriate and I didn't see much
point in arguing.' He waved a hand towards a vast and heavily
cushioned chair in which even Mrs Duvallier might have felt a
mere slip of a girl. 'Sit down, dear boy. Make yourself at home.'
His hand glided back to one of the telephones. 'Did you have
anything to eat on the way? I can ask the chef to have a salad sent
up in no time.'

Carl shook his head. He couldn't have sounded more hospitable, but it was bad enough having to try to keep the holes in his
socks out of sight without worrying about dropping lettuce
down the side of the chair. At home was just what he didn't feel.

Father Gerard leant forward across the desk. 'And how is our
dear Mrs Calman?'

'Oh, fine. Still writing away. But it's like I told you on the
telephone. She got really upset about the science fiction magazines I had in my room. And now she's got someone else in
there, a new lodger. Only he pays.'

'Renting rooms? I didn't have the impression she needed to
do that.' Father Gerard's expression altered to one of lively
concern.

'She doesn't. She's just renting it to make sure I stay out.'

Father Gerard's smile was benign. 'And isn't it time, Carl?
Shouldn't you be trying to stand on your own two feet again by
now? Excuse me.' He flicked a button in response to a flashing
light on one of the telephones. 'Fine, Dino. Tell her I'll be ready
to see her in ten' – he glanced at Carl – 'no, make it twenty

minutes and don't let me be disturbed before then.' He pressed his hands together. 'You've no idea how hard it is to find a little time for myself nowadays. So many calls on me, so much to be done – but I mustn't burden you with my worries. Tell me now, how's the painting going? I always felt that was where your future lay. You've no idea how it upset me when they papered over those lovely blue walls, Carl – but it's your sketches I'm thinking of.'

Who were the 'they', Carl wondered? But he felt his anxiety slipping away. The place might have changed, but Father Gerard was still himself, kind, concerned, always ready to look for the best in everybody, even in someone as worthless as he felt himself to be. He had not been wrong to come back.

'It all seemed to work when I was here, Father, but I just lost the impulse when I got back to London. I couldn't paint when I was spending all day designing bathroom units, but I've chucked that in. I thought that if I came back here a bit, you could help me get going again.'

'I see.' Father Gerard's face had grown stern. 'Creativity isn't the product of a place, Carl, it's a state of mind. What kind of an artist is it, I ask you, who has to come running back here every time he loses his confidence? The talent's in you, boy. All I ever did was to encourage you to use it.'

'Oh, you did!' Carl interrupted. 'You were fantastic! Being at the Retreat was the best thing that ever happened to me. Honestly. I just thought that if I could stay a month –'

'A month, eh?' Father Gerard smiled and shook his head. 'And how were you thinking of paying for all that time, Carl lad? I gather you haven't involved dear Mrs Calman in your plans.'

'Paying?' Carl stared at him.

Father Gerard chuckled. 'Now, you aren't going to tell me you thought it was all for nothing? Why, she must have given the community something in the region of £8,000 for that little visit of yours. Oh, you've no idea how the money gets eaten up – food, supervision, accommodation, medical treatment.'

'I didn't have any medical treatment, not unless you count a couple of aspirins and some cough syrup.'

'Now if it was in my hands, I'd take you in tomorrow and see what we could do for you,' Father Gerard continued smoothly. 'But you have to understand my responsibility to the board of directors. I couldn't justify it. I'd be asking them to set a precedent, you see, and once it's been set – no, I'm afraid it can't be done, Carl. I'm very sorry.'

Eight grand! And this was the same man who had sent them all out into the local villages and towns to beg for funds for their charitable institution. His eyes went back to the Chippendale mirrors.

'I can see why you don't want to upset the board,' he said. 'They seem to be looking after you very nicely here. So. No money, no room at the inn. Very bloody charitable.' He stood up. 'I'm sorry to have used up so much of your valuable time. I'd hate to keep Mrs Duvallier from getting her money's worth of interviews.'

'Sit down,' Father Gerard said. 'Now you know I wouldn't want you walking out of here in that frame of mind.'

'Try stopping me.' Carl folded his arms. 'I've got the picture. You made a mint out of keeping us on baked beans and lentil soup and telling us that cold rooms made for a healthy mind, and then you turned it into a frigging health farm. And don't bother telling me who's the chairman of the board of directors. I've guessed. The man who taught us that money was meaningless.' Carl leant forward across the desk and stared into Father Gerard's clear blue eyes. They met his without a trace of remorse. 'How could you do it? You were the one we trusted. You were the one who said that you'd never give up the Retreat while there were people like us to be helped and while there was good to be done. You call this good?' He hit the desk so hard that the telephones jangled into life. Father Gerard flinched.

'Try to control your feelings, dear boy. I did my best to make things clear to you when you rang. It's hardly my fault if you chose not to listen.'

'You never said you were running a health farm.'

'Indeed I did not. You said it, Carl, not I.' Evidently feeling that he had regained control of the situation, Father Gerard leant comfortably back in his chair. 'I always taught you not to underrate the importance of the body as well as the spirit. This wasn't an easy decision for me to make, Carl, believe me, but I came to realise that I had my priorities the wrong way round. First the body and then the spirit.'

'You're telling me that lump of lard I met in the hall came here to improve her spirit?'

'Money can lock people into a very special kind of loneliness.'

'Don't tell me who's got the key.'

Father Gerard looked at him with a sad smile. 'We ask people to give what they can. If some of them choose to be generous in their gifts, I take it to be an expression of gratitude for what we do. I'm not going to apologise to you for the work we try to do here. I'm proud of it,' he said, offering the nobility of his profile as he turned to gaze out of the window at the smooth stretch of lawn on which some kind of gymnastics class was now in progress. 'Yes, proud, and – let me be perfectly frank – it grieves me to see a fine young man like yourself begrudging a little attention where it's needed. It makes me want to ask myself how much you learnt when you were with us. Not too much, it seems. When I talk about charity, you see, I'm talking about something much more important than money. I'm talking about the giving of oneself to others. That's what I've always tried to do, lad, as you well know.'

Carl said nothing.

'Well now.' Father Gerard's smile was benevolent and all-forgiving. 'I certainly didn't mean to end by giving you a lecture. No hard feelings, eh?' He did not rub his hands together so much as gently slide one palm over the other. Tabula rasa. 'Now, it occurs to me that our dear Mrs Calman might benefit from a spell in the countryside. September's always a quiet month.' He pushed a shiny coloured brochure across the desk. 'Tell her not to pay too much attention to the figures. I'm sure we can arrange a little discount.'

'You said it was donations only.'

'For the extras, dear boy. But I'm told that our rates are very competitive.'

'Depends on what you're competing with,' Carl said. 'From what I've heard so far, I'd have thought she might have a cheaper week in Hawaii. In fact,' he said as he stood up, 'the only donation you'd get from Fay is a kick up the arse. I'd do it myself, but I don't fancy contaminating my socks. Here.' He felt in his pocket and brought out a handful of coins. 'Donation. Buy yourself a poppy to go with the cock. And I want my bike back.'

Father Gerard shook himself free from a dignified contemplation of the orchids. 'Your bike?'

'My bike. I bloody paid for it. Don't you remember anything?' He would have cried if he hadn't been feeling so angry. 'We bought it together. You helped me choose it. A Raleigh Supreme. I couldn't take it back because Fay came down in Spiro's new car and it wouldn't fit. And you said I could leave it here and you'd keep it safe for whenever I wanted to come back for a visit. You don't remember, do you?' He leant over the desk and grasped the lapels of the good father's finely striped grey suit. 'You give me my bike or you give me my mother's money back.' He was pleased to see that Father Gerard was, for the first time, looking scared.

'Take your hands off me, lad. No need for violence. I dare say you'll find the bike out in one of the sheds at the back. Ask Lorraine to take you round there and tell her I said so. Be reasonable, Carl. There's no cause to go destroying my suit.'

'Why not?' Carl asked as he walked towards the door. 'You destroyed my illusions. And those aren't replaceable.'

'You're not staying then,' said Pink Tunic as he held out his hands for the shoes. Looking at her satisfied little smile, he didn't think she merited an answer.

'He said you'd show me round to the back. There's a bike I want to pick up. If, that is,' he said as her eyes went back to the magazine on her knees, 'you can spare the time.'

'Pleasure.' She minced ahead of him to the door and out on to the crunching gravel where a chauffeur was polishing the snub black bonnet of the ultra-stretch. Normally, he would have been over the moon, feasting his eyes on the twitch of her neatly rounded bottom and the lean brown legs. Today, she could have been a walking broomstick for all the interest he felt. All he wanted to do was to sit down somewhere quiet with his head on his knees and howl. Sod sex. Sod the Retreat. Sod everything.

'Pardon?' She glanced over her shoulder.

'I didn't say anything.'

'Well.' She stood on the edge of a puddle in the cobbled yard, keeping her little white shoes clean as she pointed towards a wooden shed. 'That's the only bike here. The door's open. I ought to get back.'

'Not until I know it's there, you don't. It's all right. I'm not asking you to get your shoes dirty.' He pushed the shed door open and there it was, twisted over on its side, barely recognisable as the gleaming machine that had once been his. He picked it up and held it between his legs, straightening out the handlebars before he led it out into the air, squeaking with protest after long disuse.

'Well.' She looked at him with dislike, resenting him for keeping her out here, for wasting her time. 'You're set up, then.'

'Yes.' So much rust in the cogs he could hardly get the wheels to turn. Watching her go, he toyed with the idea of some kind of revenge. Tell the chauffeur they'd got a legionnaires'-disease case they were trying to hush up? Come back later and smash a few of the windows in the new pavilion? Tempting, but pointless. It wouldn't make any difference. The insurance would pay up. The new windows would go in and Father Gerard would continue to coin in the money, just as he always had.

Fay should have told him. Forking out all that money and letting him think Father Gerard was doing it out of the goodness of his heart. She'd meant well, of course, wanted to spare his feelings. There wasn't any reason why he should feel angry with her, and yet he did. Why did she always have to be so bloody protective? Even now, when she'd thrown him out, he knew it was only a question of a few days before she'd be getting at him through Spiro, checking up on whether he was looking after himself, wanting to know what he'd had for breakfast. Playing Mummy. Technically, she'd let him go; emotionally, she was as close to him as a limpet on his back.

And he wasn't bloody well worth it. Certainly not worth the eight thousand she'd shovelled uncomplainingly into Father Gerard's account. What was she ever going to get out of that but the knowledge that she'd wasted her money on trying to help a failure, a drunken, sex-crazed, no-good flop?

Except, perhaps, with that girl. Harriet. Little Miss Goody-Two-Shoes. He'd been all right with her.

No point in thinking about that. Harriet had chosen to be Mrs Grenderlyn. She'd got her wish and if he hadn't, it was his own fault for not knowing what it was that he wanted. He'd thought as far as the Retreat, no farther. And now?

The air was warm and the sky a soaring arc of blue, but Carl tucked in his head and hunched up his shoulders like a robin in a snowstorm as he pedalled through the gates and out, blindly, into the road.

A scream of brakes and blasting horns warned him back to the side of the road where he stood, crying and shaking, his legs buckling under him, soft as rags. A man, red-faced, furious, thrust his head out of a car window to bellow at him.

'Are you off your head? Kill yourself where you please, but don't get a poor sodding motorist to do the dirty work for you. Selfish little bastard.' Something in Carl's ashy face checked his rage. 'Life's never that bad,' he said more gently. 'Thank your lucky stars you're still here to enjoy it.'

He drove on without waiting for a response. Slowly, Carl lifted his head and tilted it back, staring up at the blank depth of blue. Something, somewhere, had chosen to save him. He was not alone.

15

'Straight into A.'s hands. Is this your idea of a joke, Sartis? Because if it is, I can assure you that it's one with a limited appeal. Grief was what you were asked to cause. Nothing drastic. Nothing difficult. Just a little common or garden misery. And you can't even manage a road accident without leaving the victim in a state of mindless joy.'

'Fœdora said I could have a month,' Raphael said stubbornly. 'I haven't even been granted a week. And how can you expect me to serve you when I'm cooped up in a police station?'

'Serve me?' S.'s laugh was not agreeable. 'I'm humouring you, Raphael. You're not serving me and you're certainly not pleasing me.' His tone softened and grew cajoling, soft and melancholy as the sigh of a summer wind. 'Raji, Raji, you who I always loved, what do you think you can ever gain by this? The friendship of a few little earth-creatures? What is it can be worth more to you than the love of your Master, your friend?'

'I wanted to make people happy,' Raphael muttered.

'And have you? Far be it from me to lecture you on something so alien to my taste, but if the preservation of one worthless young man is the best you can do –' His silence prompted an answer, but Raphael was silent. 'Did you think that I would have been so tolerant if I had not foreseen your failure? We are the Masters, Raphael, and you, my foolish little earth-lover, are the pawn. However,' S. went on after so long a pause that Raphael thought he had been abandoned, 'I am, as always, ready to be generous. You will be freed. I have spoken to Fœdora and it is arranged. You have the rest of today to redeem yourself. If, at the end of this day, I see no sign of improvement, action will be taken. You understand?'

Miserably, Raphael bent his head. 'Yes, Master.'

'And remember,' S. went on inexorably, 'that life in the

Hundredth System is worse than anything you might presume
to imagine. You are not a fool. Do well by me, and I shall do well
by you. Remember that.'

The Thwarting
of Expectations

1

Although Raphael can only see into the shadowed well of a concrete court from the window of his cell, the promise of early morning has been fulfilled by one of those brilliant summer afternoons when the newly cleaned buildings of London gleam like sea-polished quartz. Outside the palaces of Westminster, the sentries and guards wheel and march with the mechanical elegance of figures on an automaton; sunlight turns the spires and domes of Whitehall into a Bavarian fantasy-castle. Children scatter bright patches of colour across the wide country slopes of Richmond Common and Hampstead Heath and, under the shading trees, the summer lovers lie twined in sleepy gratitude for a day when everything in nature seems to have drawn together in a conspiracy of happiness and undisturbed serenity. Leaves flutter and shift in the warm southern wind and, in the neatly divided gardens of the suburbs, lawn mowers purr and rotate in throbbing harmony.

Happiness is there for the taking. Only a few people who had anticipated the happiest day of their lives are oblivious to the easy pleasures of a summer's day. Lucy, trapped in a traffic jam on her way to execute vengeance at Flite Holdings, is drumming her fingernails on the side of the wheel in a frenzy of rage as she recalls the ignoble manner of her beloved's flight. Lily, all dressed up and knowing she is already late, is waiting anxiously at the end of the street, wondering why Raphael hasn't come back and whether she should go to her father's without him. Harriet, pacing up and down the dark narrow passage as she recites the lines which are meant to quell Victor's wrath, is beginning to wonder if they are not more likely to fuel it. Harry Carpenter, while never lacking in confidence, is wishing that he was back outside the supermarket as he struggles in his whisky-befuddled state to remember even one of his poems for his first (and probably last) television performance. Only Miss Press and Victor Grenderlyn are, at this moment, basking in a state of self-congratulation. But for them, too, the granting of wishes has been ordained to lead to a cruel thwarting of their secret hopes.

2

Lily had always thought of her father's house as a place where the clocks were against her, a constant and clamorous testimony to her failure to have achieved anything remarkable. She felt it again today as each smartly echoed its chime from the next, from the mantelpiece to the bookcase to the desk by the window and out to the soft boom of the grandfather clock on the stairs, each of them crying the same song of accusation: late, late, late! How could he have done this to her?

'Well now.' Her father stirred in his chair and, as if he hadn't known it already, took out his gold repeater watch and held it towards the light. 'Half-past four, Lily.'

'I can't understand it.' Her face was scalding with mortification. 'I gave him the address. And I waited until nearly four at the house. You don't think there might be another Palace Terrace?'

'There's just the one Palace Terrace, Lily, and this is it.' Sarah, immaculate in harmonised shades of grey, looked at her sister's flushed face with the pitying smile that always made Lily feel like strangling her. How typical it was of Sarah suddenly to find time to be present when she was least wanted. Only Daddy's intervention had saved her already from another how-to-be-a-successful-person-like-me lecture. Not that his intervention had been of a comforting kind. 'I'm not sure success would suit Lily,' he had said. Why not, she wanted to know?

'I don't want to put any kind of a damper on the romance,' Sarah went on, pausing only to frown as Lily lit a cigarette and looked round for an ash tray. 'But it does all sound a little bizarre. Don't you think, Daddy? We don't know what he does. We don't know who he is.'

'I told you his name.'

'His name.' Sarah smiled. 'All we know is that he rents some kind of a basement room and that Lily thinks it's quite serious. If it's that serious, the man ought to be here.'

Mr Franklin opened his eyes half a crack and closed them again. 'Lily thinks,' he said. 'But Lily married Nigel Tremain.'

Lily looked at him with fury. 'Raphael isn't anything like Nigel. For a start, he isn't bald.'

'You are so frivolous, darling. Baldness was the least of the objections I had to your ex-husband.'

'And he's not a fortune-hunter.' Why should she have to sit here and defend him like this?

'I'll say one thing for Mr Tremain, he was always punctual.' Her father's eyes blinked open again. 'I don't want to be tiresome, Lily, but we must think of poor Mrs Havers. She likes to be home by five and it really would be rather maddening to lose her over something as trivial as this. Anyway, it's long past time for my tea. Go along to the kitchen and tell her to bring it in anyway, will you? And if your friend condescends to turn up, he'll be very welcome to join us.' He patted her hand as she flung past his chair. 'Poor love. Nothing more unpleasant than being left in the lurch, but it's better to find out now than later, don't you think?' He smiled up at her and, dimly, through her rage, she realised that he was far from displeased. He had always liked to have his daughters to himself. 'To tell you the truth,' he said, speaking as always as though he had pro-prietorial rights over it, 'I did feel it was all a little quick. A few years on your own would do a power of good to you, my darling.'

'Daddy's absolutely right,' Sarah chipped in, although nobody had asked for her opinion. 'It's just what I was saying to him before you came. And God knows we don't want any more trouble with difficult husbands.'

Lily looked at her sister with loathing. 'I'll go and tell Mrs Havers,' she said. 'If you're sure you can trust me as far as the kitchen.'

Sarah laughed. 'Oh Lily dear, never let it be said that we aren't optimistic. You'll grow up one day.'

3

Francis Wainwright looked up from his desk, and, following an instinct of self-preservation, ducked swiftly down behind it as he saw the bulky silhouette of Marvin Hackett, Star Channel's newest director, loom up behind the glass panel of his door. A hand rapped on the glass and, a moment later, he saw Hackett's shoes marching inexorably towards him across the carpet. Crouched out of sight though he was, he sensed that Hackett's gimlet eyes were boring into his exposed back. 'And it tolls for you,' he thought as he straightened himself and looked up with an air of surprise and, he hoped, pleasure.

'Marvin! How – how nice of you to drop in.' The words died on his lips as he saw the expression on Hackett's face. This was not a man who had dropped in for a pleasant chat. 'Nothing wrong, I hope?'

Hackett lowered himself into the interview chair and stared at him. It was a chair which was cunningly designed to make the interviewee feel instantly conscious that he was in the presence of a superior being, but Hackett did not look deferential. His massive brows were drawn together into a scowl which might have served him well in an audition for the role of Heathcliff, King Kong or the transformed Jekyll, and his arms were folded in a way that suggested he was struggling to restrain himself from causing considerable damage to the desk, or its owner, or both. Wainwright leant a little further back in his chair and comforted himself with the thought that it was a very wide desk.

'Coffee?' he inquired. Hackett responded with a small but decisive shake of his head.

'I'll be brief,' he said. 'I've just had a word with Julia.' This did not bode well. Julia, Hackett's only personal appointment so far, was the director of the weekend arts programmes and she had, to date, been singularly lacking in the respect and enthusiasm Wainwright felt to be due from a woman half his age and with no more knowledge of arts programmes than he had of the advertising world from which she had been tempted. He had to struggle to keep his interested and helpful smile in place.

'We're all glad Julia's settled in so well.' Just a hint of superiority of the kindest sort, just to remind Hackett he was dealing with a man of experience. Hackett did not seem to have heard him. Wrapping his arms a little more tightly to his chest, he leaned towards the desk. 'Julia tells me that the drunken oaf I saw coming out of your secretary's office shouting for a bottle of whisky is here on your authority. She tells me, furthermore, that you are proposing to let this man loose on Star Channel viewers, live, at six o'clock. I do trust, Francis, that Julia has misunderstood you.' He leant a little closer. 'I know you wouldn't make a decision like this without consulting your own programme director, unless the circumstances were quite remarkable.'

Reminding himself that Marvin Hackett, for all his ruthlessness, was the man who had once asked him to think about a programme on 'that bloke who wrote the adventure stories, Monserrat Caballay', Wainwright leant forward to meet him and looked him bravely in the eye.

'Now, Marvin, you know I've always expressed an enormous admiration for Julia's administrative skills —'

'You can leave off the icing,' Hackett said. 'Who's that man and what the hell do you mean by running a programme on him without a word to anybody?'

Search me, Wainwright thought bitterly. Couldn't the old idiot at least have obeyed instructions and kept himself out of sight in Shirley's office if he had to drink himself stupid? 'Harry Carpenter,' he said, 'is one of the most exciting performers you're ever going to see on Star Channel.'

'Go on,' Hackett said. 'Excite me.'

He did his best. His tongue, loosened by terror, rattled into a defence of Harry Carpenter's genius so larded with superlatives that Marvin Hackett's eyebrows shot upwards into his fringe. But not for long. As Wainwright, panting, came to the end of his speech, he saw that the director's face had resumed its scowl of rage. Pushing back his chair, he glared with such ferocity that it was all Wainwright could do not to fling himself on his knees and beg for mercy.

'I hope you're right, Francis,' Hackett said slowly. 'But if you're not, Harry Carpenter isn't the only person who won't be coming back to Star Channel. And I'm not talking about holidays or departmental changes. Got it?'

'Absolutely.' Wretched, cringing, Wainwright followed him to the door before creeping back into his chair. Feebly, he mopped his sweating face. What in the name of God had ever persuaded him to risk a comfortable career with retirement only five years away for a man like Harry Carpenter? Neither God nor his own intelligence seemed able to come up with an answer.

4

Millicent had made up for a recent lapse in attention to Sir Hubert's needs with an extra half-hour of weeding, when it struck her that she had been rather trusting in leaving Pat alone in the house for so long. Not that she had anything worth stealing, but one couldn't be too careful and she was, on this occasion, forced to accept that she had been downright careless. Picking up her trowel and wicker basket and pausing only to wave a brief farewell to the bronzed padre when normally she would have accepted an invitation to join him in a glass of sweet sherry and hear tales of his pilgrimage, she hurried round the corner and down the street.

She was not sure whether to be regretful or relieved when, on opening the door, she found the sitting-room empty and the envelopes for the hospital lying, unfilled, on her desk. Gone! Well, perhaps it wasn't a bad thing. She hadn't much cared for all that nonsense about womanwise or womankind or whatever it had been, and she certainly hadn't liked all those prying questions about her love-life. Still, unforgivably rude to go without so much as a by-your-leave or a thank-you note after that nice beef, she thought as she filled her glass and sank into her chair by the fire. No manners. Now, if she'd had the bringing-up of the girl – forgetful of the fact that she was the one who had chosen not to do so, she drifted into a reverie about the excellent mother she would have made.

'Mom.'

Millicent jumped. 'Pat! Where on earth were you? You gave me quite a fright.' She patted her heart. 'I've never been able to bear the thought of people creeping about the house like that.' Glancing up, she felt herself grow quite faint with alarm. 'What's that you've got in your hand? You've been poking about in my drawers.'

'It's your will, Mom,' the wretched woman said as though she hadn't got two eyes in her head to see what it was. And she never had got round to leaving the second copy with the bank. 'No need to worry. I just thought I'd take a look and see what you had in mind.'

'Nothing for you, my girl,' Millicent said sharply. She put her hand towards the telephone.

'I wouldn't bother,' Pat said as she sat down in the opposite chair. 'I thought it would make things easier if I disconnected it. You see, Mom, I didn't feel very happy when I saw this. It's not exactly a testament of affection to your only daughter, is it? Now it may sound funny to you, but I took a liking to this house as soon as I saw it. And I can't say I'd appreciate your leaving it to an old people's trust when you've got a daughter of your own to love and cherish it.'

'Sell it for all you can get, you mean,' snapped Millicent. 'I thought you were the one with the social conscience. I'll leave it where I please, madam, and I'll thank you to put that document back where you found it.'

Pat smiled. 'I wouldn't like you to think I'm threatening you,' she said. 'I'm just going to sit here and let you think about it. Think about what a house like this could mean to Womanwise.'

'I've thought,' Millicent said. 'And if you don't put it back this minute, I'll –'

'No need to get excited,' Pat said. 'I'm in no hurry.'

Looking at her, Millicent realised that it wasn't the threat to her safety that she minded, not even the will. It was the fact that she, the woman who took such pride in never being outwitted, had been trapped more easily than a child. She wasn't frightened. She was mortified.

'I think,' she said, 'I'll have a little drink.'

'Be my guest,' said Pat. With no humour at all.

5

Fay was in bad shape. She had lost the new coat even before she got home. She hadn't been able to find a thing that she wanted to wear. Her hormones were in massive rebellion, the director of her new screenplay had been on the telephone for twenty minutes to suggest alterations to the minor role to be played by his girl-friend – no use telling him that a girl who couldn't act and didn't have a union card was only going to be allowed to play the rear end of a donkey if she didn't keep her mouth shut – and Charlie Everest hadn't shown up. She wasn't even sure that she wanted him to show up, so exhausted was she after the past three hours.

The real mistake had been her decision to drop in on Gally – Madame Galina Marakova to her less favoured clients – and see what she could get on the meeting with Charlie. She had, she was ready to admit, also wanted to show off the new coat and to impress Gally with her news. She had known it was a bad idea as soon as she was called out of the waiting-room into the vast and expensively spartan penthouse studio room in which Gally examined the futures of the rich, the famous and the useful. (Fay's list of film contacts put her high in the third category and any resentment she felt was modified by the thought that the rich and famous paid more.)

'Well?' She posed in the door. 'What do you think of it?'

Gally leant forward to study her in silence for a long minute before shaking her head.

'Dahling, you know that I am always honest. It is not kind to your complexion. It makes you look fifty, maybe more.' Gliding forward with the silent swiftness of a cobra, she paused to pounce on one of the broad lapels. 'Ugly – and look at the cut of these shoulders. So heavy, so unflattering. We take it off.'

Crestfallen, Fay allowed herself to be disarrayed and folded into a soft and richly scented embrace. 'There. Now you are pretty again,' Gally cooed. 'How many times do I tell my little Fay to take me with her when she goes to buy clothes?' Gally's face grew dreamy. 'We have a nice snack at the Caprice, then we go to Stomakake and put you into something black or deep blue, not this ugly yellow –'

'Gally, I came for a reading, not for a fashion lecture. I've got Charlie Everest coming to see me today. Just look and see what you get on it. You know how I feel about him.'

Gally pinched her cheek. 'My little sweetheart. Always so much of the optimist. Come to the sofa and take the cards. So, how did you fix it? Shuffle and pick.'

'I didn't. It was really extraordinary. I've got a man renting my back bedroom and –'

'Yes, yes, I see him.' Gally nodded energetically. 'Fate has drawn this man to you.'

'Never mind that. I told him I wanted to meet Charlie Everest, and the next thing was my agent rang and said he was coming round to discuss one of my scripts. He's coming this afternoon.'

'So the new coat is for Mr Everest?' Gally smiled. 'I am so glad you let me see it first. OK. I tell you what I see. Business. A good deal.'

'I don't want a good deal. Gally, he's Mr Wonderful! He's coming to my door! It's what every clairvoyant in London's been telling me for years.'

Gally sighed. 'What are you telling me, dahling – that you are going to fall in love with every man who comes to your door? And this silly name. You are too old to be talking like a schoolgirl. Of course you want a good deal. First you get the money, then you get the man. Now. You want to know what else I see?'

Saying yes had been the second mistake of the day. Gally drew the cards towards her and snapped them shut with a triumphant smile.

'Now I tell you the truth. Dahling, you are not yourself. Today, you are not ready for your Mr Wonderful. I am not even sure you should try to do a deal.'

'You mean I'm ill?' Fay faltered. Already she could sense the throbbing step of the invading forces, the dreaded viruses, marching through her body.

'Not just ill, dahling. Terrible.' Gally shook an admonitory finger. 'How many times I tell you to go to the sun and rest – ten? Twenty? You forget about Mr Everest. You go home, you ring to cancel and you get quickly into bed. This is what I see for you. Truly, dahling.' She put her hand to the neck of her silk blouse. 'I tell you here, from the heart. You are a sick woman.'

To say that Fay was upset by this news would be a cruel understatement. By the time she was half-way down the stairs, she was weighing up the pros and cons of her favourite hospitals. By the time she had emerged into the heartless daylight, she could barely raise her arm to flag down a taxi. The cab driver was not in the mood to show compassion to a dying woman when she discovered, half-way home, that she had left her new coat in Gally's apartment.

'You won't be needing coats for a bit, if you're that ill,' he said. 'I'm sorry, madam, but it's the last ride of the day. Why don't you call your friend and ask her to bring it round?'

But Gally, when she rang, had taken her telephone off the hook.

She was, by this time, a helpless victim, a mere husk of flesh inhabited by the marauding armies. The pendulum confirmed the gravity of her condition with a swing so vicious that she was almost tempted to skip the hospital and go straight down to Kensal Green cemetery to book herself a burial spot. This, on second thoughts, seemed a bit premature. Steps could still be taken to avoid the worst. Carefully, she wrote down the symptoms – aching arm, hot forehead, stabbing pains in the area of her stomach – she knew what *that* meant – and rang the first of the typed list of doctors which occupied pride of place next to the telephone.

It wasn't her day. Doctor Pindar was away at a conference,

Doctor Sharpe said, quite unpleasantly, that he couldn't be at the beck and call of every woman with a touch of gastric flu (she crossed his name off the list at once), Doctor Carruthers couldn't fit her in until early the following week and Doctor Eugenia was rude enough to say that Fay didn't have any means of knowing that the pain stemmed from her ovaries. She went on to doubt that Fay knew where her ovaries were.

'They're my ovaries,' Fay shouted. 'Do you think I don't know where they are? I could give you enough information about my ovaries to fill a book. All I'm asking you to do is –'

'Feel free to ask me anything you like, Mrs Calman,' the unfeeling woman replied before she had finished speaking. 'I'm telling you that it's medically impossible for you to identify them as the source of a stomach pain. It sounds to me as though you've eaten something which disagreed with you.'

And this to a woman who never touched so much as a potato crisp without checking it out with her pendulum! She slammed down the telephone. Alone, neglected, unattended and mis-understood, Fay rubbed her hand over the disdained and suffering ovaries before turning for comfort to her favourite photograph. There he was, her familiar Charlie, sauve, smiling, muscular and lean as a hungry wolf. Fondly, she patted her stomach. 'That's what you need, you poor starved little things. Feast your eyes on that and tell me it isn't what you need to perk you up.' For a moment, she allowed herself to dream, until she found herself looking at the table, still strewn with yesterday's dishes, and the sink, a wobbling Pisan tower-load deep in dirty dishes.

By five o'clock, she had cleared the table, washed the plates, squirted the cats with flea-powder, apologised profusely to the director whose screenplay had arrived on his desk adorned with Max Medway's drawings, and promised to write in a cameo scene which would give his girl-friend a chance to roll her eyes at the camera for a good ten seconds. But she had, while talking to him, allowed Dora to jump up on to her lap and now her only smart skirt looked more like a hairy dishcloth and her best silk shirt had turned out to be at the cleaners. And Charlie Everest was late.

'Don't worry,' the agent said when she rang for encourage-ment. 'You're doing fine. Just get a sweater on instead. He isn't going to notice. He's coming to do a deal. And just remember what I've told you. Under all that cheap Charlie Everest charm, there's a cold little computer mind ticking up the bank credits. Don't let him fool you.'

'Got to go,' said Fay as the doorbell rang. 'He's here.'

Wasn't it how life always was, after a whole week of worrying about how she was going to look? No time to think about being ill, no time to get the cat hair off her skirt, no time to do more than aim a swift kick at the kitty-litter tray to skid it out of sight and pull on the top of her workaday track suit as she sped towards the door.

'Mrs Calman! Let me just say that I know I'm late and I feel terrible about it. Are you going to forgive me?'

Forgive him! Dazzled, she gazed at him, so cool, so elegantly and effortlessly at ease from the white sweater casually draped over his shoulders to the shoes that gleamed like polished mirrors. This was the kind of man before whom any sensible virus would lie down and die. True, he was only as tall as her shoulder, but she had always had a soft spot for small men. His eyes were azure slits and his skin was as soft and unwrinkled as a child's. This was a man who looked after himself, and she liked him the better for it. Maybe she could work the conversation round to health and find out which vitamin pills he was on. Behind her back, the telephone started to peal.

'I think somebody wants you,' said Charlie Everest and Fay, before she had stopped to think, beamed back at him and said that was how she felt, too.

'Your telephone,' he said gently. She could have wept, but then he smiled again, and it was that same gorgeous smile he always gave into the camera just before the credits started to roll, and it was just for her. He walked in ahead of her, picked up the phone and held it out, brushing his hand over hers as he did so. Fay was shaking so much that she could hardly hold it up to her ear.

It was only Lucy from a pay phone, saying something about doing what she knew she had to do and could she do a quick check on the cards to see if they confirmed that she had made the right decision? Fay sighed. Why did Lucy always have to be so frantic?

'Sure you have,' she said, not even bothering to look round for the pack. 'I'm looking at them now. You're doing the right thing.'

Lucy seemed dissatisfied with this answer. Her voice rose to a familiar wail of demand. Any minute now, and she'd be pouring out the whole Lloyd-Evans saga again.

'You go ahead and do it,' Fay said firmly. 'I've got company here, Lucy. We'll talk later. Bye.'

Turning to apologise, she felt a tremor of joy as she saw Charlie Everest seated at the table with Dora nestled in his arms.

'You like cats?' This was more than she had ever dared to hope. No clairvoyant had gone so far as to say Mr Right was a cat-lover.

'Like them! Here, let me show you. Easy there, sweetheart. You're going to have all the attention a beautiful creature like you deserves.' (This, although addressed to Dora, was accompanied by a glance and another dazzling smile which seemed to hold out the same promise to her owner.) From his breast-pocket, Charlie Everest drew out a small leather case and flicked it open to reveal a photograph of a large white Persian cat sunning itself on a terrace. 'Meet China. I took this when I was visiting my mother this spring. Would you believe that lovely creature is fifteen years old?'

'Never!' But Fay's attention had been caught by the background, not the subject. 'What a beautiful place. It couldn't be Italy, could it?'

'Smart girl.' (Girl!) He looked at her admiringly. 'Spot on. Now how did you work that out?'

It wouldn't do to tell him that Mr Wonderful had always been alleged to have Italian connections. 'I suppose it was the olive tree. So your family come from Italy?'

He tucked the photograph away. 'That's where I was born, forty-two years ago.'

Fay nodded. Why blame him? There were worse faults than vanity. 'And you go back there quite often?'

'That's where my heart is,' he said gravely. 'In a quiet little hillside village just a couple of miles inland from Naples. Matter of fact, I was back there just a couple of weeks ago. Bought myself a property near Caserta for when I settle down. Just a little white villa and a couple of hundred acres.' He was looking deep into her eyes again. 'Just olive trees and rolling hills as far as the eye can see. It's a funny thing, you know – maybe I shouldn't be saying this when I've just met you – but I can picture you in that kind of setting.'

'You can?' How many times had she not dreamed of this, the smiling man from the south, the little white house on the hill? 'Well,' she said faintly, 'I suppose we ought to start talking about the script. How much do you –'

'Fay.' He put Dora down gently on the ground and gave her another of his warm, slow smiles. 'Your agent told me you were a good business woman, and I respect that. It suits you. We know there's more to this than the script, don't we? The minute I started reading it, I knew I had to see you. I'm not talking business. I'm talking about spiritual affinity.'

'Of course you are. We're linked,' Fay said unthinkingly. She reddened. 'Psychically.'

He nodded. 'Your agent told me you do the tarot.'

'Some men don't like it.'

'But I like everything about you,' he murmured. 'She says you're good.'

'Good as gold.' She gave him a sliver of a grin. 'It's just a shame I never get paid in it.'

'Don't be too sure,' he whispered. And then, from the back of the house, a pretty girlish voice rang out a peal of laughter. His head turned.

'What a beautiful voice!'

'I didn't hear anything.' Fay resisted the impulse to jump to her feet and slam the kitchen door shut. Blast the girl – why couldn't she stay indoors and keep her mouth shut? She couldn't afford to let a man like Charlie Everest see her young, pretty neighbour sunning herself among the flowers. 'Give me your hand.' She ran a finger over the palm, willing his interest to return. 'The visionary and the sensualist – that's quite a combination, Mr Everest.'

'Just call me Charlie. Your telephone.' He shook his head. 'I can see my work's going to be cut out if I want to keep you to myself.' But the words were only words and she didn't need psychic powers to know that he was itching to get a look at the laughing girl. 'Don't move.' Frantic with apprehension, she picked up the telephone and snapped at it.

'Yes – *who*? Max, haven't you got a mother of your own to ring?'

'So hot, I think I'll just get a breath of fresh air.'

Agonised, she watched him move towards the door and out of sight, drawn like a magnet by that idiot giggle. What could have made Lucy's child choose such a moment – but then Max said something so alarming that she forgot all about Charlie Everest and sank down on a chair.

'Your mother did what!'

'I just told you. And Daddy's just telephoned to say there was a muddle and it wasn't his boat and he's going to come back and find Mummy in prison and it's all my fault —'

'Never mind whose fault it is. Did Mummy say where she was going?' Fay tried to remember what it was that she had said when Lucy rang her. Hadn't she told her to go ahead and do it? 'Max? Stop crying and answer me, can't you?'

'She's gone to shoot him. And I've looked up all the Lloyd-Evanses and none of them start with a G.'

'Do you know where he works?'

Max sniffed. 'Something Holdings in the City. He's an executioner. She must have told you. I thought you'd know. Can't you see it like you see things for Mummy?'

Not as well as I can see what's going on over my garden wall, she thought bitterly as the sound of mingled laughter murmured through the door. 'I'm doing my best.'

'You've got to see it.' He was crying again. 'It's all because of me. I only wished she could be happy. I didn't mean any of this to happen.'

'Of course you didn't, pet,' Fay soothed him. Realising what he had said, she suddenly stiffened. 'What do you mean, you wished it?'

'I made a wish. And then we heard Daddy was drowned and Gareth came round and it all went wrong and I know it was my wish.'

'And I rather think I know who granted it,' Fay thought grimly. She took a deep breath. 'Now listen to me, Max. Everything's going to be fine. I'm a witch, remember. Not a very clever witch, but I'm going to do my damnedest. All right?'

His voice was no more than a whisper of hope. 'You promise?'

'I promise.' Putting down the telephone, she ran out into the garden. It was empty. Stacked against the wall was a neat pile of magazines which had patently served as a step. Trembling, she stood still and listened for a moment before, fearing detection, she knelt down on the magazines.

'Sweetheart, I'm telling you that when Charlie Everest says he's going to make a star of you, he isn't talking about Christmas trees. You know, Lily, it's the strangest thing, but I came here knowing that woman was going to lead me to something wonderful. I knew I had to come. And here we are.'

'It's what I wished for. I made this wish and somebody told me it was going to come true. And here you are, telling me I'm going to be a film star!'

What she had wished for! So the love of a lifetime – well, a good five years – was to be snatched from her grasp at the wish of a silly little giggling blonde who fancied herself as a film star. And Raphael Sartis was responsible for it. With murder in her heart, Fay kicked the magazines back into the nettle-patch and returned to the kitchen to wait for his return.

She had no doubt now that Raphael was responsible. She had, now she came to think of it, felt that there was something odd about him from the start. That stranger from over the water she had seen in Lucy's cards had been her first warning. And hadn't he asked her what her wish was, and hadn't Charlie Everest come to her door?

A Frenchman called Raphael who could grant wishes; and hadn't that woman's name been the Countess Fœdora? It rang a chord in her mind which took her to her bedroom bookshelves. Eyes closed, she stood still. Her hand moved past Austen to Böll and returned as if of its own volition to Balzac. *La Peau de Chagrin.* That was the one. Frowning, she took it down and held her pendulum over the cover.

6

S. had kept his word, but he had taken his time about it. It was almost five o'clock when Raphael was told that Miss Wattle had announced that she wished to drop all charges against him and go home. He had, he hoped, heard the last of Fœdora, but evening was falling and his time was running out.

It was six o'clock before the taxi set him down at a tall, imposing building whose barred and shuttered windows offered no hint of welcoming light as he ran up the steps to the front door. A sharp female voice, nothing like Lily's, asked what he wanted. He found himself stammering like a schoolboy as he offered his fictitious excuses for the delay. A bolt was drawn back and he found himself looking at the dark girl he had first seen coming out of the house in Selena Street.

'You must be Raphael,' she said. 'You're very late.'

'I know. I'm terribly sorry. Is Lily here still? I tried to call, but the number –'

'My sister's gone home,' Sarah Franklin cut across him. She looked him up and down as though he was a piece of merchandise which carried no guarantee of its quality. 'You're to come in. My father wants to meet you.'

Raphael felt no responsive eagerness. He looked at his watch. 'I really ought to go back and explain to poor Lily. Perhaps another time –'

'This time will do fine. I don't suppose Lily's going anywhere. She seldom is.' She held out her arm. 'Give me your coat. It's the last room on the right.'

Walking into a sombre book-lined room in which the yellow lights flickered like fog-lights in the gloom, Raphael sniffed appreciatively, catching a trace of Lily's flowery scent. He started at the touch of a hand on his arm. 'Your father – ?'

'Over there.' She took up the position of observer by the fender surrounding a handsome marble fireplace. Walking towards the recess to which he had been directed, Raphael paused to glance at a painting, framed, but placed on an easel. It surely couldn't be what he thought it was?

'Of course it's a Rembrandt,' Sarah Franklin said scornfully as he murmured his incredulity. 'You don't think my father would bother with showing off reproductions, do you?'

'So you're Sartis.' Mr Franklin's gaze was penetrating and far from friendly.

Raphael smiled. 'De Sartis, really, but my parents decided to keep it simple. It's an old name. My father came from –'

'Never mind that.' Mr Franklin waved his genealogy away with a languid hand. 'Are you in the habit of turning up for your engagements three hours late?'

He offered the obvious explanation, the most acceptable, of a crisis at work. Mr Franklin stopped him with a snort of disgust.

'How old are you – thirty? Old enough to be able to organise your life and stick to your commitments. It's common courtesy, Mr Sartis, and we in England set some store by it. What the French do, I neither know nor care. No need to keep looking at your watch. I won't be keeping you for more than twenty minutes. Sit down. Not there. That's my resting chair. There.' He indicated a tall oak chair with a carved back designed to cause excruciating discomfort to anybody whose spine was not kept in a position as straight as a poker. 'Now. Lily tells me you've got a good job. If that's so, I'd have thought you could do a bit better for yourself than a bedsitting room in a basement. I was twenty-six when I bought this house for £500. Today, you'd be lucky to get it for less than a million. Follow my drift?'

'A very good investment.' Raphael winced as he leant back. 'I ought to say that in Paris –'

'We're not talking about Paris. This job of yours. Broadcasting. Well, Mr Sartis, it so happens that the house next to this belongs to the director of the BBC. I took the liberty of asking him about your work – I always take an interest in these things, for reasons I'll come to shortly – and he said he'd never heard of you. Anything to say for yourself, Mr Sartis?'

The room was not hot, but Raphael felt his forehead beginning to prickle with perspiration. 'French broadcasting, Mr Franklin. We don't have anything to do with the BBC. I don't want to seem in a hurry to leave –'

Mr Franklin's smile was not reassuring. 'I'm sure you'd very much like to leave, Mr Sartis. You don't like questions, do you?'

'You are being a bit like the inquisition, Daddy.' This mild intervention came from Sarah. 'Don't you think Lily's old enough –'

'Lily's never going to be old enough,' Mr Franklin said. 'If I don't ask the questions, I'd like to know who will.' He leant forward and looked intently at Raphael's face. 'I dare say my daughter's been telling you a lot of fine stories about the money she stands to inherit. I thought so. Well, let me tell you this, Mr Sartis. That money is being looked after for her by me, and if I don't like the husband she picks for herself, I'm going to make very damned sure he doesn't get his hands on it. Understand me?' He leant back again. Taking his own watch out of his pocket, he laid it on his knee. 'You've got fifteen minutes to change my mind about you. And don't waste any of it on telling me how you love and respect my daughter. I've heard it all before and it doesn't impress me. It's the facts I want.'

Raphael turned at a rustle of paper. Pen poised over her pad, Sarah Franklin smiled at him. 'Don't look so worried, Mr Sartis. I'm just the recording angel. Her first marriage was so very unsatisfactory – and you know how it is – once bitten, twice shy. You can't blame us for being cautious. Ready?'

7

Harriet heard his footsteps on the stairs and, trembling with apprehension, rose to her feet. Get it said as quickly as possible, that was the best way.

'Here we are, then.' He sounded jubilant. An arm came round the door and waved an envelope at her. 'Tickets for Venice and –' (the other arm came into sight) 'a bottle of champagne seemed to be in order.' The rest of him appeared. 'Do I deserve a kiss?' His smile faded as he saw her face. 'What's happened? What have you done?'

She couldn't say it. She couldn't imagine how she had ever thought of speaking as Pat had suggested. 'You'd better look in your study,' was all she could manage.

'Oh, my God,' he whispered. Dropping the bottle and tickets on the sofa, he turned and rushed out of the room. Listening, she heard the light go on. She heard the click as he turned on the computer. Then, for quite a long time, she heard nothing at all. Braced for a roar of anger, she was more frightened by a silence from which she could interpret nothing. Shaking, she sank into a chair and buried her face in her hands. Perhaps a miracle had happened. Perhaps, after all, she had only pressed a wrong switch. Please God, that was all it had been.

She looked up. He was standing over her and the look on his face was like that of no Victor she had ever seen before. Whimpering, she shrank away from him into the back of the chair.

'I didn't mean to do anything wrong, Victor.' Tears started to pour down her face and splash on to her lap. Foolishly, cravenly, she gave in to them, hoping that he might be sorry for her.

'I can't see what you've got to cry about,' he said. 'It wasn't your book. You're only Herostratus.'

Wiping her eyes with the back of her hand, she looked up at him fearfully. 'Herostratus? I thought he wrote history books. Do you mean you want me to help you rewrite it, Victor? I'll do anything, honestly –'

'Herostratus burnt the temple of Artemis on the night Alexander the Great was born,' he said. 'To immortalise himself. And perhaps one day, you too, Harriet, will be remembered. I can promise you that I, at least, will never forget you.'

She smiled at him uncertainly, wondering if he had paid her some obscure form of compliment. He looked so peculiar that she couldn't be sure what he might or might not mean.

'It's very kind of you –' she began. His lip curled.

'Kind? You stupid, interfering, meddling little bitch.' As he spoke this last sentence, he bent down and twisted her head back so violently that she thought he was going to kill her. 'Get up,' he said. 'Get out of this room and pack your clothes and go. I don't care where you go. I don't care what you do. All I know is that I never, never want to set eyes on you again. Now go!' And he gave her such a violent push that she fell clumsily on all fours, sobbing at his feet.

'Please, Victor.'

'Get out!' He almost shrieked it.

Too terrified even to stand up in case he struck her down again, she crawled across the floor to the door and fled into the bedroom. Blind with tears, she started pulling her clothes off the hangers and throwing them into paper bags, plastic carriers, anything in sight, cramming them in and crushing them down before she realised that all her precious revision books were in the other room. He had already shut the door, as though he couldn't even wait for her to go down the stairs before shutting out her presence. But outside the door, the books were neatly stacked in a cardboard box and on the top, neatly clipped to a note, was a £10.00 note. 'For your fare,' it said and he had signed it, Victor Grenderlyn.

She thought at first, as she came out into the dusky street, that he had taken one more step to be sure that he was rid of her and ordered a cab. But as she started to limp towards it with her armful of ramshackle bags, the girl from the next-door house came out with a handsome grey-haired man. The man had his arm round the girl's waist and as they walked past her to what was evidently their cab, not hers, they paused and glanced at her and whispered to each other. Then the blonde girl came towards her.

'Can we give you a lift somewhere? We're going to Heathrow, but if you want to be dropped on the way? It wouldn't be any trouble.'

Harriet looked at her and shook her head. It was selfish, she knew, but she didn't think she could bear the proximity of anyone else's happiness. 'I'm going in the other direction.'

The girl looked at her for a moment. Then, most

unexpectedly, she leant forward and kissed Harriet's cheek. 'Miracles do happen,' she said. 'You'll see.' And then she turned back and climbed into the taxi-cab and it rumbled away down the street. Harriet watched it out of sight with a hostile face. She was in no mood for fairy godmothers.

8

Lucy toiled up the seventh flight of stairs to Gareth's office – she had not wanted to lay herself open to the risk of an encounter in the lift. (Killing at such short range would be unnecessarily messy and she didn't want to ruin her clothes.) She entered the reception area just in time to see the coffee-skinned beauty behind the desk blowing a kiss into the telephone. Lucy gritted her teeth. This, without a doubt, was Melissa, the fiancée to be. Or rather, not to be, she reflected as she approached the desk.

'Mrs Marlowe,' she announced in her most silvery tones. 'I wonder if you could be good enough to let Mr Lloyd-Evans know that I'm here. I was just passing by and I thought I'd drop in on the off chance –'

'No problem,' the girl said, indicating a red banquette in the corner. 'He won't be long. He's just picking up a suit from the cleaners and then he'll be back. Take a pew.'

Dreadful voice. 'Too kind.' Settling herself in a position which allowed for an elegant crossing of the legs and a pleasing display of her new Italian shoes, Lucy stroked the cold muzzle in her pocket. She would do it, she decided, as soon as he came through the door. Then she would shoot the girl and then she would ring the police and give herself up. Tomorrow, it would be in all the papers. There would be photographs. TRAGIC LOVE TRIANGLE. REVENGE OF THE WOMAN HE SPURNED. Perhaps, if they were feeling charitable . . . OF THE BEAUTY HE SPURNED.

The girl was looking at her with a puzzled stare. 'You did say, Marlowe? It's funny, but you sound just like another lady Gar – Mr Lloyd-Evans knows.'

Lucy bestowed her most gracious smile. 'Such a pity we can't all have such unusual voices as yours, dear. Do get on with your copy-typing and don't let me disturb you.'

Flushing noticeably, the girl went back to her work. She typed quite well, Lucy noticed. She prided herself on giving credit where it was due.

9

It was a quarter to six when Francis Wainwright got the news he had been dreading. There was a cold grain of comfort in the fact that the harbinger of bad tidings was his secretary and not Marvin Hackett, but the sympathetic look on Shirley's face told him to expect the worst. He grasped the side of the desk with both hands.

'Gone?'

'You could say that,' she said. 'I've just had a message from Katie in make-up. She and Erroll got him into his suit and he was just going on about how he needed a drink to rev him up a bit when he keeled over. They've tried putting a cold cloth on his face and giving him a good shake, but he won't budge.'

'No chance of his coming round in a few minutes?'

'Oh, Mr Wainwright,' she said sadly, 'if you'd seen him before I took him down! He couldn't do so much as a nursery rhyme in that state. Poor old chap. He was really looking forward to it when he first came in. He kept telling me how he wished his mother could be alive to see him.'

'Just as well for her she isn't.' He was in no mood to shed tears over the Carpenter family. 'Does Mr Hackett know about this?'

She shook her head. 'I told Katie to keep it quiet until we'd decided what to do. But I don't know how long she can keep it from looking suspicious. Julia always likes to go down and have a chat with performers before they go on and –'

'Once she knows, he knows. And once he knows –' He looked up at the clock over the door. 'Fifteen minutes left. What are we going to do, Shirley? What are we going to do?'

'You ought to have done it on tape,' she said reproachfully. 'I did say. I've never known you be so reckless before.'

'Don't tell me that now!' Clasping his hands over his head, he lowered his face to the desk, seeking comfort in its smooth, cool surface. 'Think, Shirley! Think!'

'Animal Crackers? Tom and Jerry?'

'In the person-to-person spot?' He swivelled round in his chair and stared out of the darkening window at the brightly lit rectangles of the matchbox skyscrapers which stalked across the skyline. 'Somewhere out there, there has to be an answer. And if there isn't, Shirley, you and I are going to be under the banner of the unemployed by this time tomorrow.'

'You know what they say,' Shirley offered. 'A change is as good as a rest. And you've been saying for ever so long how you wanted some time at home to get your orchard looking nice – oh, good evening, Mr Hackett.'

Marvin Hackett brushed her to one side with no more attention than if she had been a moth. Brows lowered and arms folded, he advanced on the desk.

'Is this what we employ you for, Francis, to sit prattling about orchards? Are you or are you not a producer for this channel? Don't sit there twittering. Are you?'

Feebly, Wainwright nodded his head.

'Well, then,' Hackett said through his teeth. 'Produce. And if that slot isn't filled when I sit down to look at the screens in twelve and a half minutes, you won't just be out of a job. You'll be walking back to Sevenoaks or wherever it is that your miserable little body crawls out of every morning with more broken bones than a squashed chicken. That's not a warning, Francis. It's a promise – and I'm a man who likes to keep his promises. Got it?'

If Wainwright made a response, it was not an audible one. His lips were seen to move, but no sound came from them.

'I'll get you a cup of tea,' said Shirley as Hackett swept past her out of the room. 'You mustn't worry, Mr Wainwright. Men like him always sound a lot worse than they are. I'm sure he didn't mean it.'

Francis Wainwright gave her a dismal smile. 'That makes one of us.'

10

'I can only tell you that I ask for nothing more than to make your daughter as happy as she makes me.' He felt as though he had been talking for an hour, but the hands on Mr Franklin's watch showed that he had not yet completed the allotted twenty minutes. 'Have I said enough yet to convince you?'

'You've certainly said enough.' Mr Franklin carefully replaced his watch in his pocket. 'As to convincing me – Sarah, give our guest his coat and show him the door, will you? I'm sure he's anxious to make his apologies to your sister.'

Sarah Franklin was more sympathetic in her farewells. 'You'll have no trouble getting a cab at the end of the street,' she said as she shook his hand at the door. 'Don't worry about my father. He's always been like this about Lily. He's never been able to trust her to get on with her own life. She's a dear girl, but she's always been impractical. I'm afraid it was this silly business about being a film star that set him off this evening. You know,' she said as he looked at her blankly, 'her wish. What on earth made her think anything was going to come true just because she'd wished it I can't imagine, but –'

'She wished *that*!'

'You should know,' Sarah said, surprised by his expression of horror. 'Weren't you the one who said you could make it happen? That was what got Daddy so worried – he thought you were going to be some kind of an impresario. He doesn't like that kind of thing. Are you all right, Mr Sartis? You wouldn't like to come back and sit down for a bit?'

'No.' Giddy with dismay, he shook his head. 'No. I should never have left her. Your father was right. I – I thought she'd wished for something quite different.'

'Cheer up,' she said. 'It was only a wish. Lily a film star! That'll be the day.' Laughing, she went back into the house and closed the door.

11

In Miss Press's sitting-room, Pat put down her glass of water and looked at her watch. 'You've had long enough, Mom,' she said. 'I think it's time we brought a little reality into the situation. You've got the pen. You've got the paper. All I'm asking you to do is alter a couple of words. It's not very difficult. You do that and I'll walk out of the door and you won't have to worry about ever seeing me again. Just cross out that old people's home and write in "Womanwise". I'll deal with the rest.'

Millicent drained her glass and folded her arms. 'And what if I don't?' The brass knuckleduster was an arm's reach away. If she could only succeed in distracting Pat's attention for a few minutes. Through the window, she saw a taxi come rumbling down the street and halt outside the door of Mrs Tremain's house. 'I wonder who that could be,' she said. 'Perhaps you wouldn't mind taking a peek?'

Pat smiled at her. 'Perhaps I would. I'm waiting, Mom. I hate to sound threatening, but I'm not planning on sitting here all night. Violence is something I deplore, but if you're going to insist on being difficult, I just might be driven to use it. So, please, don't insist.' Slowly, she raised her hand to her neck to loosen from it a flowery silk scarf and, smiling still, she twisted it over her wrist and pulled it tight. 'Long enough,' she said. 'And strong enough. Don't look so frightened, Mom. It's your choice. I don't have to use it.'

12

'Love it,' Fœdora murmured as she leant over S.'s shoulder for a better look at the screen. 'Are you going to let her do it, Master?'

S. flicked off the pictures and lay back on the black cushions with a sigh. 'I, my dear? I don't have to do anything. It's exactly as you so perceptively remarked yourself. Give them their wishes and they do all the rest themselves. Poor Raphael. I wonder if we ought to give him a little credit for his efforts, since they've worked out to such a pleasing end.'

'Credit?' Fœdora's voice grew sharp. 'For trying to promote happiness? For working against us?'

'Gently, my dear Fœdora. You must allow your Master to have his little whims – as he allows you yours. Was it in my interests that you tried to excite his desire for you, my pet? Did I ask you to languish on his bed in black silk stockings or to exhibit yourself to him as a model in a dress shop?' Leaning back, he looked up at her face. 'Admit it, my sweet. As Clegg, he was of no more interest to you than a lump of rock. Would you have shown yourself in silk stockings to Clegg? You want me to punish him because he failed to gratify your own wishes. Even you, my exquisite, my superb Foedora, are not entirely deficient in the weaknesses of the female species. Guard yourself against them, my dear.'

Foedora bowed her head. 'The Master is too kind to his unworthy slave. He will not see such weakness in her again. I was drawn to him, I admit, but only as one of your creations. May I peel some more of the grapes for my noble lord?'

'You may –' S. broke off and looked into the darkness. 'Yes, Opal? I see you lurking there. Come forward. Entertain me. Tell me tales of earthquakes and famines.'

Opal shuffled forward and looked at the master with his large pale eyes. 'I've been with the porter at the gate.'

'Well?' S. looked impatient. 'You surely didn't come and disturb me to tell me that? Get on with it and use your sleeve if you haven't got a handkerchief. You know how I detest the sight of running noses.'

'Sorry, Master.' Opal wiped the cuff of his black jacket over the offending nose. 'I can't seem to shake it off. It's all this night-travelling. The porter seemed to think you ought to look at the earth-screen again. There's a bit of trouble with Sartis. Someone's got control of him.'

'No rest for the wicked.' S. lifted his foot and neatly kicked Foedora to one side. 'Forgive me, my lovely one. You're blocking the screen. Now, let's see what all the fuss is about.' Yawning, he registered the screen into movement while Opal and Foedora crept to his side to look. 'Well, well, well,' S. said in his most mellifluous tones. 'We seem to have suffered a small reverse. I thought, my sweet, that you told me that the woman was powerless. Didn't you?' Turning to Foedora, he pinched her cheeks between his long fingers and pressed in. 'Didn't you? Answer me.'

'Please, Master. You're hurting me.'

'Answer me.' His voice was still soft, but neither Foedora nor Opal were so foolish as to draw any comfort from that. Feebly, she nodded her head.

'Did I not tell you she was dangerous? Did I not tell you she was one of that detestable breed of spirit-meddlers I want wiped out? Look at the screen and tell me again that she is powerless. Look!'

'Master, I can't see anything,' Fœdora whispered.

'And why can't you see anything, my sweet?' he hissed. 'Because that woman is upsetting the waves. She's got our friend Sartis and I rather think she means to use him.'

'But Master,' Fœdora stammered. 'Surely you, the supreme ruler, the lord of systems —'

'Silence!' S. leant towards the screen. 'Concentrate on Sartis. Will your strength to him and help him to resist. And if you fail this time, my dear —' He laid one burning finger on her forehead. 'None of my followers is indispensable, not even the fairest of them all.'

13

As for Doing-good, that is one of the professions which are full. Moreover, I have tried it fairly, and, strange as it may seem, am satisfied that it does not agree with my constitution.

Lying on the kitchen floor with Spiro Vathos's considerable weight on his legs, Dora chewing at his left ear and his landlady dangling her silver pendulum over his face, Raphael was obliged to recognise that his position was not a strong one.

'You don't look so happy,' Spiro said amiably. 'You not expect we catch you so easy, eh? Wicked man!' He bounced on Raphael's thighs. 'You pay for hurting all these good people.'

'I didn't,' Raphael said, 'hurt anybody. Is it my fault if they hurt themselves? What's she grumbling about? She got her evening with Charlie Everest, didn't she?'

'She get to see him going away with this girl,' Spiro said sternly. 'When I come here, I find my little Fay crying and saying she going to kill herself. This make me very upset. And then she say you make it happen —'

'Never mind that now, Spiro,' Fay said, as Raphael opened his mouth to protest his innocence. 'It's the things he's done to other people I'm worried about. Get off there, Dora.' She knelt beside his head and bent down until her face was almost touching his. 'Now you listen to me, Raphael. I know your game. And you're not the only Balzac-reader around here. You put this mess right or you'll end up a lot worse off than Raphael de Valentin.'

Raphael allowed himself a weak smile. 'Don't I know it? But not through anything you can do to me.'

'You think not?' She was busy chalking lines and circles round his body. 'You think I don't know what I'm up against? But I'm ready for them. They won't break through this in a hurry.'

He decided to appeal to Spiro. 'She's mad.'

Spiro grinned at him with infuriating serenity. 'Sure she's mad. I like her that way. And like I said, Mr Surteess, I don't like Frenchmen. I don't like the way you come in here. I don't like it when I hear how you try to kiss Fay. I don't like the way you walk around here like you own the place. What you ever do for me to make me want to help you?'

Fay had lit two large blue candles which gave off a thick, sweetly scented smoke. Holding one in each hand, she bent down again and stared into his eyes. Dimly, wavering in the mist above her, he saw the face of S., dark and terrible. 'Raji,' he was saying, but so faintly he could hardly make out the words. 'Remember all there has been between us. Remember what I can give you. Trust me.'

'You wanted to do good,' Fay said. 'Do you think you won't be punished for it? I'm giving you your chance, Raphael. Do what you meant to do and I'll do my best to save you.'

Agonised, he looked from her to the proud and beautiful face of S. which hung behind her shoulders. 'They'll destroy me.'

The face of Fœdora came into sight, pale and frightened. 'Don't listen to her, Raphael darling. Do this and you'll never escape from the Hundredth System. What do they matter to you, these foolish creatures? Doing good is doing harm. You know the rules.'

'Do it,' Fay said. 'You were one of us once. Do it for your own people.'

Wearily, he closed his eyes. 'Not for you,' he whispered. 'Against them. I will do it. I did wish to bring happiness.'

'Meddling termites!' Uncoiling himself from the gloomy splendour of his cushioned throne, S. leant towards the fading images on the screen and blew, while Opal and Fœdora wailed with terror and covered their ears against the noise. Blackness fell over Selena Street as deep as a winter night and, for more than a mile around, cars shrieked to a halt and people flung themselves down on their faces in expectation of the final disaster as the wind roared down on them.

The room rocked and spun and shuddered with the strength of S.'s fury, but Fay's eyes never left Raphael's face as he flailed and twisted inside the chalk marks. His body began to change shape, to shrink and then to stretch and glow, filling the chalk marks with a pulsing, phosphorescent light. The cats fled squalling to the corners and Spiro flattened his bulk under the table. And then there was a silence and a sudden darkness as the light went out. A rank and fishy odour filled the room. The blackness pressed down, closing them in as if they had been enveloped in the belly of a whale. Trembling, Spiro groped his way to the door and felt for the switch. Beyond the passage, he saw where the front door had been ripped away to open an arch to the night. The bulk of fallen trees straddled the pavement. He turned and looked down at the floor.

'Fay, where is he? What have you done? Are you all right?'

Unsmiling and ashy-cheeked, she stood up and rubbed her hands as if she was washing away some invisible stain. 'I'm fine. You'd better go and see what's left of the door. Sybil, out of that cupboard. Dora, dinner-time, my precious. It's all over. Let's see what the pendulum says about a nice bit of liver for three frightened old ladies, shall we?'

'Please, Fay. Where is he? You got to tell me. I don't understand none of these things that are happening.'

Turning, she shook her head at him. 'I haven't got to tell you, and I'm not going to. He kept his word, and I'm afraid he'll have to pay for it. That's all I'll say.'

'He'll come back again?'

When she closed her eyes, she could see a small figure being sucked forward through a long glass tunnel, battered and hurled against its walls as though it had no more weight than a leaf in a furnace. 'I doubt it.' The liver having passed the test, she started slicing it up for the pan. 'I'll tell you one thing, though. I'm not staying here. I'll give old Grendel a week's notice first thing in the morning.

Spiro blinked. 'You got anywhere special in mind to go?'

She grinned at him. 'Somewhere with space for three cats and a welcome for Carl when he's around. Any ideas?'

A large, slow smile spread across Spiro's face. 'You meaning what I think you mean?'

Fay left the liver and put her arms around his massive shoulders, squeezing him. 'And how do you suppose I could know that, my precious? What do you think I am – psychic?'

*Putting Things
to Rights*

From Melissa Allbright to Shirley Clayton

Dear Shirley,
Sorry to have cut you short on the phone yesterday, but we had a bit of a scene going on in here. So did you, from the sound of things! Has old Wainwright gone round the twist at last?

Here's an extract from daily life in pensions and insurance, just to show you that Star Channel doesn't have all the dramas. (Joke!) This tiny little blonde woman tripped in here just before you rang, calling herself Mrs Marlowe and asking to see Gareth. I knew who she was as soon as she opened her mouth. Lucy Medway, that housewife I told you about who's been running after Gareth for years. I reckoned she must have come in to give him a piece of her mind for not marrying her. I could tell it wasn't just a friendly visit.

Anyway, Gareth didn't get back to the office until about six. (Talk about the life of Reilly!) I didn't want to seem rude, so I told her he was just coming up in the lift. Well! Talk about a cat on a hot tin roof. I thought she must be ready for him to do a bit of bonking on the office floor from the way she started jumping round and twitching at her pockets. I asked if she was feeling all right and then she gave me this look. Real hate.

'You leave me to do what I have to do,' she said. 'And I'd advise you to keep behind that desk, Miss Zimbabwe or wherever it is you come from.'

I suddenly realised it wasn't sex she was after at all. She'd come to the office to do something terrible. It was the way she kept slipping her hand in her pocket and grabbing at something. It could have been a small gun, maybe some kind of a bomb. And you know what the office is like. No alarm system. No security. Honestly, Shirley, I was so scared I thought I was going to throw up. I heard the lift stop and Gareth come down the passage and turn the handle, but I couldn't have moved to save my life, let alone his.

He went white as a ghost when he saw her, but he sounded quite calm when he spoke.

'Now, Lucy,' he said. 'I thought I told you I didn't want us to meet again. I hope you aren't thinking of doing anything stupid.'

'You don't think you can get rid of me just like that, Gareth,' she said. 'Not after all the years I've devoted to you. Well, I've got something for you and your fiancée here – my wedding present.' Then she pulled her hand out of her pocket and whipped round on him – and do you know what she was holding out? A little bunch of freesias! I've never seen a woman look so sick. Her hand went all limp and the flowers just hung there and we both stared at her.

'Well,' Gareth said after a bit. 'No hard feelings about the past, then. I did you an injustice, Lucy. I didn't think you'd be so understanding.'

'Understanding,' she said. 'Understanding! Do you think I drove all across London and waited here half the afternoon just to give you a bunch of flowers!' And she threw them down on the carpet and rushed out of the door.

I mean, weird. Gareth said she'd been going through a domestic crisis because they thought her husband had been drowned. Married to her, I should think it was a choice between the devil and the deep blue sea! Still, since he seems to have opted for the devil, I'm hoping we've seen the last of her.

Must rush. Love,
Melissa

From Victor Grenderlyn to Francis Wainwright

Dear Francis,
Unexpected though your call upon my services was, I have no qualms about saying that I thought the talk went very well indeed. I will go further and say that I think I have demonstrated my ability to give the Star Channel audience what they want: knowledge, wit and entertainment. I shall look forward to hearing your thoughts about my attached proposal for a series of half-hour talks in which I can extend and expand some of the notions I raised last night.

I was greatly taken by your young director. What a charming and intelligent woman she is! I wonder if I might take the liberty of asking you to pass on my admiration, and I wonder – a matter of idle curiosity – if you can tell me whether she is currently attached?

My commiserations on your difficulties with Mr Carpenter are, I trust, forgivably qualified by the feeling that his loss was your viewers' gain. I have no intimate acquaintanceship with Mr Carpenter and fear he does me too much honour in suggesting that I could provide a reference for the job you and your wife propose to offer him. Your benevolent impulses do you the highest credit and it is my sincere hope that Mr Carpenter is appreciative of your kindness.

Yours, with warmest regards,
Victor Grenderlyn

Extracts from the
Selena Street Neighbourhood-Protection Scheme Newsletter

Shoppers in the vicinity of Selena Street last Friday have reported seeing a young blonde woman lifted into the air and carried away by the force of the wind. The woman has not yet been identified, but she was said to be carrying two heavy bags. Police are investigating.

FLYING GIRL SAVED MY LIFE, SAYS MOTOR-STAR

Miss Millicent Press, 73, former winner of the British Ladies' Amateur Racing Championship and president of the Selena Street N.P. group, was released from hospital on Monday morning. She was being treated for shock after battling single-handed with an intruder at her home on Friday afternoon. Miss Press, a familiar figure to many of our readers, was the first to report seeing the mystery blonde.

'I've no idea how she got up there,' Miss Press told our reporter, Carole Artless, from her hospital bed. 'All I know is that she saved my life. When the intruder looked out of the window and said there was a body in the sky, I knew it was now or never. I got my brass knuckleduster and hit her on the back of the head and she went down like a sack of potatoes.'

Determined to bring the intruder to justice, Miss Press courageously fought her way through the storm to her garden shed, to find a rope with which to tie her up. It was during this time that the intruder made her escape. She is described as a short, heavily built woman, aged about 40, and with a strong American accent. Police would welcome any further information from readers.

HARRY GOES TO HOPS

Mr Harry Carpenter, a familiar figure to our Selena Street readers, has finally decided to quit his crusade to bring poetry to the people.

'There's nothing to be got from going on,' Mr Carpenter said, speaking on the telephone last night to our arts correspondent, Susan Jellicoe-Jones. 'I'm sick and tired of trying to get people to appreciate beauty. I've been offered a job as a gardener in Kent and I shall be offering my collection of valuable antiques to the British Museum for a nominal sum.'

Mr Carpenter was due to have been seen by subscribers to the new cable network, Star Channel, on Friday night, but illness regrettably prevented him from appearing.

From Carl to Fay Calman

Dear Fay

Here's something for your clarevoyant records: Remember the girl who married Grendel? Well, I was on Radlett Station on the night of the storm and she blew in. Litrally. I couldn't beleive my eyes. I looked up and there she was, flying along the railway track, bags and all, right to my side. She said the wind just picked her off the bus-stop and carried her there! She was a bit shaken-up by it, but she's fine now. Anyway, it seems Grendel threw her out because she messed up his computer and she was planning on coming back to Radlett anyway. Her family live here, and they're putting me up for a bit. Her mum's fantastic at cooking and her dad's an arkitect. He thinks he can get me some design work in the town.

Fact is, I think I'm going to stay here. I never did feel

comfortable in London and Harriet feels the same. I know you always said Camomile Hill was just like being in the country, but it's not, not when you've been for a few walks in the real thing.

I saw the bit in the paper about you and Spiro. It's just what I always thought you ought to do. One good Greek in the hand is worth twenty lousy film cops in the bush! I suppose this means that you've kicked out that frog broadcaster. Good riddance.

Did you hear on the news about the Retreat going up like a bonfire on the night of the storm? All they found of Father Gerard would have fitted into a funeral urn and I can't help thinking it serves the old bugger right. You should've told me about all the dosh he clobbered you for. It's a bit late to say it, but thanks anyway.

> Love to Dora and hope to see you soon,
> Carl

From Lily Tremain to Sarah Franklin

Dear Sarah,
As you can see from the picture, I'm in California – and guess who I'm with. Charlie Everest!!

You know I told you about Raphael saying he could grant wishes and that I wished I could be a film star? Well, after I came back from tea with you and Daddy, Raphael still hadn't turned up and I thought I'd cheer myself up listening to an old Peter Sellers record and I'd forgotten how funny it was. I'd got the speaker out in the garden and I was just rolling about on the grass in fits of giggles when I looked up and there he was. Not Raphael. Charlie. He'd come to visit Mrs Calman about a script and he said I'd be just right for the girl in his new film and did I want to come to America and do a screen test? And here I am, living in the lap of luxury and waiting for my appointment at the film studio. Charlie says I'm astonishingly photogenic. He's been taking loads of pictures of me.

I bet you're looking really disapproving now, but I know you'd like Charlie if you met him. He's not a bit like they make him out to be in interviews. Daddy will be pleased

because he's really shrewd about money. Everybody says so.
He's been explaining how I can invest my money for the best
return, and he's got a brother who runs a financial corporation
out here, so they can do it all and Daddy won't have to worry
about me any more. I'm sending him the documents today. Tell
him all he has to do is sign them and Charlie will take care of
everything else.

So dreams do come true! I wish I knew where Raphael was so I
could thank him. I know that none of this would have happened
if I hadn't met him. I rang Mrs Calman, but she said he left very
suddenly without giving any forwarding address.

Must go – Charlie's taking me to sign the last papers for his
accountant and then we're flying to Vegas for a quickie
marriage. Write soon. Lots of love,

Lily

From John Medway to Fay Calman

Madam,
Circumstances compel me to be frank. Your spiritual
meddlings have caused considerable distress to my wife and
to myself. It is not yet possible for me to assess the damage
your interference may have inflicted on our son, who is
presently viewing Legoland and other significant
archaeological sites with a teacher from his school. (I would
have preferred him to be studying maritime matters, but a
father's feelings are seldom taken into consideration by
today's schools, regrettably. No matter.)

To return to the point. My wife has been under sedation for
the last two days after carrying out an (happily abortive)
attempt to assassinate a certain Mr Lloyd-Evans, known to
you, I understand, as 'Mr Right'. When my wife was in a
condition to be questioned about this bizarre endeavour, she
informed me that it had been a 'mission of destiny' and that
you had approved it.

I am a man of actions rather than words. On this occasion,
words fail me. It is, nevertheless, my duty to set before you in
plain language the disgust, the anger, the contempt with
which I learnt of your manipulation of a gentle, generous-
hearted woman. I will admit that I had for some time been

aware that my wife was under an unhappy delusion about the nature of her relationship with Mr Lloyd-Evans. I had also understood that she was consulting a 'healer' who was helping her through a trying emotional period. Healing! Is that what you call it when you wantonly raise false expectations and actively encourage my poor deluded wife to commit murder?

Clairvoyant powers will not, I surmise, be required for you to apprehend the spirit in which I thankfully sever the connection between the inhabitants of *Ocean Spray* and you and your dangerous, despicable art.

I am, Madam, yours faithfully,
John Medway

S. extended a languid hand for his early-morning aperitif. 'Just as prescribed, my sweet?'

Fœdora bowed. 'Just as you ordained it, Master.'

Smiling, S. raised and tilted the exquisite goblet of System Three crystal (premier service) until he could see the microscopic figure bobbing at its rim in its cylinder of frozen water. While Fœdora watched, he lifted the glass to his lips. But he did not drink.

'Well?' He looked at her. 'Shall I? Or shall we take a leaf from the book of the excellent Uncle Toby for a change? The final decision, my dear, shall rest with you.'

A fly climbed to the rim of the glass and circled a little distance above it, shaking the water from its gluey wings. S. waved it away. 'Go, – go, poor Raji – get thee gone – why should I hurt thee? This world is surely wide enough to hold both thee and me.'

'Not quite,' said Fœdora.

And swatted it.

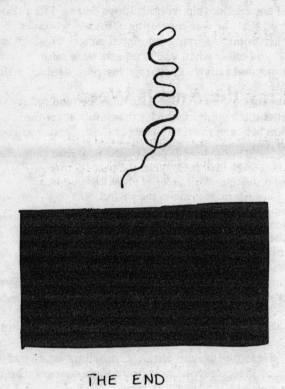

THE END

HELEN FLINT

Making the Angels Weep

Krul and Addie live in a converted Chapel at St
Boddi's, an island accessible only by the tidal road
that links it to the mainland. When the peace of this
hide-out is disrupted by hordes of uninvited guests,
Krul, a born tyrant, recognises the perfect
opportunity for playing a megalomaniacal game of
consequences to put them in their place – except
that a child is able to learn the rules faster than he
can reinvent them.

'Not the place to visit for cream teas'
   Daily Mail

'A Prospero gone bad, Krul rejoices when an August
bank holiday weekend brings an assortment of
uninvited relatives and friends to his domain . . .
Parallel to the weekend's games of humiliation is
the story of St Boddi, a 13th-century monk who
sings like an angel . . . At the double climax of the
novel, the two narratives touch, sparking an
exhilarating moment of magical realism'
   Sunday Times

FERDINAND MOUNT

Of Love and Asthma

'Gus, the narrator of this novel, and his friend Joe
Follows embark on their would-be careers as
philanderers nervous in the knowledge that their
bronchial tubes are liable to let them down.
Unfortunately they both fall for the same girl,
Gillian, a forthright lass whose softer side is touched
when her lovers are at their least successful . . .'
Literary Review

'I doubt if anyone can fail to be exhilarated by the
imaginative, intellectual and stylistic vigour which
surges through every page'
Francis King, *Evening Standard*

'An exceedingly stylish and entertaining novel . . .
The ability to combine the serious with the comic so
adroitly is rare and admirable'
The Times

'Wry, dry, sly and delightfully written'
Daily Mail

A Selected List of Fiction Available from Mandarin

While every effort is made to keep prices low, it is sometimes necessary to increase prices at short notice. Mandarin Paperbacks reserves the right to show new retail prices on covers which may differ from those previously advertised in the text or elsewhere.

The prices shown below were correct at the time of going to press.

☐	0 7493 0780 3	**The Hanging Tree**	Allan Massie	£5.99
☐	0 7493 1224 6	**How I Met My Wife**	Nicholas Coleridge	£5.99
☐	0 7493 1064 2	**Of Love and Asthma**	Ferdinand Mount	£5.99
☐	0 7493 1368 4	**Persistent Rumours**	Lee Langley	£4.99
☐	0 7493 1068 5	**Goodness**	Tim Parks	£4.99
☐	0 7493 1492 3	**Making the Angels Weep**	Helen Flint	£5.99
☐	0 7493 1364 1	**High on the Hog**	Fraser Harrison	£4.99
☐	0 7493 1394 3	**What's Eating Gilbert Grape**	Peter Hedges	£5.99
☐	0 7493 1216 5	**The Fringe Orphan**	Rachel Morris	£4.99
☐	0 7493 1510 5	**Evenings at Mongini's**	Russell Lucas	£5.99
☐	0 7493 1509 1	**Fair Sex**	Sarah Foot	£5.99

All these books are available at your bookshop or newsagent, or can be ordered direct from the publisher. Just tick the titles you want and fill in the form below.

Mandarin Paperbacks, Cash Sales Department, PO Box 11, Falmouth, Cornwall TR10 9EN.

Please send cheque or postal order, no currency, for purchase price quoted and allow the following for postage and packing:

UK including BFPO
£1.00 for the first book, 50p for the second and 30p for each additional book ordered to a maximum charge of £3.00.

Overseas including Eire
£2 for the first book, £1.00 for the second and 50p for each additional book thereafter.

NAME (Block letters) ....

ADDRESS ....

....

☐ I enclose my remittance for ....

☐ I wish to pay by Access/Visa Card Number ☐☐☐☐☐☐☐☐☐☐☐☐☐☐☐☐

Expiry Date ☐☐☐☐